JUST CAUSE

JUST CAUSE

Mike Fry

Cover artwork Angie@pro_ebookcovers

ISBN: 978-0-9758482-5-8

FIRST EDITION

www.mikedfry.com

For my daughters Peta, Danielle and Stephanie
Love you so much

1

The morning sun is yet to rise above the British metropolis. One by one the lights in the city town houses switch on as if controlled by some random program. First the bedrooms on the upper levels, small bathroom windows, then kitchens, dining rooms and finally a flash of light illuminating the front steps, as their fortresses burst open. The occupants scurry to their cars or bus stops. As if sequential, the first rays of sunlight break through the sentinels of concrete. Long shadows of movement are cast as the city comes to life.

Belgravia is one such area, populated predominately by the very wealthy and professionals in a variety of doctrines. City dwellers and city workers reside, mostly by necessity and some by choice. London is a powerhouse of industry, commerce and government with the inner suburbs providing the human resources necessary to keep the heart beating and the pulse racing to meet the physical demands of this bastion of power.

For Nick and Dianne, their townhouse is both functional and necessary for their career and lifestyle. A consultant obstetrician, Dianne caters to the demands of wealthy mothers to be in the Harley Street rooms she shares with her practice partners. Partners who also charge exorbitant fees to those who feel the greater the price the greater the provision of quality. She started her career in more humble surroundings. A shared bedsit in Southwark with fellow nurses at Guy's Hospital and following her dream to one day become a doctor. At the same time battling the chauvinistic hierarchy of high-level medicos and fighting the stigma of adult study in place of a good school followed by university. Her dream paid off after many years of study and hard work. Her degrees and further qualifications hard won while still working beneath the canopy of hospital bureaucracy and condescension. There were times of impediment during her pre-baccalaureate study in the '80s however Dianne takes pride in now providing her services at St Thomas' to those mothers less able to afford specialist attention in difficult pregnancies and deliveries.

Nick usually follows Dianne to breakfast. He insists on giving her adequate preparation room as he studies the rising morning light. That is, when he's at home. If ever there was an antithesis between the careers of two people, then the occupants of this Belgravia townhouse would be it. Where one person was a preserver and giver of life the other had the power and ability to take that away. If asked, Nick would say he worked for the British Government. If pressed, he would explain that he was a civil servant in the employ of the Foreign Office and frequently travels overseas. If pressed further about his job, even if in intimate and convivial surroundings, Nick would have no hesitation is telling the person to 'mind their own fucking business'. Nick's close friends and associates knew he held a commission in the Royal Navy and some of them knew he worked with Naval Intelligence. Very few knew he was also an MI6 operative and those that did were sensible enough not to mention it. Times had changed for Nick. Those in his line of work, approaching mid-sixties, mainly involved themselves in the administration of the agencies they worked for. Mainly, but not always.

Nick's boss was Adrian Nightingale, now Rear Admiral and a Sir to boot. "I tell you what," offered Adrian when Nick posted to Navy Intelligence back in 1979, "I'll stake you ten thousand pounds now and invest it for you. In twelve months' time you will repay that ten thousand and still have at least ten thousand to keep investing." Adrian smiled and slapped his back.

"Why are you doing this for me?" asked Nick

"Because you saved my life old boy, that's why."

That was early 1979. Adrian said that US gold was on the rise and could double or possible treble by the end of the year. Nick's investment, staked by Adrian, got Nick over £33,000. Adrian took his £10,000 investment back and gave Nick £23,000. Nick never knew how much Adrian invested or where he got his tips from but whenever Adrian gave him a tip, he took the advice.

It was Adrian who encouraged him to get into his own inner-city house back in the early days after Nick and Dianne became an item. He had a friend in the banking industry who would arrange finance for him. By 1982 interest rates had dropped to ten percent in the UK and Adrian told him he should make the move. Nick protested at first as the price even then was a fair hike above his pay grade. Adrian insisted and followed up with some investment advice. Nick protested again and once again Adrian insisted and staked his first investment with the Paternoster Square crowd.

Today Nick and Dianne were extremely comfortable. They bought the three Mews cottages behind their townhouse giving them garage space for their cars and a double entrance. One on Eaton Square and the other in the Mews. The cottages and the townhouse had cellars which Nick was able to cross connect when they joined the back of the houses together.

Nick came down and joined Dianne at the breakfast table. Their children had moved out some time ago. Jeremy was a diving instructor in the Bahamas and Julie somewhere in the Himalayas studying wildflowers.

"I've decided," said Nick reaching for a coffee cup.

"Decided what?" asked Dianne as she scanned the morning paper for something of interest.

"You know whether to pull the pin and retire."

"Well, I've heard that before Nick."

Nick looked out of the window onto the green reserve across the road. "Too much crap and political correctness these days."

"So, what will you do then?" asked Dianne, "you're not going to hang around here and drive me crazy."

"You're so busy you wouldn't notice." Nick leant over and kissed her neck as she flipped the paper over to another page.

"I would so Nick, you have to get a hobby or something."

"Well, I'll have a chat to Age this week."

"How is Adrian, I haven't seen him for ages?"

"To be honest he's been a bit distant lately. He's getting a lot of crap from Downing Street these days."

"Well that can't be anything new," replied Dianne munching on a piece of toast with a generous dob of marmalade. "They're all a bunch of tossers in the house." Dianne threw the paper down on the table, "and I mean both major parties, and the rest are looneys in my book."

Nick drew his gaze away from the park and turned towards Dianne. "Anyway, it's time to go. I think I'll have a chat to personnel and see where my pension's at."

"What are going to do with your diaries Nick?"

"I've been thinking about that as well." Nick met Dianne's inquisitive gaze. "I met a chap a few years ago when I was in Australia. I stayed at his hotel, part time writer of sorts, ex-military so he would understand some of my stuff."

"Why do I get the feeling that I'm going to get a job."

"I'll arrange something with our solicitors, keep it at arms-length so to speak, but I might get you to do the meet and greet."

"Thanks, but you're not usually that trusting Nick."

"I knew I could count on you sweetheart."

"Not me you goose. Him. Anyway, you'll be lucky to get a pension with our investments. Isn't it asset based?" Dianne ran her tongue over her lips collecting the last remnants of the home-made marmalade. "And there's the house down the coast. Maybe, you could spend more time down there, fishing or something."

"Maybe you could go down with me, you know, take some time off. It's been a while since we had a holiday."

"Make me an offer I can't refuse sweetheart and I'll think about it; but right now, I'm in a gynaecological frame of mind and I have to go." Dianne jumped up, grabbed her bag, kissed Nick on the lips and headed for the front door.

Nick stood there looking at the closing front door, holding his cup of coffee and vacantly wondering if today would be the day that he really was going to submit his resignation.

2

Across the river, the day started as most other days for Detective Chief Inspector Nigel Connelly in his one-bedroom flat just off Waterloo Road in Newington. It was all he could afford after his second marriage of thirty-five years suddenly evaporated in front of his eyes. He shared the bathroom down the passageway with a reclusive academic whom he barely saw. Thank goodness the toilet was in a separate closet and, as the academic was a younger man, he had less use of the facility at night. Nigel kept a chamber pot aside for emergency use in a homemade commode but hated the damn thing. His doctor said it was to be expected at his age, that his waterworks would eventually need some attention. Some plumbing work was mentioned but for the moment Nigel was content with a little inconvenience.

He'd given up smoking many years ago, but a morning cup of coffee was mandatory as were some bacon and eggs for breakfast with a fresh tomato and fried bread. To his way of thinking all the food groups were there on the one plate, a plate that would be left in the sink, with yesterday's plate, and the day before, to be washed at some other time.

Nigel was an old-fashioned copper. He preferred his creased gaberdine mac to the trendy Berber wool coats of his younger contemporaries. The beige trench coat had been his constant companion for more years than he cared to remember. Underneath, he would wear one of his three rather out of style suits. Nigel was philosophical about his lot. He enjoyed being on the streets of London, as he had for most of his life. Jurisdictions had changed and in recent years he found himself being called out further afield. In his halcyon days he would enjoy a bit of ruffing it up with the local crims but in these past few years he spent more time behind a desk than on the street. They'd given him a smart phone and an iPad, although he conveniently left them in the car and preferred taking notes in his crumpled notebook. He also enjoyed experiencing an antiquated pheromone by using a public telephone box.

One day was rolling into the next for Nigel and he was quite happy to give the married men time off with their families on weekends, while he covered their shifts. The last thing he wanted to do was sit in his flat, alone. There was no garden. He disliked most of what was on the television networks. Most of all the news with frantic bad-mannered reporters trying to elicit as much sordid detail as they could from those unfortunate enough to have become fodder for the masses. Yes, this weekend was just another weekend.

3

Stella lay panting on the floor of her contemporary flat in Frithville Gardens. Grabbing her towel, she wiped the sweat from her face and shoulders. Her 'Sweaty Betty' Lycra leggings and scrunch top were wet and clinging to her ripped body. She gasped, and sitting up, took a huge gulp of her energy drink. She was exhausted. A full two-hour workout was not what she had planned however the phone call that afternoon had unnerved her. She had to work it out of her system. Why would the recruitment officer of MI6 call her on a weekend requesting she come into their office first thing on Monday morning for an interview? She had applied to their organisation over a year ago and had not heard from them since. *Why now?* she thought.

4

The Cotswolds can be beautiful in spring. The smell of fresh rain on the grassy slopes. The misty valleys and coloured refractions of light filtering through the moisture in the air. The lack of haze and the pure air make wonderful conditions for an assassination. Finding an elevated position is paramount to an objective; as essential as access to a rapid exit from the location once the execution of the mission had taken place.

Small cottages inhabit the landscape among the fields and narrow laneways. Trees populate the countryside alongside the hawthorn hedges and broken fences. The walking tracks along old disused railway easements provide arterial access, once the prerogative of the hiss and clickety-clack of steam driven trains.

Bishop Julian Borthridge, recently retired, sits in seclusion in one of those cottages. He sits comfortably every evening, reading from his extensive library in a leather Chippendale wingback chair. Life is not too bad for Julian, considering that 12 months earlier he faced an uncertain future in the custody of Her Majesty's government.

The verdict was guilty of child molestation, multiple sexual penetration of minors and a sentence of thirty-five years behind bars. Whilst in confinement, in a secure and isolated area of the prison, the lawyers for the church were able to secure an appeal. The result was a reduction in the sentence due to age and perceived health issues. Further conditions were relaxed by an accommodating judge, due to the two years he had been confined to a cell in an area protected from other prisoners. Lawyers made further applications to the judge regarding his health and the sentence was further reduced to home isolation for a period yet to be determined, with an electronic monitoring device including regular visits from court officers.

This evening he sat, as usual, next to the open fire with a reading lamp above his right shoulder. The housekeeper, employed by the local vicarage, had left sometime earlier after her daily chores. Julian was clearly visible through the pane glass windows from the adjacent hillock where the man was setting up his equipment.

A plastic sheet was laid down on the grassy top of the hillock beside the tripod and camera. No-one would pay too much attention to a wandering photographer amongst this picturesque landscape. From his position he had a clear view of at least 500 metres in all directions. Observing no other roving individuals, he unpacked his belongings. The AXMC rifle with .338 calibre was built for this task. The bipod settled firmly on the grass in front of the plastic sheet and the man lay down, carefully adjusting the Schmidt & Bender scope and rangefinder. For no other reason, other than habit, the man pulled a camouflage cape over the rifle and himself. The suppressor was clear of the fabric and his sight was clear and uninterrupted.

Julian was a man of habit, and this evening was no exception. He had finished his dinner by six-thirty as the sun behind the man on the hillock was casting its last rays of sunshine. As was his usual routine the Bishop kept one window slightly open for a little fresh air. Julian had moved to his chair, turned the light on and opened the pages of the leather-bound book. While the bishop was turning the first page the man made the final adjustments to the focus. The sky was still light and the distance to the target of seven-hundred metres was anticipated by the man as a perfect kill shot. The crosshairs were set to Julian's left temple as the man gently squeezed the trigger until the mechanism's fired the modified lock base bullet. The projectile made a clean entry through the partly open window and into Julian's left temple, expanding and removing most of the right side of his face and the back of his head. The effect was instant, brutal and bloody. A tower of blood sprayed the bookcase behind the chair. Bone, brain and blood spray combined with other tissue hissed and burned in the open fire. The arterial blood continued to pump for a few seconds, saturating his body, the book and the chair.

Satisfied with his work, the man packed his equipment into his bag, folded the camera tripod under his arm with the camera still intact, and headed off down the hillock to the disused railway easement. Once there it was only a short walk in the dim light of dusk to his plain white van parked in the laneway on what used to be a railway platform. Rock music was heard as the van travelled along the country by-ways.

At 8am the following morning the housekeeper arrived.

"Hello Bishop Borthridge. I'll put the kettle on?"

Without waiting for a reply, she boiled the kettle and made a pot of tea. She took the pot to the kettle, not the other way around, and poured the piping hot water over the English breakfast tea leaves. She arranged the silver tray as always with a small jar of cream, a bowl of sugar and an English Rose cup, saucer, teaspoon and ornate tea strainer. Feeling extremely proud of her first chore, smiling and humming to herself, she carried the tray into the library, screamed and dropped the tray. The scene was very disturbing.

5

Cheltenham detectives investigated the incident. They concluded that a high-powered rifle was fired from outside of the building the previous evening, penetrating an open window and hitting the Bishop in the head. They found no apparent clues around the building nor any tangible evidence that the building had been entered until the arrival of the housekeeper the following morning. There were other cottages in the area however the occupants had neither seen nor heard anything unusual. The elderly occupants of those cottages were cleared of suspicion. A SOCO from Gloucester attended the scene and the Cheltenham branch awaited the results of the forensic and ballistic report from the attending forensic investigator.

6

The private laneway outside the local manor house was deserted in the early Sunday morning. The man erected the detour signs at the nearby intersection of narrow country roads. His white van was parked on the grassy kerb. Inside the high stone walls surrounding the manor house the engine of the maroon Bentley Continental GT pulsed as Judge Benedict Ryder settled into the plush white leather seats. Religiously proceeding to the Sunday morning service at the Parish Church of St John the Baptist, he fastened his seatbelt, released the brake and coasted towards the opening automatic steel gates. One hundred metres along the road the man stood alongside the detour sign dressed in an iridescent yellow safety coat watching Judge Ryder turn left out of his driveway slowly driving towards the detour sign.

The man held up his hand as Judge Ryder slowed his car down, placed the gear lever into Park, and opened the driver's side window.

"Good morning. Is the road blocked?" asked the judge.

The man leaned towards the open window. "I'm afraid so Judge Ryder, you won't be able to get to church this morning."

"Really. Oh dear, was it an accident, was anyone hurt?" asked the judge.

"Yes, a fatality," the man replied, as he pulled the Glock revolver from his pocket. Pushing the silencer against the right side of the judge's head, he pulled the trigger.

The bullet made a clean entry; however the exit wound resulted in a large spray of dark red blood and bits of bone and grey matter splattering the interior of the Bentley. The colour of the blood a stark contrast to the white leather as Judge Benedict Ryder's heart continued to pump blood out of the gaping wound on the left side of his face. The judge slumped forward but the weight of his body was held back by the man to avoid the horn sounding. The man unlatched the seat belt and pushed the judge to the left across the console. The Bentley remained stationary in the middle of the laneway with the motor quietly idling as the man walked away, stowing the detour signs into the back of the white van. The man drove away from the scene with the radio volume on high.

It was sometime later that an inquisitive Sunday driver passed by and discovered the deceased judge and the gory interior of what was once an immaculate maroon Bentley Continental GT.

7

Detective Chief Inspector Nigel Connelly of New Scotland Yard arrived at the grisly scene in the Oxfordshire laneway. He parked his BMW Series 5 some distance back from the tapes across the road and walked towards the constable standing guard. Showing his warrant card, the constable waved him through as his phone rang. A veteran of the force for some forty years he had some idea why he had been called in.

"Yes, I've just arrived. Tell the Assistant Commissioner I'll be in the office later this afternoon. I'll call you when I leave here."

Nigel placed the phone back in his overcoat pocket as he walked towards the Bentley. A group of officers wearing white forensic suits were combing the crime scene. The judge's body was still slumped across the console. Samples were being taken of the blood spatters and the exterior of the car was being dusted for prints. Nigel approached one of the plain clothes officers standing beside the Bentley.

"DCI Connelly of SCO, Met Ops," showing his ID card, "who's the senior officer attending?"

"That would be me, DS Spencer sir."

"Where's your DI then?" asked Connelly.

"Broken leg sir."

"Has the coroner been informed?"

"Yes sir."

"Right," Connelly paused as he looked around. "You're working for me now. I'll clear it with region. I'll be SIO, but I'll leave you to look after this end of it. Run me through what happened?" Nigel peered through the open driver's door. "Professional hit?"

"Looking a bit like that sir. Victim is Judge Benedict Ryder, lives just down the road, circuit judge with the Crown Court. According to a neighbour goes to church every Sunday, lives alone, divorced. I was planning to do a full check on his recent trials, and his personal life," Spencer hesitated, "or will you be looking into that sir?"

"No, you complete your incident investigation Spencer, have a good look around his house and send the full report to me at the Met, here's my card. Anything unusual, give me a call. Who's the SOCO attending this scene?"

"Fred Majors sir, the CSI, he's over there by his van."

Connelly glanced over as Fred Majors looked up from his iPad and gave Connelly a nod.

"Oh yes, we call them CSIs now. Ok, tell him the body's to be sent to the Coroners Morgue at Horseferry Road and as I said report, my desk, asap."

Spencer knew better than to ask too many questions of a DCI, but he did wonder why the Met was on the job.

Connelly drove off as Spencer walked down the lane with a constable toward Judge Ryder's home. The automatic gate was closed. Spencer had the foresight to bring the judge's keys and remote for the gate and garage. One press and both opened. Once in the garage they were able to access the house and proceeded towards the living area.

Spencer scanned the garage, "Constable, look for the security system and see if it's armed, I don't want another team of coppers coming down on us."

Unsurprisingly the house was furnished in quality furniture and fittings; a healthy combination of antique and contemporary items befitting the judge's station in life.

The constable returned, "the control unit's inside the front door, but it's turned off."

"That's odd," retorted Spencer, "the gate was closed, I would have thought the judge would have turned it on."

The front of the house on the ground floor was dedicated to a living room, dining room and study, each resplendent with items of art, the likes of which one would expect to see in a gallery or museum. The study had a large desk set in front of a bay window, glass panes with a heavy tapestry curtain half drawn. On the desk was an Apple MacBook together with the usual trappings of writing paraphernalia. Spencer put on a pair of blue nitrile gloves nodding to the constable to follow his lead as they examined the office for any possible clues.

While the constable concentrated on the bookcase Spencer leaned forward and pushed the start button on the computer and waited. A password was required. Spencer noticed a piece of notepaper sitting under the laptop. Pulling it out he was surprised to see a four-digit number.

"I don't believe this," said Spencer half laughing.

"What's that boss?" enquired Constable Hargreaves.

"There's a piece of paper under the laptop with what looks like it could possibly be the password to opening the MacBook," replied Spencer. "It'll be a fucking miracle if it is."

Spencer punched the numbers on the keyboard.

"Fuck me, its opened," gasped Spencer, "who in their right mind leaves the password to a computer right next to it?"

The screensaver flashed up with a picture of the judge's house. Spencer moved the cursor to the documents folder and pressed the touchpad. The file list opened with a library of mainly word documents. He then clicked on images and the screen came alive with a myriad of thumbnails.

The constable called out. "Hey Sarge, there's a heap of VHS tapes and DVDs in the bookcase."

He moved the cursor to slideshow and stood upright in surprise. A collage of images of children and men in what could only be described as confronting situations started to roll over in sequence. He opted out of that folder and pressed videos whereby an index of video thumbnails indicated material analogous to that of the still images.

Spencer called the constable over.

"Jim, I want you to witness some of these images for me and record these on your phone in real time."

Constable Jim Hargreaves commenced video filming while Spencer described the scene and the contents of the MacBook. "The time is 1335, at The Manor, 352 Church Lane, Whitecross. Owner of the premises is Judge Benedict Ryder, recently deceased. DS Chris Spencer and Constable Jim Hargreaves in attendance. An Apple MacBook on the desk containing explicit child pornography and a bookcase containing a number of VHS and DVD tapes which could possibly contain similar material."

The constable continued with the video while DS Spencer detailed the location and nature of the contents of the study. When completed he went back to the computer and inspected more of the files and directed the constable to do a quick inspection of the other rooms in the house. Spencer clicked on a few recent emails together with the attachments and he reeled back in shock. Aside from the nature and content of the images he also recognised some of the male persons in the photographs. He shut the computer down as the constable returned to declare the rest of the house empty and nothing unusual. Spencer picked up his phone and called the forensic officer currently at the murder scene.

"Fred, it's Chris. When you're finished there, you'll need to do a full house internal down here at the judge's home. I also want you to witness the contents of a MacBook found in the judge's study. I'll see you back at the car in a few moments."

Once back beside the Bentley, Spencer showed some of the computer images to the forensic investigator Fred Majors and DC Shane Fellows, while Constable Jim Hargreaves filmed the witnessing.

"Do you chaps know why I'm filming this?" Spencer looked directly into the eyes of the three officers as they stood motionless. "I'm doing this because I don't want some bastard in a pinstripe suit saying this never happened or this computer and the filth in it never existed. I want you chaps to be very mindful and accurate in your reports as to what you've just seen. Is that clear?" Spencer met their gaze once more as they nodded their heads.

"I'm heading off to the office to copy this hard drive and then I'll be driving to the Met and sitting down with DCI Connelly later today." Spencer headed to his car and took a deep breath before he fastened his belt and pressed the ignition button. He drove towards his fellow officers and called out.

"Constable Hargreaves, I'll need your phone as well." Taking the phone from Hargreaves, "Jim, I want you to stay at the house until relieved. Shane, you finish up here. We'll be putting an officer in that house 24/7 for the next few days at least.

8

From where he was sitting opposite the police station at Abingdon the man in the white van could see DS Spencer exit his car carrying the MacBook into the front door of the police station. He smiled as he pulled away from the kerb.

Spencer copied the contents of the hard drive onto a 3TB portable hard drive with the duty sergeant watching the procedure. He had been in the same situation some years earlier as a DC where crucial electronic evidence in a case somehow disappeared and he was adamant that there would be no repeat this time. He gave the sergeant the task of ensuring the portable hard drive was logged in as evidence and placed in the safe in the evidence room. The sergeant was also tasked with rostering on a constable at the judge's house for the next few days. Returning to the car, Spencer then copied the images and videos onto a memory stick, placing the stick into the glove box. He also sent a copy of the phone video to his home computer.

If the traffic on the M40 was reasonable, Spencer estimated he could make the Met in about an hour and a half on a Sunday. Enroute, he called DCI Connelly.

"Sir, DS Spencer."

Connelly cut in quickly. "What's up. Didn't think I'd hear from you for a few days."

"New development sir, something you need to see today." There was no hiding the tension in Spencer's voice.

"I'll get the desk to send you straight up." Connelly grunted and frowned as he put the phone down.

By the time Spencer knocked on Connelly's alcove it was close to 4pm. It was Sunday with the usual rostered officers around the corridors and spaces. The Saturday night offenders had mostly been processed and the Met was relatively quiet. Connelly was alone in his department as he called for Spencer to come in.

Spencer showed Connelly the contents of the laptop. Many expletives were uttered during the viewing. After about an hour Connelly spoke.

"Right Spencer. I take it you had a copy of the hard drive placed in evidence?"

"Yes sir, with the duty sergeant at the station and locked in the safe." Spencer was breaking out into a sweat.

"Now, who else has seen or is aware of the contents of the computer?" Connelly was making notes.

"Constable Hargreaves, who was taking a video of the initial inspection of the study on his phone." Spencer passed the constable's phone across the desk to Connelly.

"Also, SOCO Fred Majors and DC Fellows." Spencer fumbled with his handkerchief as he wiped the sweat from his brow. "And also, the duty sergeant at Abingdon station."

"Right," said Connelly, "Now the shit's going to hit the fan on this one Spencer, and I can tell you that some people aren't going to be happy. In fact, once this gets to the top there'll be pollies who'll want this quashed, hidden and buried. Thankfully, we've got enough officers that've seen this, and enough reports will be in the system by tomorrow that a grave robber's dog couldn't bury."

Spencer nodded.

Connelly continued. "Were there any reporters or media in the vicinity when you left."

"No sir, we had the roads blocked off."

"That won't stop the bastards. Tell the other officers in attendance that any statements will be made through the Met, understand? You did well Spencer. Now piss off back to wherever you call home, clean up the details and make sure the forensics come directly to me. I'll appoint you as my Deputy SIO, so clear your desk of anything else you're doing and pass it on. I want you back here tomorrow after you've collated any relevant material. I'll keep the MacBook. If anyone gives you shit, point them in my direction, understood?"

"Yes, understood sir."

Connelly's next job was to contact his superiors and organise a briefing. He sent an email to the Assistant Commissioner requesting a meeting on Monday afternoon. This would give Spencer time to collate what was required and get all the ducks in a row for Connelly. The meeting would be a tad premature but given the volatility of the evidence, Connelly felt he would get a rocket if he didn't present the evidence so far. He called the coroner's office to check when the post-mortem was scheduled although there was no doubt on the cause of death. Connelly was, however, interested in any ballistic results.

Monday morning was a frantic one for DS Spencer. As directed, the interim report on the forensic inspection of the crime scene and the house was sent directly to DCI Connelly, with Majors sending Chris a copy. Fred Majors and Spencer met at the Abingdon station at 9am and discussed some of the initial findings. The most surprising comment by Majors concerned the judge's house.

"We bagged all the tapes, CDs and DVDs Chris but we found something interesting." He opened an evidence bag and placed a small camera on the desk. "Wi-Fi camera, motion activated, high definition with a memory card installed." Fred continued, "we found it behind the pole pocket on the curtain header in the bay window. It was installed to focus on the writing desk in the bay. I played the video files on the card, and it clearly showed the judge using the computer and viewing the files."

Majors stopped and took a deep breath. "It also showed the judge logging on and off and clearly showed which numbers were used for the password. Equally disturbing old chum is this."

Majors pushed the SD card into his laptop and played some of the files. The two officers gasped in alarm as the video files showed the judge masturbating whilst watching the videos on the laptop: videos of men and young children.

"Fucking hell."

"Exactly my sentiments," offered Majors as he closed the files and placed the SD card and camera back in the evidence bag. "Look Chris, this is explosive and somewhere along the line it could blow up in someone's face. We need to make sure it's not us. I agree, everything we find, every little detail, must be passed on and we leave nothing out." Majors stood up and went to the jug and poured two cups of coffee. "White and two?"

"Yes, thanks Fred. I got a call from Connelly this morning before I left home. He said that all officers attending say nothing other than put the details on the report, leave nothing out but speak to no-one. No scuttlebutt, no reporters, no media. Scared the shit out of me."

Spencer reached for his cup as he continued. "I've spoken to the duty sergeant and the constables about the confidentiality, and I believe that the investigation is contained so far."

"Right. The lab will have more results back today and I'll be sending those directly to the DCI." Majors took a sip of his coffee. "He seems like a reasonable chap, been around a few years."

"Yeah, old school. Can't be too far away from his pension. Can't say I envy him right now." Spencer gulped down his coffee and grabbed the evidence bags. "By the way Fred, did you make a copy of the SD card?"

"Yes Chris, logged in as evidence and a copy in the safe with the copy of the hard disk."

"Who do you reckon put the camera behind the curtain Fred?"

"I could hazard a guess and say the same person who wrote the password on that piece of paper."

"The killer?"

"That's my guess."

"If that's the case then the killer or killers went into the house after the murder, wrote the password down but left the camera there." Spencer frowned. "Hang on, the judge was the only one on the video camera."

Majors stood up and faced Spencer. "That's right. The camera was operated by Wi-Fi. They deactivated it while they were in the room and re-activated after they left. And my guess is that they did that deliberately, so we'd easily find the evidence on the computer. Someone is playing a dangerous game here. Be careful."

"Could the evidence have been planted?" asked Spencer.

"Looks too authentic Chris, he was definitely having a wank." Majors shrugged.

"Fuck," said Spencer as he walked out of the staff room.

"Oh, Chris," shouted Majors as Spencer turned around. "By the way, for what it's worth, the judge presided over that case with the bishop. You know the one who got murdered last week over near Cheltenham."

"Fuck," said Spencer once again.

9

Spencer arrived at the Met just before 2pm. Connelly came out of his office and met him in the corridor.

"Follow me." Connelly shuffled down the corridor with the MacBook and a heap of files under his arm.

"Where are we going sir? I have something I need to talk to you about," commented Spencer.

"We can talk about it later." Connelly turned as he was walking. "Meeting with the Commissioner, my boss the Assistant Commissioner and other brass hats," Connelly pressed the lift button. "I only hope the pollies keep the fuck out for the moment."

The lift opened on the Commissioner's floor and the two made their way to the conference room.

The room was empty aside for a civilian technician setting up audio visual equipment. Connelly and Spencer took seats next to each other.

"Look chum, let me do the talking. I'll answer all questions, even if they're directed at you." Connelly looked Spencer in the eye. "They can be a pack of bastards Chris, and at the end of the day the further up the ladder, the more they cover their arses."

"Thank you, sir, but I need to talk to you now." Connelly dismissed him and pulled Spencer to his feet.

The Commissioner, Sir Alex Connaught-Sinclair came into the room closely followed by Deputy Commissioner Celia Graham, Connelly's boss Assistant Commissioner Horace Larkin, Connelly's immediate superior in the Specialist Crime

Unit Commander Gerald McIntyre and Corporate Services Manager, Assistant Commissioner Ron Hatchett.

Gerald McIntyre sat next to Connelly as the others spread around the table. All officers attending were in uniform, excepting Connelly and Spencer.

"You should've gone through me first Connelly," whispered McIntyre, bristling with rage.

"You weren't answering your phone Gerald, this couldn't wait. Golf, was it?"

The Commissioner called the meeting to order.

"I called this meeting as a matter of urgency," Sir Alex scanned those attending with icy cold eyes. "And I've kept it to a small number on the recommendation of AC Larkin. Whatever is said in this room goes no further without my authority. Is that clear."

There were nods all round with each attendee making eye contact with the others.

"Right," continued Sir Alex, "AC Larkin if you could begin."

Larkin stood up.

"Thank you, Commissioner." Larkin nodded to Celia Graham, "Deputy Commissioner Graham and gentlemen. Some of you may have heard that there was a murder committed yesterday, the scene of which was attended by the two officers present DCI Connelly and DS Spencer. The victim was, now the late," Larkin paused, "Judge Benedict Ryder, Circuit Court Judge."

There was a mixture of reactions at the table from furrowed brows to a look of horror.

Larkin continued. "The victim was shot from close range by a handgun, to be confirmed by forensics, to the head. The victim was in his car at the time and was found by a passer-by yesterday, in the late morning, close to his home. The scene was also attended by a forensic officer from the Oxford division and local constables. For further details I'll hand over to Unit Commander McIntyre and DCI Connelly."

McIntyre stood up as Larkin sat down.

"I'll hand this part of the conversation to DCI Connelly sir." McIntyre directed his conversation to the Commissioner as Connelly stood up.

Connelly proceeded with his preamble and overall description of the murder scene and conversations, with those present. He then detailed the findings in the home of the judge.

"If it were not bad enough that a respected member of our judiciary has been murdered the crime is compounded by the evidence found at the home of Judge Ryder." Connelly spoke directly to Sir Alex, "If it would please the Commissioner, I would like to connect the MacBook, owned by Judge Ryder, to the projector and I would advise also that the device contains extremely distressing and offensive content."

The Commissioner looked around the conference table, halting his gaze in front of each individual person. "Are there any of you, who for any reason, feel this would be inappropriate or would like to leave the room?" As expected, there was a conclusive shaking of heads.

"Proceed Chief Inspector Connelly."

The technician took the MacBook and connected it to the projector. "The password please?" asked the technician as the screen came to life.

"0916", replied Connelly.

The Deputy Commissioner cut in. "How did you come by the password Chief?"

Connelly shuffled and faced Celia Graham, "there was a note next to the laptop on the judge's desk with the password written on it, ma'am."

"Who found the note Chief?"

"DS Spencer Ma'am, sitting here next to me." Spencer moved uncomfortably in his chair.

Celia Graham gave Spencer a look that could chill a keg of beer. "Carry on Connelly."

"Thank you, Ma'am." Connelly opened the manila folder in front of him.

"Upon noticing the piece of paper next to the laptop DS Spencer typed the numbers in and surprisingly the password was correct."

Celia Graham interjected again, "A little unusual would you not think?" Once again giving Spencer a steely stare.

"Unusual Ma'am, but as my presentation will show, the dots do come together." Connelly once again continued a little taken aback by the surly attitude of the Deputy Commissioner.

Again, Celia Graham interrupted the presentation. "I hope we're not here to cast aspersions on one of our most respected judiciary or embark on some kind of witch hunt."

This time Sir Alex took the floor. "I think we'll let Connelly complete his presentation before we interrupt him further Celia." Sir Alex motioned towards Celia and then waved his hand at Connelly, "Please proceed Connelly and this time without any interruptions," looking back at the Deputy Commissioner.

"Thank you, Commissioner. As we'll see the desktop is routine with the usual icons and a quantity of libraries. We'll go to the images file, and I do warn you again that some of the images and videos are extremely disturbing."

Connelly scrolled through the thumbnails stopping every now and then to blow the images to full size amid gasps and shuffling in seats. He then switched to the video files and showed an ordinal number of segments to which there were mutterings of disgust.

Connelly paused the screen. "Aside from the disgusting acts, you will note that some of the people in these images may be familiar to you." He looked at each officer in turn as they returned his gaze then mostly looking down at their hands. Celia Graham maintained eye contact, with Connelly detecting her gaze showed equal disgust of him as she did the images on the screen.

Connelly inserted the SD card showing the video of the judge masturbating in front of his laptop and stared back at Celia Graham whereby she immediately got out of her chair and left the room.

"Was that totally necessary Connelly?" asked Sir Alex, clearly himself shaken by the images.

"I believe it was sir," replied Connelly, "I thought it was necessary to make it specifically clear to everyone present that this evidence was not contrived or falsely planted or in any way presented for the purpose of a false accusation or a witch hunt. The discovery of this evidence was witnessed by officers and confirmed in writing, throughout their investigation.   In addition, the procedures inside the house were videoed by one of the officer's present and that video has also been logged and entered as evidence. I will add that not all of the evidence, tapes, DVDs and CDs have been viewed yet and will be part of the ongoing investigation."

Sir Alex looked around the room before speaking. "Is there anything else you wish to say or show us before we conclude this meeting Connelly?"

"Yes sir, there is. We believe that the camera used to film the desk, MacBook and the note with the password were placed in the office by the killer or killers for our benefit." Spencer nudged Connelly's arm and pulled him towards him.

"Is there something that officer wishes to say, if so stand up so we can all hear it." Sir Alex sat forward in his chair.

Connelly frowned at Spencer.

"I told you to keep your mouth shut," whispered Connelly out of the side of his mouth.

Despite the obvious hostility Spencer stood up and spoke.

"I do apologise to DCI Connelly sir, but some new information came to light just prior to this meeting and I've not had an opportunity to tell Chief Connelly sir."

"Out with it then," said Sir Alex impatiently.

"We just found out this morning that Judge Ryder was the presiding judge in the successful appeal made by council representing Bishop Julian Borthridge, who was shot last week in his cottage in the Cotswolds sir. The charges were that of sexual penetration of a minor and other charges of a sexual and perverted nature sir."

Sir Alex stood, "Meeting closed," turning to AC Hatchett. "I want a lid kept on this Hatchett. No media, no journalists. Understand?"

Hatchett gathered his paperwork. "Absolutely sir."

Sir Alex turned to Connelly and Spencer. "I want you two in my office now." He turned to AC Larkin and Cdr McIntyre. "You two as well."

10

The four officers gathered in Sir Alex's office. Larkin and McIntyre sat in the two available chairs leaving Connelly and Spencer to stand. Sir Alex leaned back in his chair.

"This is going to get messy. I can't see any way out of that." Sir Alex rolled forward and put his head briefly in his hands. "Am I to believe that there's a serial killer of some kind?"

Connelly replied first. "I think it's too early to say sir. It's now looking like we have two connected murders, so we'll continue our enquiries with that in mind. I might add, following Spencer's comments, during the past twelve months, as in previous years, there have been around sixty unsolved murders around the country. I think we need to take a closer look at some of those crimes."

"Horace, McIntyre. Comments?" Sir Alex opened his hands.

Larkin answered as McIntyre sat motionless. "I agree with DCI Connelly sir, we need to broaden our scope and continue enquiries per standard procedures as with any other investigation."

Sir Alex leant forward with a degree of frustration. "But it's not just another investigation, is it?" He continued without waiting for a reply. "We'll need to mitigate the issues with the media at some stage. When they get hold of this child molestation business all hell's going to break loose and there are the other persons of interest in the videos and images that we'll have to deal with."

McIntyre saw his opportunity to get involved. "Sir, with such a complex case it would necessitate an appointment of a task force to deal with the various streams of enquiries, and."

Sir Alex interjected. "That's exactly what we won't do McIntyre. The whole house would come down on us like a ton of bricks. Setting up a task force would bring the pollies and the media all over us like swarming ants."

Connelly gave Spencer a kick under the table and a look that could kill. Spencer considered it a warning to keep quiet.

"Might I make a suggestion Commissioner?"

"Go ahead Connelly," replied Sir Alex.

"I understand Commander McIntyre's suggestion and under different circumstances I would agree. Perhaps a smaller group reporting directly to you sir. Those present together with a few specialists in this type of crime," offered Connelly.

Larkin and McIntyre exchanged looks with what could best be described as half nods, hoping for a pathway through the impending impasse.

"And what specialists are you referring to?" asked Sir Alex.

Knowing full well that he was overstepping the mark and quietly incurring the wrath of his immediate supervisors Connelly continued. "Well sir, we should include a profiler. One of the consultants we have used on previous complex cases would be appropriate. I would also like another person with whom I have worked on occasions over the years, Nicholas Hood."

"Who is this Hood fellow, Connelly, I've never heard of him?" questioned Sir Alex.

Connelly tilted his head to one side. "He," hesitating a little, "he works rather anonymously most of the time sir. He has at times worked for us, some years back, also MI5 and 6, holds a commission in the Royal Navy as a Commander—."

Sir Alex jumped in as Larkin and McIntyre turned in their seats scowling. "Look here Connelly, are you suggesting we use a damn spy? This is the Met, Connelly. We're policemen, not some spy circus. No. We have our own specialists. The media will have us for breakfast".

Having gone in far too deep already Connelly persisted. "That's exactly my point sir. We need someone who moves in the shadows, sir. We may even be dealing with a killer or killers with military experience. Hood worked for Navy Intelligence when I first met him. He knows how to gather evidence without being obvious. He can be as elusive as the people we're chasing, and he's as sharp as a tack. He's been in this business as long as you and I have sir, and that has to mean something." Connelly thought that appealing to Sir Alex's longevity in the force might do the trick.

"I'll tell you what Connelly, I'll make a few calls. Not that I doubt you." Sir Alex fixed his gaze over the top of his reading glasses to Larkin and McIntyre which they saw as their queue to nod. "Well, let's call it quits for now. Horace, I'll be in touch with you after I've made those calls. Thank you, gentlemen."

Sir Alex rose out of his seat, grabbed his papers and walked to his adjacent office.

Larkin turned to Connelly and Spencer. "Well Connelly, you did your best to make me, and the Commander, look like a couple of Toby Jugs. This had better work, and if it blows up, the shit will come down on you. For goodness's sake Connelly, it's not long before your pension and you could have left on a high note."

"I'm hoping that won't be the case sir."

"Well, you can hope all you want man, I thought you were better than this. A fucking spy of all things. I'm actually looking forward to meeting this Mr Hood."

"Commander Hood, sir," offered Connelly.

"He could be Admiral fucking Hood for all I care. Make it work Connelly. Anyway, the Commissioner may knock it on the head after he makes some calls." Larkin and McIntyre shuffled out leaving Connelly and Spencer alone in the room. Very alone.

"That went well," said Spencer.

Connelly walked out. "My cubicle, now."

11

Admiral Sir Adrian Nightingale had just finished briefing the Foreign Secretary as he made his way to his armoured, chauffeur driven, Range Rover Sentinel outside the King Charles Street Whitehall building. The trip back to his office via Millbank was a little over a mile and with no traffic hassles would take about five minutes. He settled into the back seat as his private phone rang.

"Adrian, it's Alex, how are you old chap." Sir Adrian Nightingale and Sir Alex Connaught-Sinclair, whilst not close friends did however meet regularly at White's, the club on St James St. They would also bump into each other at official events although Sir Adrian loathed public officialdom.

"Alex, yes I'm fine. Is this official, do I have to scramble?" asked Sir Adrian.

"Might be best I think, I have a couple of questions."

"OK Alex, I'll call you back on the secure phone."

Sir Alex picked up the return phone call.

"Alex, Adrian again, what's up?"

Sir Alex shuffled the papers on his desk until he found his scribblings from the recent meeting.

"We're working on a case Adrian, and one of our officers suggested a fellow that has worked or is working for you. Nicholas Hood. I was wondering if you could comment old chap?"

The silence was deafening. After a few seconds Sir Adrian answered.

"Alex, we have a policy of not commenting on the subject of who does or does not work for us. That's all I can say I'm afraid." There was a coldness in Sir Adrian's reply.

"I had an idea you might say that, but thanks anyway Adrian."

"Sorry old boy, by the way I'll be calling in to White's for a sherry on the way home. Perhaps you could join me, say six-thirty?" Adrian anticipated the reply.

"Why yes, I could do that. See you then." Sir Alex hung the phone up and frowned. "Damn," he muttered under his breath.

Sir Adrian pocketed his secure mobile phone, scribbled a few lines on his notepad and gazed out to his left as they cruised down Millbank towards the Vauxhall Building.

Whites was moderately busy for a Monday evening as diplomats, politicians and senior bureaucrats chatted over their 'after-work before heading home' drinks. Many of them lived close by in the stately townhouses and apartments of Belgravia, St James, Mayfair and other inner-city suburbs during the week, but on weekends migrated to affluent leafy suburbs further afield or private estates outside the M25.

Sir Alex settled into a cushioned wing-back leather chair and ordered a cream sherry grabbing a copy of the Times, scanning the back page in preference to whatever the front-page headline had to offer.

Sir Adrian swiftly acquired an adjacent chair and outstretched his arm. "Good to see you again Alex." The two shook hands firmly as the waiter approached with Sir Alex's sherry. "I'll have one of those as well thank you."

"Sorry about our conversation earlier today," Adrian hoped his sincerity came across as intended, "but we're pretty tight when it comes to declaring who our operatives are."

Alex nodded in acknowledgement. "Yes, old chap, understand."

Adrian continued. "But if there was such a chap, and I'm not saying there is, mind you, he could be like another chap I know. Exceptionally good at his job, likes to act independently, doesn't suffer fools lightly," Adrian paused and leant closer to Alex, raised his eyebrows and lifted his chin, causing his bottom lip to curl over. "Conversation can be a little colourful at times if provoked, but the, er, type of chap you would prefer to have on your side rather than against you. Now I must be off," Adrian grabbed the sherry as it arrived and gulped it down and extended his hand.

Alex stood, grabbed his hand and shook it firmly. "Thanks, old man. One more thing before you go. If you were me and a chap like that turned up, would you use him?"

"Absolutely." Adrian smiled, turned and walked out of the room.

Alex relaxed back into his chair and summoned the waiter. "I'll have another one of those."

12

Eight people were seated in the rooftop conference room. The Commissioner Sir Alex Connaught-Sinclair, Deputy Commissioner Celia Graham, Assistant Commissioner Horace Larkin, Assistant Commissioner Ron Hatchett, Commander Gerald McIntyre, Detective Chief Inspector Nigel Connelly, Detective Sergeant Chris Spencer and Forensic Psychologist Dr. Stella Wilde; there remained one empty chair as Sir Alex opened the meeting.

"Good morning. I see we have one vacant chair. Could someone elaborate please?" Sir Alex drifted his gaze around the table.

DCI Connelly leaned forward. "The vacant chair is for Commander Hood, sir."

"And where is Commander Hood?" asked the Commissioner.

"I'm right here Commissioner," the door to the conference room burst open as Nicholas Hood moved towards the vacant seat. "Terribly sorry if I'm a little late. The traffic was frightful, taxi got held up, accident near Marble Arch."

All eyes were on Nicholas Hood as he entered the room and took his seat. Although in his mid-sixties, Nicholas had the demeanour of a man much younger. Tall, straight back, tailored Saville Row suit and Magnanni shoes. An obviously athletic build hardened by regular exercise. A full head of short- cropped salt and pepper hair, silver at the temples and neck. Steely blue eyes that scanned the room, missing nothing and analysing all. The two females in the room maintained their gaze: one with an icy stare, the other with quiet contemplation.

Connelly gave Nicholas a subtle nod that was returned with a smile.

The Commissioner continued without personally acknowledging the late arrival. "I'll start by reminding those present about the absolute confidentiality of this meeting and of the subject matter. Is that clear?"

The attendees all nodded as if by turn with Nicholas simply smiling as the Commissioner looked directly at each person. Resisting the urge to extract a more decisive acknowledgement from Nicholas, Sir Alex pressed on.

"It's been my decision that instead of a full-on task force, we'll persist initially with a small working group. I understand at this point in time that we're breaking away from protocol." Pausing, "For the time being I want the results of any investigations linking the recent murders of Judge Ryder and Bishop Borthridge, and any other previous or subsequent incidents to be contained within this room."

Deputy Commissioner Graham was about to speak but Sir Alex held up his hand and motioned to his Deputy. "You and I will have a chat about the changes to procedure after this meeting Celia." This seemed to shut down the Deputy for the moment however she was far from impressed and for some reason directed her contempt towards Connelly and Hood.

"Connelly and Spencer together with Commander Hood will be at the sharp end of the investigation with assistance from Dr Wilde regarding any profiling and forensic assistance required. AC Larkin and Commander McIntyre will oversee the working group and report directly to me." Turning to the Corporate Services Manager. "Once again Ron, not one word of this is to reach the media. As far as anyone outside this room is concerned, we're conducting a normal, run of the mill, investigation. If you hear any scuttlebutt here, or anywhere in the force, you shut it down. Right?"

"Right sir." Hatchett was left in no doubt at all as to where his responsibilities lay.

Sir Alex turned his attention to Commander Hood. "Thanks for your attendance, Commander. I'll leave you to liaise, as required, with the members of this group. I will, however, ask that you respect our chain of command and for the purpose of this exercise you rank alongside DCI Connelly. That may have sounded like a question Commander Hood, it was, however, a statement. Good day to you all." Sir Alex rose and left the room quickly followed by Celia Graham. At the door to the conference room Sir Alex stopped and turned to the DCI. "Connelly, I'll probably need the MacBook and other evidence at some stage. I'll have to speak with the Home Secretary before too long. Perhaps you could supply me with a list of names of those people that can be identified in the videos and images. That's all."

Raised voices could be heard from outside the conference room between Sir Alex and his deputy, as Larkin called his work group together.

"Best we leave this room now. Meet me in my office in thirty minutes. Gerald, with me." Larkin, with McIntyre in tow, left the conference room and hurried down the stairs.

Connelly spoke to the remainder. "I'd normally suggest a quick coffee in the canteen, but that might be too public. Spencer, organise some coffees in my little alcove."

"Right Guv. Where's a constable when you need one?" Spencer shuffled off to the canteen for coffees. "I hope you all like NATO standard, white with two?"

Wilde called out, "Herbal tea for me."

Hood followed, "If it's not too much trouble, black, no sugar."

Connelly smiled. Spencer turned expressionless. The three entered the lift, down two floors.

Exiting the lift they proceeded across the open plan area towards Connelly's space. Not really an office, in fact a screened corner of the general office floor.

"It's been a while, Nick. We've had some changes in recent years. Our toilets are just as colourful as our cars," smirked Connelly.

"That's comforting Nigel, so having a shit and getting arrested have more in common than we thought."

Stella Wilde smiled at the dialogue as they turned into Connelly's area. After working with the Metropolitan police force for a few years as a psychologist and profiler, the vernacular of men and women in blue was grist for the mill, in her view. Her conservative demeanour, plain, almost dowdy sense of dress shielded a different persona away from work where she pursued her daily routines in a local gym combined with her love of pole dancing.

"Sit down. Spencer can find an extra chair when he gets here." Connelly ushered his guests into his modest cubby with a not so modest view. "Quite frankly I'd prefer a back room with no windows. I'm an old-fashioned copper. I prefer to be out and about or in my own dingy office. Mind you, we're all encouraged to get out of the office and communicate profusely on electronic gadgets. Emails instead of a knock on the door, texting between units in the field and there's been no reduction in paperwork as they said there would. Look at my desk." The computer took centre stage on the desk however the remainder of the space was cluttered with bundles of paper with stacks of files scattered around the office floor.

"Do you ever see a solicitor, or a barrister, walk into a court or an interview room armed with just a smartphone?" Connelly eyeballed Nicholas and Stella, "No you don't. As much as our new generation of bureaucratic senior cops tell us to 'get with it', the fact is our legal system is still built on reams of A4 and foolscap."

The coffees and herbal tea arrived. Spencer telepathically fetched himself a chair from an adjacent station.

"You were a bit quiet at the meeting Nick?" asked Connelly as he settled into his chair.

"Nothing to say at this stage, Nigel. But don't worry, when the time comes, I'll speak my mind," Nick smiled as he took a sip of the black brew, a little surprised at the colourful mug with the Met logo. "Really into branding these days aren't we."

"Yes," said Connelly, "Glad you like the livery, and I can't wait for your contributions."

Stella smiled as she crossed her legs. Nick had been watching her body language since arriving, but not as closely as Chris Spencer, he observed. Nick was eager to get her input once the group moved to examining the evidence. There was more to this woman than just her 'thirty-something' professional façade. In Nick's view she had already assessed each one in the group, just as he was doing. His assessment was, however, far from complete.

He knew Connelly from years ago. They first met when Nick was a young Lieutenant with Navy Intelligence in the early 80s and Nigel was a bobby on the beat based at the older Scotland Yard on Broadway. There had been a discreet number of cases, over the years, that had brought the two together in some form of collaboration, during which the level of mutual respect had grown. Spencer, although young and newly promoted to Detective Sergeant carried himself well.

"So, you two chaps have known each other for some time?" Spencer questioned the two older men.

Connelly answered first, "Yes we have Spencer, Nick and I go back a long way."

Nicholas nodded. "Yes, a long way, and yet here we are again. Before we go into this next meeting Nigel could I ask a favour?"

"Well, that does depend," replied Connelly.

"Nothing too drastic. I wondered if I could borrow Spencer for a few days. I'd like him to do some research." Nick gulped down the remainder of his coffee.

"Can I ask what research?" Connelly enquired.

"I need someone who has access to records. Recent unsolved murder cases in the UK, say from the past twelve months." Nick looked Connelly in the eye. At the same time watching Stella Wilde's expressions.

"Can't see why not." Connelly turned to Spencer. "Spencer, you'll spend the rest of the week with Commander Hood."

Spencer nodded.

Nicholas turned to Stella. "Dr Wilde, can I call you Stella?" without waiting for a reply as Stella shuffled in her seat. "After Spencer checks out the records, I'd like you to go over those records with him. Would you be amenable to that arrangement?"

"Well, yes but aren't we getting ahead of ourselves. AC Larkin and Commander McIntyre may have different plans." Stella straightened her skirt as she moved forward towards Nick.

Nick stood up. "I wouldn't worry about that Doctor," Nick paused, "er, Stella."

13

The furniture in Larkin's office, up one floor, had been rearranged to allow for the extra seats. To Nick's surprise even Spencer was afforded a chair. The group were seated in a rough circle with Larkin and McIntyre together and the others spaced out. A low occasional table was in the centre of the circle where Larkin had placed some files. The others sat with a notepad on their laps. Nick sat relaxed with his legs crossed, a notepad obviously absent.

"Commander Hood, I see you don't intend to take notes." Larkin's acid tone did not escape anyone.

Connelly shuffled slightly, as did Stella. Spencer's mouth dropped open with McIntyre motionless.

"That's correct," replied Nick, straight-faced.

"We have a fair amount to go through Commander."

"I'm sure you have Mr Larkin."

Larkin interjected, "That's Assistant Commissioner Larkin, not Mr."

"As you wish." Nick paused, "I have a photographic memory and one hundred percent recall so I suggest you continue with the meeting so we can get out of here and get some work done." Nick changed the position of his legs and pretended to brush some lint from his grey suit.

Stella struggled to control a chuckle as Connelly put his head in his hands. Spencer's mouth remained open, and all McIntyre could do was look at the colour of Larkin's face go from bright red to purple.

The silence was deafening. Connelly decided to break the ice.

"If I may sir," Connelly spoke directly to Larkin who was struggling to contain his anger. The colour in Larkin's face started to fade as he adjusted his gaze. Connelly continued without waiting for permission.

"Perhaps, myself and Spencer should get Commander Hood and Dr Wilde up to speed with the two cases that brought us here today. I would also suggest that I take Commander Hood to the crime scenes. Commander Hood has also expressed interest in any recently unsolved murder cases and DS Spencer would be able to do any research required. Would that be appropriate at this point sir?"

Larkin was still bristling with anger as he regained his composure. "Yes Connelly, initially, that would seem to be the best course of action." Turning towards a tentative McIntyre. "I suggest we meet again in 7 days, unless there are any serious developments."

Larkin collected his papers and rose in his chair "By the way, and to add insult to injury, I've had a call from the NCA. They've taken an interest in these two murders and from experience I fully expect them to appoint one of their own to head this investigation. This group will only be temporary. Apparently, they know something we don't. Well at this stage anyway." Larkin turned to McIntyre, "Carry on Commander, and Connelly, how's that list going?"

"Still working on it, sir."

"Well, I don't have much time before Sir Alex has to front the Home Secretary. We can't keep this under wraps for too much longer. The Secretary will want to see the Prime Minister as soon as he sees it. Get me a list of names by Wednesday 9am at the latest, understood?"

"Yes sir," replied Connelly in a sweat.

"Right," said McIntyre, "we'll see you next Monday, meeting closed. I'll send an agenda later in the week, and

Connelly, there's a chain of fucking command you know. Give the list to me and I'll pass it on".

The four left the room.

"That went well," uttered Spencer.

"Very well, I think," said Nick, "But I'm not so sure about the NCA. They have their own investigation teams and maybe there's more to this judge murder than we currently know. As for the fucking chain of command, I don't like the idea of too many people seeing that list."

"By the way sir," ventured Spencer, "do you really have a photographic memory and one hundred percent recall?"

"Of course not," smirked Nick, "but they think I do."

"I was going to ask you about the journalist in the courtyard near the main entrance?" asked Spencer.

"The redhead?"

"Yes."

"How do you know she's a journalist, Spencer?"

"Just a hunch, cigarette, notepad, untidy dress."

"Well, she's not a television journalist," remarked Nick, "not dressed well enough, hair isn't groomed, and don't the TV channels only use glammed up tarts?"

"Really," stammered Stella, "that's such a chauvinistic, insulting statement."

"Yes, it probably is," Nick replied, "but that doesn't make it a false statement. So, what's your opinion Doctor?"

Stella gazed through the window at the figure below. "I'd say there's a good chance she's a journalist so we might assume that for the moment. Is that a problem?"

Nick considered that the question was directed at him. "It depends on what she's fishing for. When we leave, we leave separately. If she approaches, politely tell her to fuck off. If she has a contact in the force, she won't be waiting out the front for them. She'd be meeting them in a pub somewhere."

"We have our own media department that looks after these people anyway, just point her to the main entrance and she can speak to one of Hatchett's people," offered Connelly.

The four left the building separately as agreed, the last was Nick. He was halfway across the courtyard when the lady with the red hair approached him.

"Commander Hood, I'm Emily Chancer from the Daily Mail can I have a chat please?"

Nicholas stopped, surprised that she had approached him by name. "There's a media department in that building Miss Chancer, it is Miss?"

"Yes, it is Miss and I know, I've already spoken to the media officer, but you're not with the police, are you?"

"No, I'm not Miss Chancer but I have an old friend who is, and I was catching up with him, not that it's any of your business." *What's her game?* thought Nick.

"I'm surprised you didn't just meet up with him in a pub Commander?"

"I'm surprised you didn't meet up with whoever your contacts are in a pub Miss Chancer. Maybe nobody wants to talk to you." Nick kept walking towards the Victorian Embankment.

Emily ran past Nick and jumped in front of him. "Something is going on, isn't it? Those murders are linked. I checked, and the Judge presided over the trial of the Bishop and got him his parole."

Nick stopped. "Look Miss Chancer. Emily. You'll have to ask a representative of the police force about any police matters. I don't work for the police, never have done, never will. I suggest your time would be better spent going through the proper channels."

"Are you still employed by British Intelligence Commander?"

"What has that got to do with anything and right now you're standing on very dangerous ground Emily."

"No, I'm not, I'm standing on the corner of Richmond Terrace and the Victorian Embankment."

"You know exactly what I'm talking about Emily. Don't be a fucking smart arse."

"I could report you for using offensive language Commander."

"I don't give a fuck Emily, and who do you think you're going to report it to."

"I could try MI6, the Foreign Office, The Police Commissioner or I could call the Mayor."

"What the fuck is wrong with you. I could make a phone call as well, and just maybe you'll end up writing obituaries for the Sacred Gardens Crematorium."

"Can we start again?" asked Emily, smiling.

"We haven't started Emily, go away." Nick hurriedly crossed the Terrace leaving Emily standing on the kerb, stamping her feet.

14

Spencer, as a matter of urgency, was given the job of trying to identify as many people as possible in the videos and images on the MacBook. The DVDs and VHS were given a low priority and were probably dated. Meanwhile Connelly and Hood ventured into the Oxfordshire and Gloucestershire countryside to examine the crime scenes of Bishop Borthridge and Judge Ryder. The stations at Oxford and Cheltenham were informed, where it was confirmed that both crime scenes still had a constable in attendance 24/7.

The drive from London into the country gave the two seasoned veterans an opportunity to catch up after some years.

Nick initiated the conversation. "Did you get accosted by that redhead Nigel?"

"No, I walked straight past her. She didn't even blink."

"I think she was waiting for me."

"Why would that be Nick? How would she know who you were?"

"I don't know," Nick paused, "so, tell me Nigel, why exactly did you call me in? You guys are perfectly capable of murder investigations. You've certainly had plenty of experience."

Connelly concentrated on his driving for a minute or so before answering. "The fact is Nick, and I didn't want to stick my neck out in front of the AC, these last two murders look like professional hits."

Nick responded, "Still, you guys have a serious crime unit for that sort of stuff."

"Yes, we do," Connelly paused as he overtook another vehicle, "I have a feeling, call it a copper's gut if you like, we might be dealing with someone with military experience."

"Why do you say that?"

"You'll see when we visit the crime scenes. Not the easiest of shots on the Bishop, and whoever killed the Judge must have been cool and very collected." Connelly settled into the outside lane. "If I didn't know better, it could be the sort of stuff you guys get involved in."

"You've been watching too many movies Nigel. We don't do that kind of stuff." Nick shrugged off the inference.

"You know exactly what I'm talking about Nick. There are people trained to do this stuff. I'm not saying your associates have anything to do with it, but the fact is we know they're out there." Connelly paused again. "The other thing is that in both murders, in my view, the killer is likely to have used weapons that both the military and police would have in their arsenal."

Nick shifted in his seat and made the seatbelt more comfortable. "So, not just a sociable get together then? Look Nigel, a lot of hardware is on the black market, the dark web. People don't just go out and buy them over the counter. Not in UK, maybe the USA, but not here. If the perpetrators are foreign, they certainly wouldn't bring weapons in their cabin baggage. The sources for professionals are endless."

"You're probably the only one I know who can investigate this quietly without causing a fuss or making any waves." Connelly continued, "even the amateurs can pick a copper snooping around, and besides, we also have a duty of disclosure. The days are gone when we could smack 'em in the head until they squeal or stick a baton in their mouth. I'm limited in my techniques but you're not."

"Oh, I see." Nick smiled, "I don't do much of that these days Nigel, but I get your point. How's life in the new building?"

"New building, new structures." Nigel half looked to his left, keeping an eye on the road. "I'm an old-fashioned copper. I used to have an office. I like having an office. Now it's open plan. I have a cosy corner with a view. I like my pencil and paper, now I have an iPad. It's changing and the flavour's gone out of it. I know the crooks are getting more sophisticated, but I still believe in old fashioned policing."

Nick nodded as Nigel continued.

"Coppers are spending too much time on computers, and we're like meat in a sandwich with all this political correctness. Every corner you turn some bastard gets offended and then some senior constable with a hat full of scrambled egg tells everyone to take a pill and go to therapy if you can't handle the heat." Nigel took a deep breath. "I liked it much better when, if you got a bit of lip, you gave 'em a smack and threw them into the clink for the night. Can't do it anymore."

Nick considered his friends comments. "It's a changing world Nigel. I know that sounds cliché, especially coming from someone you call a spy. Basically, and this is how I see it, the crimes are still the same crimes, murder, fraud, extortion, sexual assault, whatever. The categories haven't changed, but the means by which they're carried out, well they have changed. That doesn't mean there's not still a role for old fashioned police work. There is, but if the MO of crimes change then so too must the MO of policing and investigation. I see where you're going, and perhaps we're seeing too much bureaucracy and top-heavy administration. Too many officers more concerned with climbing the ladder, heavy on theory but light on street cred."

"There used to be a time," Nigel continued, "when what went on in the Yard was strictly police business. Now it's all over the internet. Just log onto the Met website. Most of our investigating procedures laid out, organisational structure, floor plan of the new building. For fuck's sake, it a bloody joke.

Now we're recruiting constables, with a degree, straight out of initial training as detective constables. No regular police experience required except basic training. Some of the smartest detectives I've known never even contemplated getting a degree. They'll be getting their warrant cards in cornflake packets next. Spencer did his time in uniform and even though he's young he got street smart very quickly."

The two continued in silence for a while until Nick spoke. "OK, let's see what these crime scenes tell us. How far to our first call?"

Connelly replied, "We're doing the Bishop's cottage first then back to Abingdon. The DCS at Cheltenham was quite chummy and happy to hand the case over. Absolutely no leads. As I said, a clean hit."

15

There's something quite tranquil about thatched cottages nestled in tree clad valleys. A meandering brook of filtered spring water close by with the odd rainbow trout rising to take a midge or damsel fly. The cottage gardens of flowering perennials and seasonal herbs creating its own bouquet of natural remedies. Then to be presented with a blood-spattered room, like some grotesque scene from a horror movie, was almost comically repulsive. Such a startling contradiction with the tapestry of nature just a few feet from the front door.

Nick didn't flinch when he entered the room. Almost mechanically he walked around, firstly executing a three-hundred and sixty-degree panorama, then moving back to the doorway. He glanced up at the ceiling almost admiring the pattern of blood spray on the pressed metal plafond. After this preliminary perspective, he moved to the view across the cottage garden, closely inspecting the aspect from the window before speaking.

"Nigel, was there any ballistic information in the forensic report?"

"Let me check the iPad Nick. I hate that fucking thing. Cheltenham was emailing me the complete report."

Connelly left the cottage and walked back to the car, grabbing his briefcase. Opening the case, he pulled out the tablet and logged on.

Inside the cottage Nick was standing behind the bloodstained wing back chair. He crouched down against the back, picking up the smell of the iron in the blood. Closing his left eye, he squinted so the top corner of the chair, where the Bishop's head had been, was lined up with the open window. He focused on the window space which then gave him a rectangular portrait of the grassy hill beyond.

Connelly came back into the room. "Says here a medium calibre projectile, possibly .338. Projectile not found."

Nick nodded and moved to the window.

Connelly scrolled down. "The fatal wound was caused by a high velocity projectile consistent with, but not exclusive to, .338 calibre."

"Yes, I agree Nigel. We need to find that bullet and I think I know where it is." Nick walked back to the wing back chair.

"Let's look at the entry wound."

Connelly opened the images file on the report.

"Yes," pointed out Nick, "see the wound, clean entry point. I would think a jacketed hollow point or expanding type that opens-up inside the target. It hits the bone, and all hell breaks loose as the projectile rattles around the inside of his head in microseconds. This would mean that the projectile line becomes diverted as the side of the chap's head tears away from the rest of it. Death is instant, he didn't feel a thing."

"That would be very comforting for the victim, I'm sure. So, where's the bullet Nick?"

"I love these old antiques; they're made so well. Solid timber frames and heavy tapestry fabrics. Not like modern crap. This one's antique mahogany. Imported from America, part of the chinaberry family."

Grabbing a butter knife from the chiffonier, Nick scraped away some of the hard, crusted blood around the edge of the fabric where the studs fasten the fabric to the frame. His finger pushed through a small tear in the fabric and probed into the coir filled cavity.

"There was so much congealed blood covering the top of the chair I'm not surprised that the person inspecting the scene didn't remove it all. It would've been a jelly-like mass and disguising any holes in the fabric." Still feeling around, he felt something solid. "Got it."

Nick extracted his finger and thumb holding a misshapen bullet. "Yes," he said with satisfaction, "we now know the calibre and the location of the killer when he pulled the trigger."

"We do?" ventured Connelly.

"Yes, my friend, we do," smiled Nick, "let's take a walk."

Nick led the way up the side of the hill looking left and right as they made their way.

"You know Nigel," Nick stopped and turned to look down at the cottage. "If you want to stay on this investigation or should I say we, it might be pertinent to keep some aces up our sleeve."

"That could get us in a bit of trouble Nick. Withholding evidence, and there goes my pension."

"No, nothing like that. You and I have been on a few unusual cases over the years. I'm just saying that we keep our conclusions and opinions to ourselves for the moment. We ensure we disclose any tangible evidence and make sure we dot the i's and cross the t's. That's all." Nick looked at Nigel for a response.

"Seems fair Nick. I do get a bit prickly when someone from the top floor takes the kudos from my hard yards. Not this time, eh?"

"No, not this time."

The two continued up the grassy slope until the hill plateaued out with a scattering of wild blackberry and hawthorn bushes. From this position there was a 360-degree vista. A clear and uninterrupted view for at least five hundred yards in all directions.

"What would you estimate the distance to the Bishop's chair from here?" asked Nick as he crouched on the grass.

Nigel squatted next to Nick and squinted to focus on the midday light. "Around eight hundred yards."

"Pretty close. I would put it at seven hundred metres, so seven hundred and sixty-five yards would do it." Nick lay down on the ground facing the cottage holding his arms in a rifle holding embrace. "Yes, this is the spot."

"How do you know exactly?"

"It's where I would take the shot."

Nick and Nigel scoured the area for clues.

"I'm not expecting to find anything tangible." Nick bent down on one knee, "but look here."

There were two small indentations in the ground under the grassy cover, about forty centimetres apart.

"I'd say he used a pic-rail bipod here, probably a ground sheet to lay down on." Nick ran his hands over the grass. "A big chap I'd say, quite heavy. There's a couple of dents in the damp soil where he came down on his knees. The ground must have been quite wet at the time."

"Looking very professional," stated Nigel. "Military?"

"Hard to say old chap," Nick got to his feet, "So many gun clubs these days, competition standards are high. Just look at the Olympics, any number of sharp shooters could have taken that shot."

"But not if it's a kill shot," offered Nigel, "very different when you take a life?"

"True," replied Nick, "it takes training and an icy cold state of mind to plan and execute a murder."

They walked down the hill and thanked the duty constable before driving to the judge's house near Abingdon.

"Nigel, there was no phone, television or computer in the house. If he were having an emergency, how would he contact anyone?"

"Might have been a condition of his release. Perhaps he used those devices in the perpetration of his crimes. Besides, who gives a damn what happens to the pervert."

"Mobile phone?" enquired Nick.

"Prohibited probably," replied Nigel.

"Was he wearing an ankle bracelet?" asked Nick.

"Yes," replied Nigel, "It was a condition of his parole."

"Well at least the judge got that bit right. Just a thought Nigel. It's almost as if the Bishop was a sitting duck."

16

The drive to the judge's house near Abingdon took about an hour and a half with a bit of traffic on the A419. As expected, there was a constable on duty inside the gates who was happy to have some company in the damp, misty country house.

"Bit spooky here, guv, I don't mind sayin'," uttered the constable as he closed the gate.

"Bit superstitious, are you?" laughed Connelly.

"OK during the day guv, no chance of falling asleep at night though, jumping at my own shadow." The constable stood beside the front door, "shall I just wait here then sir?"

"Yes constable, how long is your shift?"

"Hoping to get away by 5pm Guv. Missis cooks up lamb casserole on Wednesdays," replied the constable with perceived excitement.

"Lucky you," chuckled Connelly. "I'll get bangers and mash and then only if I cook it myself."

Once again Nick's eyes darted around the house as they walked towards the study. "Where's the car Nigel?"

"As far as I know forensics have it over at Lambeth, but any results would be in the report. Why?"

"We might take a look at the vehicle, at some stage." Nick continued his reconnoitre.

Connelly followed Nick as he perused the office. "I'll be leaving the officers on duty for the time being Nick. If the NCA are getting involved they may want to inspect the crime scenes and we'll have to hand over the evidence."

"Might be a good idea to have the images showing other persons of interest copied and tucked away for a rainy day." Nick turned to Nigel, "what do you think?"

"I'll call Spencer now and get him onto it." Connelly felt for his phone.

"He's looks like a smart young fellow, that Spencer?" offered Nick.

"Yes, he is," replied Nigel with a smirk, "hasn't been shaving that long either."

While Connelly made the call, Nick shuffled around the office. Carefully avoiding the areas smudged with the dusting powder. Connelly approached Nick as he finished his phone call with Spencer. Pointing to the curtain rail, Nigel drew Nick's attention to the location of the camera.

"There was a mini camera positioned behind the curtain rail, up there, Nick. It was focussed on the desk area and the memory card in the camera had some disturbing images. It clearly showed the judge logging on and logging off. Some of the videos showed him jerking off on some of the videos. The password was written on a piece of paper also on the desk." Nigel paused while Nick appeared to be taking it all in. "It appeared to us that the killer or killers made sure there was compounding evidence against the judge."

Nick turned towards the bay window. "Interesting Nigel, "it's almost as if the killer is on the case with us," pausing, "but chose to be judge and jury as well."

"What about the security system? Any cameras around the house or recorded material?"

"I'll have to get Spencer onto that. He was the investigating officer, but we can have a look around while we're here." Nigel made his way to the front door.

Nick and Nigel walked around the house noting there were four external cameras. Walking back to the house Nick examined the security system control unit and called out to the attending constable in the front porch. "Constable, were you here with DS Spencer when he did his initial inspection of the house?"

Constable Jim Hargreaves leaned in through the front door. "Yes sir."

"Do you know where the recording device is for the security cameras?"

"Yes sir, it was under the stairs. Fred Majors pulled it out and took it away as evidence when he was doing the forensics."

"Thanks Constable."

"It should be with the other evidence at Abingdon," offered Nigel, "unless Spencer has brought it to the Met."

"Make sure we make a copy of that as well Nigel, and I'd like to see any vehicle or pedestrian movements in or around the house leading up to the murder."

17

Nick and Nigel stopped for a pint and a counter lunch on the way back to the Met. It was Nick's suggestion that they call into The Hind's Head at Bray just off the M4 and pretty much enroute. Originally a hunting lodge and coaching inn dating back to the 1400s, the cosy and opulent surroundings provided an element of privacy within the leather padded alcoves. Now a Michelin-starred restaurant offering a premium menu, designed by a celebrity chef, it certainly fitted Nick's bill but not so much for a twice divorced copper approaching retirement.

"I'm glad you're fetching the bill on this one Nick my old chum. Bit posh for Mr Plod," Nigel chuckled as he slid across the deeply buttoned couch to the corner where he stretched his legs out admiring the surroundings. "Very impressive my old China, love the couches, come here often?" in a comedic cockney intonation.

"As a matter of fact, I have been here before. I'm glad you like the couches. Lord Stanhope will be frightfully grateful that you approve." Nick perused the menu and passed one over to Nigel, reclining even further back into the sumptuous leather.

"Who?" asked Nigel.

"Lord Stanhope, old chap, the Fourth Earl of Chesterfield. You see he wanted a sofa style design where a gentleman, such as yourself, could sit comfortably without creasing one's suit." Nick studied Nigel's wrinkled suit, creased tie and crumpled gabardine mac.

"You don't say. Well, give him my regards Nick, when you see him."

"That would be a tad difficult considering he died in 1773 and I've no plans to visit him anytime soon." The two of them burst out laughing as the waiter approached.

"We'll have two pints of your best while we consider the order, thanks waiter." Nick's affable nature had the ability to put everyone at ease whether they be noble, proletariat, detective inspectors or waiters.

The two spent the next couple of hours going over the possible scenarios and motives with the two recent murders. Each one contributing from many years of experience in the field and at times reflecting on some notable cases they'd been able to work on jointly.

"You know Nick, that first time we met, remember that incident near the Tower Bridge where you jumped in and saved that young boy. I was just a bobby then and from memory you, a newly promoted lieutenant from Australia."

"A long time ago. That was also the first time I met Dianne."

"Last time we touched base she was at St Thomas's." Nigel paused while he masticated a tender piece of eye filet.

"Yes, moved on since then. She has rooms in Harley Street now. Still visits St Thomas's from time to time. Works long hours, but she loves it and suits us both as I have to, you know, slip away every now and then." Nick fell silent as he studied the remains of the beef wellington with seasonal greens.

The waiter approached. "Gentlemen, would you care for another ale?"

It was Nigel who ventured a reply. "Thanks, but no, we have a drive ahead of us. Thanks for asking, just bring my friend the bill."

Nigel slid out from behind the table and stood up. Try as he may to straighten out his crumpled clothes the exercise was futile. "So much for no fucking creases Nick, that Stanhope must have been a tosser."

The black Series 5 was parked across the road as they walked past the cars in the hotel car park; a Lotus Elan, a vintage E type and an Austin Healy 3000. Close by, with a gaggle of onlookers eagerly chatting, were the owners, resplendent in their angora jumpers, mohair scarves, trinity tweed flat caps and leather driving gloves.

"Tossers," uttered Nigel as they crossed the road.

"Don't be too harsh on them Nigel," offered Nick, "I've got a vintage Healy myself."

"I rest my case," grunted Nigel as he opened the driver's door, looking up and laughing as Nick opened the passenger door.

Connelly started the engine. "By the way how's Spencer going with that research you asked him to do?" Pausing while he pulled away from the kerb. "And what was it you were asking for?"

"Nothing much," replied Nick, casually looking out of the passenger window as they turned towards the M4. "Just a few details on all the unsolved murders and suspected suicides in the past twelve months in the UK."

"Fuck me Nick, that'll keep him busy."

"I don't want all the details, just location, time, date, cause of death and occupation of the deceased."

Nigel paused to take it all in. "Are you saying that we have a serial killer?"

"In a manner of speaking Nigel, and just a theory at this stage. With just two murders with a common thread, I wouldn't jump to any conclusions. But it did cross my mind that the Judge and the Bishop may not be the only victims of the killer. I'll be interested in what Dr Wilde comes up with."

"She's pretty smart. Been on a few cases lately."

"We'll see."

18

The M4 traffic was moderately busy as they headed back to London. Connelly did his best to weave his way through the congestion. Past Heathrow it started to choke up as the traffic slowed to a crawl. Nick decided this was a good opportunity to call Spencer to see how he was going with his job list.

"How's that list going for DCI Connelly, Spencer?" asked Nick as the car inched forward slowly.

"Going well sir. Sick sons of bitches, I nearly threw up a few times. I might have nightmares tonight."

"Well, make sure that MacBook is locked away and secure for the night."

"Yes sir."

"Now you're a bright young lad Spencer, I'm sure you understand that it would have been totally against protocol to have made any additional copies?" asked Nick.

Spencer fumbled a little, "That's correct sir, it would have been most inappropriate."

"Very much so," continued Nick, "So let's hope none of the original or the back-up files go missing whilst in police custody or those perverts could get off Scot free."

"That's correct sir. It would be devastating if the evidence was lost."

Nick flicked the phone off and turned to Nigel, "I reckon young Spencer had already thought of that."

"I think you might be right Nick."

Spencer was on the computer in Connelly's alcove when the DCI walked in the next morning.

"Early start eh Spencer?"

"Yes boss, finished that list but I haven't given it to Commander McIntyre yet." Spencer reached for a manila folder on the top of closest stack.

Connelly scanned the list. "Shit. How the fuck did you get all these names so quickly?"

"I used a facial recognition software. Hope you don't mind. I downloaded it yesterday afternoon. Worked here 'til 2am, had three hours kip on the couch and back into it this morning."

"Fuckin' hell Spencer there's three politicians, two judges and a copper in that mix."

"That's not all boss," Spencer grabbed the list and pointed to a group of names, "these here are foreign diplomats and half a dozen business leaders, one of which is CEO of a defence weapons contractor, and there's more. Twenty-three in total that I was able to identify."

"So, what are you onto now Spencer?"

"I'm doing research for Commander Hood. I had to get clearance from Commander McIntyre so I could access all the regions. Did you know that in the past twelve months we've had 650 homicides and nearly 6,000 suicides." Spencer shuffled papers as he continued, "and detection rate for homicides is running at about 80%, so I'm going through the 20% of unsolved cases as we speak."

"Let's narrow it down to just gun related homicides Spencer and forget the suicides for the moment. Work on location, time, date and the occupation of the victim. Might be handy if you can get the ballistics on those 20%."

Connelly decided that his alcove was too crowded and headed down to the canteen for breakfast.

Spencer was now relieved that the data search was focussed on the unsolved gun related homicides. At the same time, he found himself reflecting on the statistics of violent crimes and suicides, wondering how society had got so fucked up.

McIntyre was sitting at his desk and looked up when Spencer tapped on his door.

"The list of those pedos on the images Commander," offered Spencer as he was signalled to sit.

McIntyre sat motionless as he scanned the list and counted the names.

"Twenty-three?" Looking up at Spencer

"That's all I was able to identify. I think a specialist might be able to identify more. More than enough for the Commissioner to work with I would think."

"Has anyone else seen this list?"

"DCI Connelly gave it a quick look this morning, no one else."

"OK Spencer, good job."

"Thank you, sir."

Spencer beat a hasty retreat happy to get back to the homicide stats and away from the shit storm that was brewing.

McIntyre took a deep breath and made his way to AC Larkin's office, poking his head around the corner of the open door.

Larkin looked up. "Come in Gerald, what have we got."

"A fucking nightmare sir, if you pardon my French. Twenty-three names and maybe more on the way. Pollies, business CEOs, diplomats, judiciary and a fucking senior copper would you believe."

Larkin's complexion went a ghostly shade of grey as the blood drained from his face. "My god, this has been going on under our noses and we knew nothing about it?" Larkin looked questionably at McIntyre.

"Looks like it, sir, but perhaps the NCA or another branch might be investigating, and we wouldn't know."

"I have to see the Commissioner right away. Ok leave it with me Gerald."

McIntyre sauntered off to his office quite thankful for once that the chain of command had moved into overdrive.

Larkin phoned the Commissioner's office insisting to the PA that he have an immediate meeting with Sir Alex.

"It's worse than I thought Horace." Sir Alex pushed his face into his hands, his elbows firmly on the desk as he raised his head and sighed. "I've already arranged a meeting with the Home Secretary for tomorrow morning, way above the Mayor's head, and I expect we'll be at No 10 within the hour." Looking up at Larkin, "Thanks Horace, I'll take it from here."

19

For most people Wednesday morning was another day at the office but for the Commissioner of the Metropolitan Police it was a day when dark storm clouds were approaching fast from the chilly north. His driver had picked him up from the internal car park so as not to attract any untoward attention. There were always expectant journalists lurking close by eager to log some breaking news into the network and inflate mediocre incidents into matters of national security. Never to let the truth get in the way of a good story, their cameras were at the ready seemingly at every street corner.

It was a five-minute drive to the Home Office where the Right Honourable, Wilford du Maurier was totally oblivious of the fact that his day and that of many others was going to turn into absolute shit.

"Good morning, Sir Alex, I'm hoping this unscheduled meeting won't be a long one. Rather a busy day coming up."

You've got no fucking idea, thought Sir Alex.

"Sir, good morning, something of a rather important and sensitive nature has come up."

"Really? sit down." He offered Sir Alex one of two upholstered lounge chairs covered in a ghastly floral fabric that had seen its best days.

Sir Alex sat and reached into his black leather portfolio. Pulling out a manila folder he extracted a plain white typed sheet of paper and passed it to Wilford.

Placing his reading glasses on the bridge of his nose, Wilford briefly scanned the list of names. "What do we have here, an invitation list?"

Sir Alex leaned back in the chair, taking a deep breath, then leaned forward. "Yes, you could say that Home Secretary, an invitation of sorts. These are people who have been identified in pornographic images and videos of having sexual activity with children and others."

"But many of these people listed are in the upper echelon of society, pillars of the community?" Wilford's face was distorted in disbelief.

"Yes, they are Home Secretary and, based on the evidence we hold, they will very soon be issued with arrest warrants."

"But this will be disastrous for the government; for the bastions of power that we hold so dear." Wilford grasped his throat as if he was choking. He reached for a glass of water, gulping down a mouthful, "We must speak with the Prime Minister at once."

"Yes, I thought that would be the case Secretary." Sir Alex was unusually calm as the Home Secretary reached into his top drawer for his medication.

20

Three minutes after leaving the Home Office, Sir Alex was sitting outside the office of the Prime Minister at 10 Downing Street. The Home Secretary had insisted on speaking with the PM first. Sir Alex was used to the posturing of politicians and in any case it was academic.

The evidence was all but conclusive. He had an obligation to issue warrants based on the existing evidence. Ethically, he could not delay past the process required to speak with the Crown Prosecutor to whom he must show the evidence, which should provide a realistic prospect of prosecution. The fact that members of the judiciary are also involved should not in any case delay the process. It would be very unwise for any politician, or member of the judiciary to seek to delay or obstruct due process, or in any way intimidate officers in the execution of their duty under law.

For Sir Alex his pathway was clear. Crystal clear. He was prepared to allow the Prime Minister a short amount of time to prepare and brief his cabinet however justice had to be seen to be done in a timely fashion as everyone taking part in this process would be held accountable for their actions. This would be of even more importance to the political sphere who cannot be seen to be operating in a bubble.

The Prime Ministers aide approached. "Sir Alex, the Prime Minister will see you now."

There had been many light-hearted meetings within these hallowed walls but today was not going to be one of them. A decided sombre atmosphere prevailed with a frowning PM sitting in a leather studded chair gazing at the ground as Sir Alex approached. The PM stood up and extended his hand with a firm shake. *A little too firmly*, Sir Alex thought, *but no matter*. He was directed to a chair as he looked around the room. The Home Secretary was seated closest to the fireplace, the PMs policy adviser, Crispian Goodfellow, lounging almost horizontally on a three-seater couch, but pulling himself upright as Sir Alex sat on a vacant wing back opposite. The PMs media adviser decided to stand up and rest his arm against the mantlepiece. The Chancellor of the Exchequer sat uncomfortably on an Edwardian dining chair adjacent to a small round coffee table.

"Well Sir Alex, this is a fine how do you do," offered the PM, making some effort to appear accepting of the situation, however poorly executed. "I'll come straight to the point, how long have we got?"

"Well PM, in terms of police processes and protocols, as soon as I have spoken with the Crown Prosecutor and he accepts the evidence as we have it today, my officers will issue warrants for the arrests of the known British individuals that we have so far identified. The overseas diplomats are immune from prosecution, but it would be our recommendation that they be issued with expulsion orders and placed permanently on our blacklist. That would also include members of their families." Sir Alex paused a moment. "Given the nature of the crimes, as evidenced in the videos and images, I would be inclined to provide Interpol with copies of the evidence, and I would not be surprised if there were similar conduct in their own countries, but that would be a matter for those jurisdictions."

Sir Alex looked around at the long faces in the rooms.

"It would be pertinent to cancel the passports of those to be charged as I would consider them to be a flight risk. I'll action that as soon as I leave this meeting and speak to the Passports Office and Border Control." Sir Alex sat back in his chair. "It

71

would also be very improper for anyone in this room to speak with those identified on the list I have provided, and I must caution anyone present that alerting those persons to impending arrest could be construed as an 'accessory after the fact.' I don't know if you've noticed, but there is also a Baronet on the list although his title was not included."

"So, how long have we actually got Sir Alex?" asked the PM again, his shoulders stooped, arms outstretched with his palms facing inwards, fingers apart and fingertips touching lightly.

"I will meet with the Crown Prosecutor tomorrow around midday, warrants will be issued tomorrow afternoon and I would expect arrests to be made tomorrow evening. I have no doubt we will have QCs out in droves tomorrow evening seeking immediate release, bail and God-knows what. The press will be onto it from the onset even as the warrants get issued, so get ready."

"And there is no way we can, you know, quieten it down a bit?" offered Crispian Goodfellow.

"Well, I'm certainly glad you said that Mr Goodfellow, rather than the PM. The answer is no. I have no wish or inclination to defray the consequences of breaking the laws of this land and considering the heinous nature of the offences nor should you." Sir Alex stood upright, "I will leave you to your deliberations and bid you good day."

"Have you spoken to the Mayor, Commissioner?" asked Goodfellow.

"The Mayor," replied Sir Alex, "fuck the Mayor." Sir Alex turned and left the room, leaving it somewhat more sombre than when he entered.

21

The warrants were issued and, as expected, by the time police officers knocked on the doors of the offending participants in the videos, there was a herd of photographers and journalists in each location.

"How the fuck do these bastards know who's being arrested and when?" asked one of the officers present.

"If you ask me, someone's on the take mate," replied another.

One by one embarrassed aristocrats, CEOs, one red faced Chief Constable from the Essex Division and other pillars of the community, twenty-three in total, were arrested during that evening. Distressed family members, most of them unaware of what charges might be laid, cried and remonstrated at the doorways. Most of them more concerned with their standing in the community than of the welfare of the arrested persons. These crimes were committed by the upper echelons of a class society that continues to look down at those who don't live in the right neighbourhoods or speak with a clipped fine British accent. Those who do not reflect the hallmarks of a fine university education or who came from the wrong side of town.

The head of the NCA met with Sir Alex late that evening to tell him they would be assuming control of the child pornography case. He requested information and evidence collected prior to and during the arrests to be handed over to their officers during the next few days. The meeting was cordial, as it should be, however no senior police officer enjoys having cases of importance usurped by political pressure or the haughty attitude of another authority. An agency so blatant and disdainful in the execution of its bestowed authority. Yes, it would be true to say that publicly the Met and the NCA have a sound and co-operative working relationship.

22

The Friday meeting took place in the meeting room on the third level behind Connelly's alcove. Spencer had arrived early with a stack of papers and was setting up his laptop as Connelly tramped in.

"What are you doing there, Spencer?"

"Setting up the visual presentation Guv. I've collated all the stats and done a spreadsheet. Oh, by the way the NCA have taken possession of all the evidence we were holding."

"So that would include the judge's computer, camera, memory card, videos, DVDs, the lot?"

"Yes boss, and the back-ups that were made."

"That would be all of the back-ups Spencer?"

"Yes sir, I had to sign a document to that effect," Spencer winked at Connelly.

Connelly smiled at Spencer and touched the side of his nose and continued "I've no fucking idea about all this technical stuff Spencer, but it's looking good. Keep it simple son." Connelly navigated to his desk and unlocked the top drawer and pulled out a manilla folder. Shuffling back to the meeting room, he pointed to the coffee pot percolating in the corner with a questioning look at Spencer.

"I thought we could use some coffee, and there's also a jug of hot water for the tea drinkers. I pinched some herbal teas, milk, sugar and biscuits from the canteen as well." Spencer stood up looking obviously pleased with himself.

Connelly walked over to the brew point and grabbed himself a mug. "Keep it up Spencer, we'll make an inspector of you yet."

Stella Wilde made her way in, dropped her holdall on a chair and inspected the brew station. "Herbal teas, I'm impressed." She selected a Camomile herbal infusion and added the appropriate amount of hot water. Leaving the bag in the mug to infuse, she carried it to the chair next to the holdall and sat down, wrapping her fingers around the brightly coloured receptacle.

Connelly took his seat beside Spencer who was fiddling with the laptop as the widescreen tv came to life. Turning to Connelly, "it's Bluetooth sir."

"I'm sure it is Spencer; I'll take your word for it."

Nicholas Hood came in last and closed the door behind him and noticing the coffee pot, helped himself to a mug.

Connelly smiled at everyone and immediately turned to Spencer. "You can get the show going Spencer unless Nick wanted to say anything first."

Nick gestured towards Spencer. "No, Spencer can start off," and turning to Dr Wilde, "I asked DS Spencer to get some stats Stella, unsolved gun homicides in the past 12 months."

"The reason for which will become obvious I am sure," commented Stella with a wry smile.

Nick observed that Stella's attire was not quite as dowdy as their first meeting, and something was different with her hair and makeup.

Spencer started. "You'll see on this spreadsheet the basic stats on the unsolved homicides in the past twelve months. On the left is the column for the location, next column is the date and time, followed by the victim's name and lastly occupation. Of the 34 gun-related homicides in the past twelve months only 19 have been solved during that time leaving the 15 on this chart." Spencer looked around as Stella was making notes. Connelly was squinting to focus on the screen as he reached for his glasses. Nick was passively studying the screen.

"You'll see on the right-hand column the various occupations of the victims," Spencer continued, "the locations are scattered all over the UK, Scotland and Wales. At this stage nothing in Northern Ireland and I'm waiting for some statistics from our friends in Eire. You will note the variety of occupations from government, business and general community. Nothing obvious until I dug a little deeper." Spencer switched to a different data sheet. "Sorry, are there any questions so far?"

There were slight shakes of their heads around the table together with a degree of noticeable anticipation as Spencer resumed his presentation.

"The actual occupations presented as nothing unusual until I combined it with their recent activities," the other three leaned forward in their seats as if by instruction. "For example, if we look at James Albright, TV executive, nothing unusual there. However, he recently produced a series of current affairs programs that received severe criticism for what was termed 'left-wing bias'. He targeted some conservative politicians and prominent businessmen. One of the politicians resigned due to ill health following accusations that proved untrue, and one of the businesses mentioned in the report fell into receivership, once again based on unsubstantiated rumours. It was also believed that lawsuits were pending and that Mr Albright's brother, also a notable left-wing supporter is also a QC. Comment was made that it would be years before any action would be seen in a court of law."

Spencer paused to have a sip of his coffee. "By the way Mr Albright was shot in his driveway after returning home in the evening. No witnesses, nothing but a dark shape on a cheap security camera. Nine-millimetre handgun: no gunshot sounds, so probably silenced." Spencer wiped a dribble of coffee from his chin.

"We now look at Brendon Smith. Property consultant by profession. Recently released from prison. Convicted of killing his wife and three children by firstly gassing them in their bedroom and then cutting their throats. Pleaded not guilty. Sentenced to twelve years and psychiatric treatment. Served two years. New evidence and accusations of police tampering with evidence led to a re-trial and he got off. Unsubstantiated rumours that he got drunk after release telling a friend that he got away with it. Brendon had a drinking problem and got shot while walking home after the pub. No witnesses, no sounds of gun shot."

Spencer stopped and finished his coffee.

"Don't stop there," said Connelly, "Keep going lad."

Stella was making copious notes as Nick sat totally focussed on the screen.

Spencer flicked to the next case. "Nancy Green, known prostitute, drug user and trafficker. Numerous arrests, short term imprisonment. Two children, father's unknown, removed from her custody after they presented to hospital with heroin overdoses. They were twelve and fourteen. It's believed that she administered the drugs herself. She was well known in criminal circles and catered her sexual services to local thugs and drug barons in the Newcastle area. She was on bail for drug trafficking and running a property for the purposes of prostitution. It's believed that one of her criminal clients shot her. Once again, no gunshot sounds or witnesses."

Spencer paused to refill his coffee mug, followed by the others as they stood up together.

"Are we supposed to believe that the same person committed these crimes?" asked Connelly.

"I don't think we can count it out, do you Nigel?" offered Nick.

Stella decided it was her turn to contribute. "If it's the same person, and I'm not saying that it is, we could be looking at someone who's very unhappy with the judicial system."

"There's a name for that Stella," suggested Nick.

"Yes, there is, and I deliberately didn't say it. I wouldn't want to brand these homicides with the same metaphorical label at such an early stage. I reserve my opinion until we see the remainder of Chris's presentation."

The day progressed with a group discussion following each of the crimes. Spencer was awarded compliments many times during the day for his research and selection of the individual homicides, to which he would often remark that it was actually Nick who pointed him in this direction. Stella took copious notes on each case while Nick sat back in his chair in deep thought, often requesting that they flip back to one of the previous listings. Connelly made a few items on each case while frequently placing his hand on Spencer's shoulder and giving it a light shake.

"You're doing well my boy," was frequently heard during the day. One could be forgiven in thinking that there was a father and son working together.

23

The lunch break in the ground floor canteen was a quiet affair with few case words spoken. Nick and Nigel were old familiar colleagues, but the main topic of conversation was focussed on Stella and Chris. It was Nick who started the dialogue.

"So, Stella, if not too personal what does a forensic psychologist do when she is not being a forensic psychologist?"

"Well Nick, I can't speak for other forensic psychologists, but I go to the gym a few times a week and," Stella hesitated as she looked each man in the eye with an analytical stare, "I pole dance."

Chris couldn't help himself and jumped right in. "What, in clubs?"

Stella leant forward in her chair. "No Chris, not clubs. It's my hobby. I have a pole set up in my lounge room and I turn the music up. It's a fitness regime. Typical male stereotype comment there Chris."

Chris abruptly apologised as Nick and Nigel chuckled. Chris fumbled with obvious embarrassment. "I'm sorry Stella, I just had some images in my mind."

Nigel jumped in. "I'd shut up if I were you Chris, you're digging a deeper hole for yourself."

"Now you know why I don't go around telling the Met I pole dance," remarked Stella.

"I think it's safe to say that your secret is safe with us," commented Nick as he sought a nod of approval from Nigel and Chris.

The afternoon session continued with the list of fifteen. It was past 5.30 in the afternoon when the last of the 15 crimes was discussed. Nick leaned back in his chair with his hands clasped behind his head. By now the men had taken their jackets off, loosened their ties and partly rolled their sleeves up. The coffee pot was empty and most of the biscuits in the tin had been consumed by the three men, while the sensible pole dancer nibbled on a plain wheat digestive.

"Before we make some closing comments," Nick started, "I'm the first to admit that there's nothing at all linking these murders. However, and as crazy as it sounds, the one common element is that very thing. There is nothing linking these crimes." Nick stood up and walked around the room as he spoke. "Now, I don't want to influence anyone's thinking here and I can see why these cases have remained exactly what they seem to be, isolated, individual crimes. No copper, however skilled," he paused as he looked at Nigel and Chris, "no copper is going to say that these crimes have anything in common except the fact they were all murders by a firearm of some description. None of the ballistics match and no two murders were carried out in an identical manner and none of these fifteen victims seemed to be connected in any way."

Stella followed on from Nick. "If we follow your earlier unlabelled comment Nick, it's not beyond the realms of possibility, although we are drawing a longbow here, that each of the victims in some way have committed what to some, could be perceived as an act against community or fair justice." Stella paused, "However, I'm a scientist, I could not, given the information presented today, be persuaded to determine that these acts were perpetrated by a single individual on a misguided crusade of some kind."

"I take your point Stella," replied Nick as he rested his hands on the back of his chair as Nigel chipped in.

"I'm an old copper as you can plainly see," said Nigel, "but I've got an old copper's nose and an old coppers instinct. I'm prepared to accept that there's a possibility that someone out there has got a serious hard on for corrupt individuals." Nigel looked at Stella, "Sorry for that analogy Stella."

"That's OK Nigel," laughed Stella, "I've been around coppers long enough to appreciate their clinical observations; and no more comments about pole dancing, thank you."

There was laughter all round when Commander McIntyre burst into the room.

"Something's just happened in Manchester. I've spoken to the boss, and I've got a chopper ready to go. Someone has just blown the head off a Muslim cleric outside a mosque. No room for everyone so Connelly, Commander Hood, you're with me." McIntyre gave the room one fleeting gaze and rushed off.

Nick and Nigel grabbed their jackets and followed McIntyre out of the room while Chris and Stella stood there momentarily stunned. Chris played with the TV remote and quickly found the breaking news.

24

The man preferred still days. Days when the wind was almost negligible and the air was clear, as often seen after a shower of rain. On days such as these he could accurately shoot to kill over two thousand metres. Today would be easier, much easier. From his vantage point above the city, he could take his pick among the crowded streets below. Collateral damage however was not the aim. Today his target was specific and there would be no mistakes.

The top floor of the high-rise construction project was an ideal location to set up his AXMC rifle. The concrete slab provided the perfect base for the bipod and the man found himself comfortably settled in place awaiting his intended target. Friday afternoon with early 'knock-offs' was a perfect time to set up his equipment. No management on site. Posing as an engineering surveyor, he insisted that the top floor be kept clear of other personnel and vibrations while he established the new shots. New shots were going to take a completely new meaning today.

The packing case of his TST, total station theodolite, was the perfect cover for packing the rifle and provided the man with a legitimate reason to be on the worksite and the last to leave late that afternoon. The security guard had provided him with the keys to the construction lift and no-one else could have access to the top floor unless he released the cage. Beside him was a sheet of canvas spattered with dried cement in case of marauding media helicopters or wandering drones.

Twenty floors below, the city continued its pedestrian motion of commuters eager to end their working week and make their pilgrimage home to the suburbs of Manchester and its myriad housing estates. Twelve hundred metres to the north of the man's position was the Masjid Mosque where the visiting Shia Imam, Bashir Mijhak was conducting Jumu'ah along with his vitriol of violent jihad. Each Friday for the past four weeks the man had been observing the Imam's movements and routines and he now awaited his departure from the mosque. The limousine that brought the Imam to the mosque was parked at the bottom of the front stairs where a large group of Islamic men had congregated to farewell their Faqih.

The man carefully adjusted the focus on the Schmidt & Bender telescopic lens and rangefinder. He checked and re-checked the magazine holding the .338 custom built cartridges. He reached over and pulled the canvas sheet over himself and the rifle, with the tip of the suppressor just proud of the cape.

The last members of the congregation passed through the front door and down the steps as the Imam and his two minders moved towards the top of the steps where they stopped as the Imam gave his final blessing to Allah and the men below. The man took his final aim and slowly squeezed the trigger. The recoil was tempered by the muzzle brake as the rifle fired with a slight thump and hiss. The man observed the hit through the scope as the Imam's head disappeared in a huge pink spray. The headless body slumped lifeless to the top step oozing blood as both minders drew their weapons, covered in the bloody spray and pieces of brain and skull. The handmade projectile had done its job. The heart within the headless body continued to pump for nearly a minute while the man on the top floor of the building site calmly stood up and packed his rifle and equipment away as pandemonium broke out on the street outside the mosque. The minders were looking in every direction and yelling as the panicked crowd ran off in frenzied terror.

The building site was quiet as the cage came to rest on the ground floor. The security officer nodded from his hut by the gate as the man placed his cases in the back of the plain white van and then drove off, dropping keys into the hands of the security officer. The streets in this area were quiet but from a distance the police sirens could be heard as the man smiled and turned on the Bluetooth audio, Love You Like a Hurricane.

25

By the time the police helicopter arrived at Manchester there were choppers everywhere. Commander McIntyre instructed the pilot to overfly the murder scene before they landed in the grounds of Stockport Divisional HQ where the local division had a car waiting for them.

"The Chief Constable is a fly-fishing mate of mine," said McIntyre, "I called in a favour although he told me in no uncertain words to 'observe not involve'." He continued as they walked away from the chopper, "This case may be unrelated to our investigation, but it looks like a long-range rifle shot. Sniper. It pretty-well blew the poor chaps head off his shoulders. Not to mention the shit storm that will come from the Muslim community. I'm glad it's up here in Manchester and not in London."

The drive to the Mosque took a little longer than anticipated. The traffic was heavy and even with the lights flashing and siren wailing it took around 15 minutes to get to the crime scene. The driver stopped as close as he could as the three made their way to the corner of the street. The police were having trouble keeping the crowd of angry Muslims behind the tape as an investigation team worked diligently with chaos and confusion erupting around them. The Chief Constable attended the scene with a few officers keeping the media back. McIntyre, in uniform, involved the Chief Constable in discussion as he signalled to Connelly and Hood to approach. The Chief Constable nodded to McIntyre as he walked off to speak with one of the investigating officers.

"The Chief has said it's OK to look around. Don't speak to the investigating officers or any of the forensic team and flash your badge if approached by anyone. Do not talk to the media." McIntyre walked off to the Command Vehicle while Nigel and Nick made their way up the steps of the mosque, careful not to step on the blood trail and spatters.

There was a white sheet over the corpse of the dead Imam lying on the top step of the entrance. The Mosque, once a grey stone Anglican Church was now painted white with gold trim. The once proud spire pointing to heaven was now half the height with a minaret resplendent in white and gold. The stained oak panelled doors now embellished with Islamic icons in gold and covered in spatters of blood from the severed jugular. Nick found himself enough room amid the spatters and pools of blood to stand behind where the Imam had once stood, before his head was disengaged from his body. He glanced back at the door and aside from the spatters of blood and bone there was no sign of the bullet after it passed through the head of the Imam. There was no point in lifting the sheet as apart from the lacerated flesh where most of his neck had been there would be nothing to see.

Nick concentrated his gaze in the early evening light towards the visible horizon surrounding this suburban street corner. His appreciation of the crime scene and the projection of body material led him to believe that the shot was made directly towards the entrance, give or take around ten degrees. He focussed his gaze on the buildings in front of him, a visual cacophony of concrete in the form of residential low rise and office buildings but it was the space in between that interested him most. Sitting proud in prime position was a high rise building under construction. It was some distance but to the trained observer a classic FFP, Final Firing Position. Far enough from the target to quietly pack away the equipment and depart the scene without raising the slightest suspicion.

Nick turned to Connelly, "we're done here."

"We are?" questioned Connelly.

"Yes, my friend, we're off to the FFP."

"What the fuck is the FFP?"

"You'll see. Let's find ourselves a police car."

26

Hood and Connelly found the car they arrived in with the driver sitting patiently at the wheel. Nick took the front seat while Connelly launched himself into the back. "What about McIntyre?" asked Nigel.

"He'll be fine, we'll catch up with him later," replied Nick while he busily studied Google maps on his smartphone.

"He'll have my guts for garters Nick."

"No, he won't, he'll be too busy big noting himself with the Chief Constable and talking flies and the one that got away. Let's go." Nick leaned over towards the driver pointing to a road on the map. "Do you know this area?"

"Yes sir, building site over there."

"Exactly what I'm looking for and put those damn lights on."

With lights and sirens screaming they were outside the building site in minutes. They jumped out of the car to find the gates closed and no security officer in the small hut inside the gate.

The uniformed officer shone his torch around in the diminished daylight. "There's a security number on the sign sir."

"Give it a call and tell them to get someone with a key down here quick smart," Nick paced left and right. "The bastard made the shot from here Nigel."

"Well, it's getting too dark to do anything tonight, and it's a weekend, probably be some workers doing a Saturday shift I would think," offered Nigel.

The uniform cut in as he waited for the phone to answer. "Not many on the job tomorrow guv, big day at the footy."

Nick laughed. "Of course, we're in Manchester, nothing stands in the way of football."

The phone finally answered at the security firm. "Here, give me the phone," uttered Nick as he grabbed the mobile from the constable. "Hello, I want someone with a key, where are we?" asked Nick, turning to the constable.

"15 Commercial Crescent, Spacetec Towers sir."

Nick gave the constable back his phone.

"Nigel, we need a guard on this site tonight with a key and we'll come back at first light before the tradesmen come on site."

"Nick, I don't have any jurisdiction here, and even if I did, they wouldn't lock up a site on speculation."

The constable stood back as the two senior gentlemen engaged in colourful conversation.

"Well fuck it, we'll have to stay here until daylight ourselves."

The constable intervened. "I knock off in an hour. If it helps, I could bring a car back. It's going to get a bit cool tonight for a stake out."

"It's not a stake out lad," said Connelly "but sounds like a good offer." He turned to Nick, "Nick?"

"Yes, it'll have to do, I don't want anyone in that building, especially that top floor, until we look at it first."

The constable waited until the security officer turned up and provided the group with a key.

Nick grabbed the key, "by the way was there a security officer on the site this afternoon?"

"Yes, he would have finished about 6pm I would think," offered the security officer as he walked back to his car.

"Can you have that man here first thing in the morning?"

"Yes, his shift starts at 6.30 in the morning, same man."

"Excellent," muttered Nick as both cars drove off leaving the two men standing in the dark. "Pity that site cubicle's so small."

"Maybe we should wander inside and sit down inside the ground floor, at least it's undercover," Nigel pushed his hands deep into his pockets.

"Normally I'd agree with you Nigel, but this could potentially be a crime scene so I wouldn't want anything disturbed until after tomorrow morning."

27

The constable returned at 8.30 in what the two were hoping would be a comfortable car to spend the night in. Instead, it was a commercial van that greeted them with a cheerful copper at the wheel.

"Shit," said Nigel, "I was hoping the constable would come back with something a bit more commodious."

"Sorry I'm a bit late gents, I called into a takeaway. Thought you might be hungry." The constable slid the side door open to reveal a fully fitted out campervan, with table, bed, bench seats and a little kitchenette. "The missus and me use this on weekends, do a bit of camping we do. "Op in, I got coffee too. Oh, by the way, Commander McIntyre asked me to tell you to find your own accommodation as he's going home with the Chief. He said not to make it too posh, and he'll catch up with you around lunchtime tomorrow."

There was laughter all round as the three settled into a feed of hamburgers, chips and some 'not so bad' coffee.

"What no ensuite?" asked Nigel jokingly, pieces of hamburger running down his chin.

"Actually, yes guv, it folds out the back like a tent, but I left the porta-loo at home," laughed the constable.

"That's OK Constable, he'll take a piss against the fence like the rest of us. By the way what's your name constable?"

"Don't laugh guv, but it's Constable, Kevin Constable."

"You mean you're Constable Constable," smirked Connelly.

"'Fraid so guv," replied Constable as the three of them chuckled.

There was room in the van for the three to find enough room to get some form of sleep before sunrise. By the time Nick and Nigel had awoken the constable had three cups of piping hot coffee ready to go. The sun was low on the horizon when the security officer turned up. Connelly flashed his badge and the two engaged in conversation as Nick and Constable made their way around the back of the van, gulping down the remains of their morning cuppa. The guard unlocked the gate as Connelly approached the other two.

"We're in luck boys. The guard tells me that after the tradesmen left, a white van pulled in driven by a man who told him he was doing a building survey. The man stayed for about an hour and then left. He was roughly 6 feet, medium build, aged about 35 he says. He had equipment with him and said he was there to take some shots from the top floor. Apparently pleasant speaking and wait for this," Connelly paused and held up his mobile phone, "the guard said he photographed the van on his mobile, which he does for any vehicle entering the site. He's messaging the image to me now."

Nick grabbed Nigel by the shoulder, "our man might have just made a career blunder." Nigel approached the guard. "Can we have the keys to the construction lift," gesturing towards the side of the building.

Constable remained with the guard, returning the key they acquired the previous evening as Connelly and Hood rode the cage to the top floor. Twenty floors up gave a commanding view of the Manchester landscape, north to the city centre, west to the Irish sea and east to the hills and moors of the Peak District National Park. The air was still in the early morning light with a city haze blurring the distant high rise of the city itself. Almost instinctively Nick made his way to the north facing edge of the top floor focussing through the haze towards the mosque. Cursing himself for not having at least a pair of binoculars he used his mobile phone to zoom in on camera mode. Carefully he moved to the left and then stopped beside a two-metre concrete column with steel strands emanating from the top like an optic fibre lamp. Resting against the column was a soft brush broom with beads of hardened cement stuck to the stems of the bristles.

"He was here Nigel," pointed out Nick as he scanned the area in front of him. "He's run a broom over the area to take away any marks left by the rifle. There are footprints but see how there is no tread. He has slipped socks over his boots. You can dust the broom for prints and dust the construction cage on the lift, but he'll have been wearing gloves. He may have made an error by bringing the car onto the site but that'll have been his only mistake."

Nick stood up and took one last look across the cityscape and the sight of the killing. "Clever bastard, but not clever enough."

Connelly and Hood returned to the ground of the building site approaching Constable and the guard. Connelly instructed Constable to remain at the site until an investigation team arrived. He then called the Stockton Divisional HQ requesting a car and the duty DCI to come to the building site. While Connelly was engaged with the local police Nick had called Spencer and asked him to check the licence plate in the image taken by the security guard.

In less time than it took to grab another coffee, a car had arrived with the duty DCI and a driver who was directed to take Connelly and Hood to the Greater Manchester Police HQ. Before leaving, Hood and Connelly briefed the DCI with Connelly handing him the broom for dusting. With the duty DCI on site, Constable Constable was cleared to leave. Nick and Nigel made a point to thank him profusely for his help and a promise of being 'mentioned in dispatches' for his out-of-hours initiative and assistance.

28

The canteen at City HQ offered a reasonable breakfast although visitors were required to pay. Connelly was happy to return the favour from The Hind a few days ago, and at a much more agreeable price.

McIntyre and the Chief Constable arrived at the canteen both clad in plus fours, hex pattern sleeveless jumpers and flat caps.

"Morning chaps," announced McIntyre, affably grinning from ear to ear, "Jim kindly lent me some clobber and we had a quick 9 holes. I hear you chaps had a spot of luck last night."

"I'd call it something quite different Commander," suggested Nick sarcastically, "There's nothing lucky about professionally examining a crime scene and collecting evidence."

Connelly jumped in before the interchange escalated, "Sir, we have an address in Liverpool where the van used by the assailant is registered."

"Well let's go," chimed McIntyre, excited at the possibility of taking the credit for arresting a killer.

The Chief Constable had been standing close by, being briefed by another officer. He called out to McIntyre.

"Gerald, there's a jurisdictional issue here. I've been advised that one of our officers will need to accompany you and whilst I appreciate the work you and your officers did last night, he'll liaise with Merseyside to make any arrests necessary." The Chief turned to the officer at his side. "Advise Merseyside that we are coming in. I'll call their Chief Constable and square it off." Turning to McIntyre, "and Gerald, it might be better if you get back into uniform first. You and I'll stay here while the others go and rev up the Scousers."

Hood and Connelly, in company with a local DCI, left a dejected McIntyre standing in the lobby of the police HQ. Within an hour they had arrived at Merseyside HQ where they were escorted to the registration address of the white Ford Transit Custom in Ropewalks.

A squad car was positioned on each corner of the block having arrived silently with no lights or sirens. An armed tactical unit waited for instructions at an incident control point.

Hood and Connelly alighted from the vehicle and respectfully kept their distance allowing the incident controller and the tactical squad leader to do their job. The area was a light industrial site with the warehouse and associated compound clearly visible in the centre of the block. A collection of white vans could be seen in the compound with a few people loading the vehicles from a ramp on the ground floor of the building. Having secured all sides of the warehouse by armed personnel, the tactical squad was given the go signal.

The armed personnel carrier approached the compound and turned in, blocking any exit and discharging the armed squad. They immediately ordered everyone to the ground as four of the squad entered the building. Within a few minutes, and with no shots fired, the remainder of the staff in the building were laying down on the ramp. The squad commander took off his helmet, advising on his radio that the building and compound was now secure. The incident controller together with a small number of police, including Hood and Connelly, made their way on foot to the compound where the people inside were now standing and lined up by the officers. The cars at the corner of the block continued diverting any traffic away from the area.

The tactical squad commander came over to speak to the incident controller as Hood and Connelly listened close by.

"It's a meals-on-wheels charity depot," the squad commander was almost laughing, "they're all volunteers. They're loading meals for the poor and homeless. Look at them, most of them are pensioners themselves. I'll stand down my men and leave you to clean up, some of them have shit themselves."

The DCI in charge of the raid called base and requested an ambulance to assist the charity workers and if they can find a social worker to do some counselling at the same time.

"Fuck, what an embarrassment," uttered the DCI, calling over a local sergeant to disperse the units and return them to other duties.

Nick and Nigel remained silent considering they had caused this incident. They were approached by the DCI that accompanied them. "Don't be so glum old chums," he said jovially, "would have been worse if we'd shot a pensioner brandishing a ladle and a pot of soup. Deadly that. I've seen these scouse's when they've had a few at the local and they don't muck around."

"We've forgotten why we're here," Nick insisted, "there's still the question of the registration of the vehicle. Is the vehicle here?"

Connelly checked the vehicles. "No, it's not here."

Nick asked the DCI if he could see if there was a depot manager in the group. Within a few minutes an elderly man came over to them.

"Good morning, sir," offered Nick, "I'm so terribly sorry this has happened, but we need to ask you a few questions."

"You want me to answer a few questions?" stammered the elderly man, "I've got some foocking questions for you. Our lunchtime meals are late, my Doris has shit herself, Ernie has got palpitations and Eric can't hold his bladder back at the best of times; and you want to ask me some fooking questions?"

Nick held up his hands at the same time calling the DCI over. After a few minutes of discussion, the DCI went back to his car and called up the HQ communications centre.

Nick approached the man who had sat himself down on a wooden crate. "Look, we need to see the registration details of your vehicles. Have you got any paperwork or details on a computer?"

"Well Doris does the computer work, and I can't help you there. Doris is a bit inconvenienced right now, if you get my drift," the old man gestured towards the building, "but I'm sure I can find the registration papers for you. All the vans are donated you know." With that the old man shuffled off to the building only to return a few minutes later with a handful of papers. "Here you are."

Nick and Nigel checked the vans to find that three vans corresponded to the paperwork, but one van had different registration plates.

Simultaneously Nick and Nigel guessed what had happened. It was Nick who spoke first.

"The pricks have switched number plates and my guess is the plates on this van have been switched from another Ford Transit Van. How many white Ford Transit Vans are there in the UK? Fucking thousands is my guess and spread all over the fucking country." Nick screwed the papers up in his hands.

The old man came over to Nick. "'Ere, what are you doing, that's my paperwork. You'll have to replace them, you will."

Nick placed the crumpled paper into the old man's hand as four squad cars pulled up.

The old man held his hands up in the air, "Foocking 'ell what in the foock is going on here."

Nick rested his hand on the man's shoulder. "Look I know we stuffed up your day, but what if we gave each of your van's a police escort around the city so you can get your orders out in time. They'll stay with you until your rounds are finished. No parking problems, no fines. OK?"

The old man looked at Nick, nodded and then walked across to the remaining police officers. "You're all barking mad, you lot." Then he yelled out to the squad cars, "Try to keep up and don't get in our foocking way. You don't mess with a meal cart in Merseyside, ya stupid pricks."

He turned back to Nick chuckling, "I've always wanted to say that to a copper. Now foock off and let us get back to work."

29

Connelly's phone rang as the two walked out of the compound. Connelly stopped as Nick listened.

"Yes sir, yes sir, thank you sir, yes sir we'll see you back at the Yard, yes sir, I mean the Met." Connelly was ashen white as he placed the phone in his pocket.

"That was McIntyre," Nigel paused and took a deep breath. "The Manchester and Merseyside Chief Constables have told us, and I quote, 'fuck off back to London, this is our case'. We're to take a train back to London and I meet with the Commissioner on arrival. The Commissioner is totally pissed off that the NCA has taken over the Judge and Bishop case. You are to go and do whatever you do when you're not providing theories in police investigations."

"That's not very polite," expressed Nick, "after all we've done for them."

"I'll call a taxi, Nick. I somehow don't think they're sending a car for us."

The taxi drive to Lime Street station from Ropewalks should only have taken a few minutes but by the time they got to St Georges Place the traffic was gridlocked. The Sikh taxi driver was mumbling and running his fingers through his long grey beard. "Big problem, not very good," he gestured towards London Road, "big demonstration. The Muslims are demonstrating, it is not very good. Much trouble I see."

Nick paid the cab driver. "We'll walk from here."

The train from Lime Street to Euston took a tad over three hours. With over twenty trains a day to London there was minimal wait at the station. It was Nick's turn to pay the bill, so they chose first class with a sleek Virgin high speed service which gave them plenty of opportunity to both drown their sorrows and draw the positives of their case work to date.

They ordered some drinks as the train left the station.

"Looks like the shit is hitting the fan, Nick."

Nick was deep in thought as he studied his complimentary meal box. "Fancy a steak again?"

"Did you hear me, Nick? This last murder is going to start a shit storm. There's probably marches in London as well."

"I hear you, Nigel. Look, I firmly-believe that this last murder is doing exactly what was intended." He hesitated and looked Nigel squarely in the eye. "Mayhem and hysterical claims of Islamophobia, demonstrations, claiming the victim like they normally do. But I'm very damn serious here, this is not the end of it. This murder was done to deliberately cause racial unrest, and mark my words, there will be retaliations." The attendant arrived with two beers. Nick stopped talking until the attendant left.

"Look, I don't blame the local police for telling us to fuck off." Nick continued, "I'd do the same. They've got a hornet's nest to deal with and they need to be focused on their own turf. They don't want us telling them that murders across jurisdictions are connected without tangible proof because it makes life more difficult for them than they need."

"I get that. You're talking to an old copper here. We all like to look after our own turf. If our theory is correct and I'm not convinced either way yet, there is fuck all we can do about it. I'm off the case and back to harassing local crims and chasing parking tickets. Spencer will be back to the mid-west. Stella will find herself a pole to climb and you my friend are off to Spooksville, wherever that is."

They both ate in relative silence as they studied the countryside and hamlets as they flashed by. The boxes were cleared away and another two beers were ordered.

101

"Look, thanks for the first-class seat, Nick," Nigel broke the silence, "let's keep in touch?"

"Of course," replied Nick wiping his mouth with the white napkin. "It ain't over my friend. I have that feeling."

"Well, it's over for me Nick. I've got a size eleven bollocking when I get back and probably a performance assessment to boot."

"Look on the bright side, we've had some fun over the years, haven't we?"

Nigel nodded and smiled as the train pulled into Euston station. "Well, this is where we part Nick." Nigel extended his hand as he stood up. Nick shook hands as he stood and affectionally grabbed Nigel's shoulder and gave it a firm squeeze.

"I'll see you soon."

30

Nick sat back in the chair and looked out of the window as Nigel walked past and up the platform. Before he could get up another man sat where Nigel was parked a few moments ago.

"Hello Nick, old bean."

"Jeremy, what are you doing here?"

"The boss wants to see you. I've got a car waiting."

"Have you been on the train since Liverpool?"

"Can't say old man, you know the story."

"Hello Nick," Sir Adrian Nightingale rose in his seat and, walking around his desk, shook Nick's hand warmly and motioned towards the chair in front of his desk. "Take a pew."

Sir Adrian walked back around the desk with his back against the Millbank skyline of new apartment buildings.

"Quite a dog's breakfast in the north there, Nick. Were you onto something?"

"I thought so Age." With no one within earshot the relationship between the two was very informal and friendly. "It's just a theory but I can't help feeling that a number of recent murders are connected in some way."

Sir Adrian leaned back in his chair and clasped his hands together. "I happen to think you're right. I don't want us to grasp at straws here but two of the victims on your list were on a watchlist including this Muslim chap in Manchester. The other was a journalist with, shall we say, nefarious connections." Sir Adrian stood up and sat on the corner of his desk next to Nick. "I want you to stay on whatever lines of enquiry you're on. Report directly to me and," hesitating as he spoke, "keep that team you're working with together, Connelly, Spencer and Wilde."

"You knew that?"

"Of course, old chap. I've had our people keeping an eye on you and your friends ever since I met Sir Alex at the club where he asked about you. Don't worry Nick. All above board. Just curious. Seems that you're onto something after all." Sir Adrian moved back to his chair. "See if you can utilise your friends' talents and you'll need to keep an eye on what our police are up to. I don't think the various constabularies are interested in making any connections at this stage, but they will if these killings keep up, and I think they will."

Sir Adrian poured a couple of Courvoisier cognacs and offered one to Nick. "Interesting that most of the victims that you're looking at probably deserved to depart this earth or at least remain in prison, don't you think?"

"And you know what list we're looking at Adrian?" asked Nick incredulously.

Sir Adrian pressed a button on his desk. Within a few seconds his door opened, and Stella Wilde walked in. "I believe you've met Dr Wilde, Nick."

"Stella's working for you?" asked Nick in disbelief.

"Don't look so astonished. There're plenty of people working for us that you haven't met yet. Stella's only just joined us."

"Good afternoon, Nick." Stella extended her hand.

"Good afternoon, Stella, good to see you." Nick pulled up a chair for her. "By the way how did you and Spencer go after we left yesterday?"

"Actually, Chris and I worked into the evening after you left." Stella sat down and crossed her legs smiling.

"And?" asked Nick.

"And what Nick?"

"And what conclusions did you reach after Nigel and I left."

"Well, we decided we were hungry."

Sir Adrian was amused by the developing conversation and watched as the two volleyed to and fro.

"And the list Stella? Not really interested in your social life." Although the improvement in Stella's attire since their first meeting had not gone unnoticed.

"You were right about two things," she paused and gave Nick a warm stare, "firstly my social life should be of no interest to you, and secondly there's a strong possibility that we have a vigilante."

Sir Adrian decided that it was time to intervene.

"I want you two, Connelly and Spencer to continue to investigate." Sir Adrian moved forward to the corner of the expansive oak desk again, "Stella, Nick and I go back a long way and if any of this gets nasty, he's the one you and the others will want in their camp. I can't put it any other way." Sir Adrian remained sitting on the corner. "The NCA will concentrate on the child pornography and regional police will continue with their investigations but at this stage they're regarding them as individual crimes and don't see any connections other than the Bishop and Judge killings. We'll leave them in that state of mind as you continue your investigations." Sir Adrian focussed on Nick. "Make sure Connelly and Spencer know to keep quiet about this. OK?

"Absolutely sir," said Nick now more formal in Stella's presence, "I'll speak with them later today."

Stella jumped in, "I'll speak to DS Spencer myself, if that's alright sir," speaking direct to Sir Adrian, "I'm having dinner with him tonight sir."

"Mmm," murmured Sir Adrian, "very well Dr Wilde, I'm fine with that. How about you Nick?"

Nick sat back in his chair smiling, "Yes sir, fine with me." As he raised his eyebrows and turned the corners of his mouth down, looking at the carpet.

"Well, that should be all for now Commander Hood and Dr Wilde." Now in formal mode Sir Adrian stood up, giving the other two the indication that it was time to leave.

Nick opened the door for Stella to leave first.

"Oh, Dr Wilde," Sir Adrian called from his desk across the room, "I hear the Cornish Crab Salad at the Savoy Grill is splendid."

"Thank you, sir. I'll remember that." Stella half turned in astonishment.

"How did he know we were going there?" whispered Stella to Nick as they moved into the outer office.

"It's his job Stella."

31

Nick was deep in thought as the two walked down to the main foyer of the Vauxhall building.

"Penny for your thoughts Nick?" asked Stella, "you haven't said a word since we left the boss."

"I'm getting that feeling Stella. I've known Sir Adrian for many years. He recruited me back in the late 70s." Nick sat down in one of the chairs in the waiting area and gestured for her to take a seat. "In my view, if this is purely a domestic matter, he's jumped in quite quickly, albeit behind the scenes." Nick paused and unbuttoned his jacket as he leaned back. "My guess is that there could be international connections in these murders or, and this could be one or both, we have someone involved at a high level. Could be a politician or a bureaucrat."

Nick frowned as he looked Stella directly in the eye.

"It's imperative that young Spencer and DCI Connelly keep us in the loop as much as they can. We need to know where the police investigations are, at any given time." Nick leaned forward towards Stella, "MI6 have contacts at the NCA, so I'm sure we can keep tabs on them. I'll speak with Nigel this evening."

"So, what do we do tomorrow, Nick?"

"I'll organise a taxi to pick you up at 9.30."

"You haven't asked what my address is."

"No, I haven't." Nick smiled. "Not too early?"

"Is there anything that you and Sir Adrian don't know?"

"I'm sure there is. Are you offering anything?"

"Get fucked Nick." Stella stood up, half smiling as she shouldered her bag.

"Right then, I'll join you in the cab outside my place. The taxi driver will have his instructions."

32

The black London taxi was waiting outside the block of apartments in Frithville Gardens as Stella closed the front door. To her surprise the fifty something driver got out of his seat to open the back door of the taxi for her.

"Morning Ma'am," the driver doffed his flat cap with a curled forefinger and then gently closed the door.

"Good morning driver," Stella leaned forward, "you know where you're going, I take it?" This was more of a statement than a question.

"Yes, I do Ma'am. Commander 'ood and me goes a long way back. We was in the Puss toogevva. But that was a long time ago luv. I was just a young kellick then, now I own twenty hackneys, don't drive no more, just do the odd favour for the guv."

"Oh, I see," replied Stella, wondering how far Nick's network of associates extended.

Of course, Stella didn't really see. It was just a polite comment to accommodate the reply. Teddy Firkin was a third generation London cabby. His father owned and drove as did his grandfather. Following twelve years in the Royal Navy as a quartermaster gunner Teddy, when ashore, was seconded as a driver. Teddy had given the sea away to go back into business with his father. His father had died some years ago; however Teddy had continued to invest in taxis and now owned twenty cabs. He was exceedingly proud to be providing employment to many people in his east end neighbourhood. A true Cockney, Teddy was a consummate cabby and chuffed about his knowledge of the great city of London.

"Yes Ma'am, as soon as the old guv gets on the dog 'n bone, I's off in the old sherbet to nab some tea leaf. A real bubble and barf I can tell ya." Teddy started whistling as the taxi wove its way through the busy streets to the Eaton Square townhouse. Nick was waiting outside as Teddy pulled the black taxi up and waited for the Commander to jump in the back seat.

"Morning Teddy."

"Morning Guv, where to?"

"Just drive for the moment Teddy, I have a few questions for you." Turning to Stella, "morning Stella, how was the Savoy Grill?"

"Very nice thank you, "replied Stella, "and that's about as much as you'll get from me Nick."

"Fair enough." Nick leaned forward until his head was close to Teddy's left ear.

"You had crossed rifles on your cuff back in the old days Teddy. Do you still do any shooting?"

"Sure do Guv. Secretary of the East End Rangers I is."

"Got your ear to the ground Teddy?"

"Depends Commander, what kind of ground are we talking about?"

"How's the black market for military equipment these days." Nick gave Teddy's shoulder a couple of taps.

"Commander 'ood, I don't know what you mean," laughing with his head back and rolling his eyes. Teddy kept driving into Westminster eventually pulling the car over in front of the Tate Gallery. "Can't stay here long Guv, the Bill will 'ave me."

"I need to know if there's any military equipment up for grabs and who's dealing."

"There's an Uncle in Soho who owes me Guv. Got the Rex on any Stoke on Trent."

"Thanks Teddy, we'll get out here. Here's a tenner for your troubles." Nick offered him a ten-pound note as he opened the rear door.

"I ain't got no troubles Commander," laughed Teddy as he dropped his window and gave them a wave as he pulled away from the curb.

33

Stella grabbed Nick's cuff as they turned towards the steps leading to the Tate. "You know I didn't understand a fucking word he said except it seemed like he knew someone who might have some information."

"He knows a pawnbroker in Soho who has the gossip on the local criminals." Nick smiled, "You really have to listen more closely Stella. Time for some culture."

The Djanogly Café at the Tate had just opened where they ordered one coffee, double shot in a mug and one peppermint tea in a cup.

"Have you had any breakfast?" asked Nick.

"No, I don't have breakfast, just a cup of tea. I don't get hungry until midday."

"I like to start the day with a couple of eggs myself if I can," said Nick as he pulled a chair out for her at a table for two.

"So, Nick, where do we go from here?"

"We wait."

"For what?"

"The next murder Stella."

"How do you know there's going to be another murder? We could be waiting weeks and how would we know if it's the killer we're looking for?"

"There's going to be another murder in the next day or two and I am hoping it's going to be in London so that Connelly can be in on it from the start." Nick thanked the waitress as the drinks were placed on the table. "I'm hungry and that Black Forest cake looks just the ticket."

Nick rose abruptly, returning to the table with the cake, offering Stella some.

"No thanks Nick. Look, how can you be so cool and calm when some maniac is about to kill someone and even worse, it could be somewhere close by?"

"Not simply a maniac Stella, a zealot perhaps. This person knows exactly what they're doing. No collateral damage, no accidental victims, just cold calculated assassinations. Until we start finding some clues, he or she, won't be caught." Nick scooped up a slice of cake and washed it down with a gulp of coffee.

"Well, I can't be so cool about it, and the thought that a gunman could be a stone's throw away is quite unnerving." Stella sipped her tea and waited until Nick finished his cake. "I'm not a field agent Nick, I'm a scientist. I don't wait in dark alleyways, smoking a cigarette with one hand on a beretta and the other on my dick."

"Well, I'm glad to hear that, Stella." Nick finished his coffee and continued. "I don't smoke, I use a Sig Sauer P226 Elite with a rosewood grip, and it's bad practice to masturbate when you're on a stake out."

There was a hesitation before they both burst out laughing. Nick's phone rang.

"Nick, it's Age. There's been another shooting in Manchester. I'll text the report to you." The call terminated as quickly as it began. The phone clicked as the message downloaded. Nick looked around to see that no one was close by as he read the message to Stella.

"This just came in from our office." Nick moved closer to Stella and read the message quietly. "The leader of a right-wing neo-Nazi group has been shot and killed in Manchester. The victim, Sean Garrity, was killed at close range outside their club rooms in Clifton. The victim had been very vocal about Islamic activism in the north of England and his group was accused by

Islamic groups of being involved in the recent murder of an Islamic preacher. The victim was killed by a person believed to be driving a white Ford Transit van. Continued unrest within the Islamic community is now compounded by groups of right-wing activists demonstrating against what they believe is a murder committed by Islamic terrorists. 'C'."

Within thirty minutes Nick and Stella were on the platform at Euston Station making their way to the first-class carriage of the Virgin high speed train to Manchester.

34

One hour earlier

The white van waited in Rake Lane near the Clifton Railway Station. As expected, a Harley Davidson Softail Classic crossed the bridge at 9am from the north and continued down Rake Lane before turning left into Lumns Lane. Just before the tyre services building the bike turned right into the club rooms of the Northern Neos. Parking his bike outside the steel shed Sean Garrity rested his bike on the side stand and removed his helmet.

The white van pulled up alongside as Sean reached into his pocket for the keys to the club rooms. Sean looked towards the van as the driver called his name. At six feet five Sean had to lean down to speak with the driver but was met with a silenced Glock 45 auto. Two bullets were fired in quick succession and Sean was dead before his head hit the ground.

The driver wiped the blood spray from the side mirror before pulling away slowly and turned around driving back in a northerly direction along Lumns Lane and then left into Rake Lane. From Rake Lane it was Queensway and the A666. The steady thump of The Scorpions could be heard as he passed by the shops, houses and passers-by.

It would be sometime before anyone would notice the body lying on the ground beside the motor bike. Drunken club members lying around the shed were not unusual. This was an area to be avoided by those who were familiar with the neighbourhood.

35

"Why are we going to Manchester Nick? I doubt if we'll be able to get near the crime scene."

"Trust me, Stella."

The fast Virgin train was passing Stoke-on-Trent when Nick made a call. All Stella heard was that they would be meeting someone at Clifton. On arrival at Piccadilly Manchester they hailed a taxi to the Clifton railway station where they waited on the road bridge close to the ramp leading down to the platform. Within a few minutes a BMW Series 5 Estate police vehicle pulled up with the driver signalling them to get in.

"Good afternoon, Commander Hood, Ma'am."

"Stella, I'd like you to meet Constable Kevin Constable," laughed Nick.

Stella leaned over and shook his hand from the back as Nick buckled up in the passenger front seat.

"Nice to meet you Constable Constable."

"Now Guv," said Kevin as he pulled away from the kerb, "I've got you some GMP ID's and as far as anyone is concerned, you're here relative to the group's links to domestic terrorism." Kevin continued, "Which is not too far from the truth, pack of bad bastards and many around here would think whoever shot this prick, whoops sorry miss."

Stella interjected, "Continue Kevin, no problems here."

"Well, most around here would've liked to have shot him themselves, truth be known."

Within a few moments they were at the roadblock in Lumns Lane with the officer waving them through.

"I'll park here and let you walk the rest of the way in case I get asked why I'm so far away from where I'm supposed to be," laughed Kevin.

Nick and Stella walked the remaining 100 metres to the parking area next to the shed. They flashed their passes and with so many uniformed police, plain clothes and forensic officers in white suits they were left alone to inspect the crime scene. The body had been moved but the blood-stained gravel clearly indicated where the incident had taken place. Once again, the injuries must have been inflicted to create maximum trauma with a huge amount of blood present together with fragments of tissue and bone.

A plain clothes officer approached them.

"Pretty well blew the back of his head off, poor sod. Anyway, he was a total arsehole." The detective pushed his hands deep into his pockets.

Nick responded, "So, pretty well known in these parts then."

"Yeah, the whole damn lot. Drugs, prostitution, standover tactics; we found a few handguns inside as well. I was hoping we'd find a rifle like the one used on that Arab. Who are you, if you don't mind me asking?"

"London. Just interested that's all, in case it was terrorism related. Don't worry we'll check the report out when it hits the desk but thanks for the extra info. Thought we'd have a butchers 'ook while we were passing frew." Nick did his best with an East London twang.

The detective nodded and walked off seemingly satisfied with Nick's impersonation of a London copper. Nick turned to Stella, "we'd better head off ourselves, before he realizes we never said who we were and who we worked for."

The detective spoke with a uniform as he approached the shed. "They must pay those London coppers well, Saville row suit, Italian shoes, I'm wasting my fuckin' time here."

36

Kevin had the engine running by the time they reached the car and offered to drive them to Piccadilly Station for the train to Euston.

"I thought that detective was going to quiz us for a moment," commented Nick.

"No, Jimmy wouldn't worry. I saw him over there with you. He's got it together. Probably working out how to minimise the paperwork when he gets back to the station. What do you reckon?"

Nick answered, "About the killing? I would say a medium calibre handgun, probably silenced. Possibly a soft nose bullet, could have been an expansion type. If it blew the back of his head off might have been a forty-five. We need to see a ballistics report to be sure. No doubt it was a professional hit. Not much to go on. I guess you people will see what's on any security cameras in the area although all we're likely to see is a white Ford Transit van. If there's a number plate, I'd put money on it being stolen."

"Listen Guv," Kevin leaned out of the driver's window, "Been a lot of demonstrations in northern towns. The Muslims are marching almost every day and not only blaming the Nazis but also the other Islamic Sunni group. In my opinion they're all barking mad. The streets are pretty tense, and our Chief Constable is absolutely packing it."

"Thanks Kevin, I'll keep that in mind."

The trains run frequently from the Piccadilly Station at Manchester to Euston Station. Every twenty minutes or so there is a streamlined fast train ready for the two and a half-hour direct journey. Nick thought that by now the staff would recognise him as a regular considering his multiple trips in the past few days. Nick cursed Virgin for cancelling their dining car a couple of years ago and providing a meal box as a mediocre form of compensation. After all, first class passengers were probably Virgin's best customers.

"You don't talk much about your personal life Nick?" asked Stella as they settled into their seats.

The train pulled out as Nick contemplated the reply. "Was that a statement or a question, Stella? Anyway, why would I?"

"I guess it was a question. We're going to be working together," answered Stella, "but I'm sorry, I didn't mean to be intrusive."

"No, not intrusive at all," Nick fumbled with the meal box so conveniently dropped on their table as they spoke. "I try to keep my personal life away from the job. Less complicated that way."

"Well, it seems that you and Sir Adrian, and probably most of the Met, seem to know all about me."

"I'm sure that isn't true , although you should check the fastenings on your dance pole, the top ones in the ceiling are a little loose."

"You know that?"

"Just joking, Stella. What would you like to know?"

"Who is Nicholas Hood?" Stella opened her box and removed the cellophane around the ham and cheese croissant.

"Apart from the fact that I say 'fuck' more often than I should," laughed Nick.

A woman sitting across the aisle butted in. "Please don't use that word in front of me, I find it offensive, and a man of your age should know better."

Nick was quick with a reply, "This discussion is not directed at you madam, perhaps you shouldn't listen to other people's conversations; that way you won't hear anything that may offend you."

Stella remained silent and a little bemused.

A voice came from the seat behind Nick as a middle-aged male leaned forward. "I say fuck all the time."

Another lady opted in from close by. "I said fuck this morning. I don't usually use that word. I dropped a jar of strawberry jam on the kitchen floor. There was jam and broken glass all over the floor and I said fuck. My granddaughter looked at me and said *"that's another name for sexual intercourse, they told me that at school. That's when a man puts his penis into a lady's vagina."* Well, I nearly fell over and then she said, *"the teacher said there were other names for those as well."* I don't know what the schools are teaching kids today."

The carriage group erupted into laughter and then there was silence. Nick noticed the lady opposite stand up and move to another seat further down the carriage.

"Well, I'm married, happily. My wife's a Harley Street specialist physician. We have two children, a boy and a girl. All grown up and living their lives. I might add they're still a boy and girl, we're a fairly conservative family." Nick relaxed back into the seat. "I have a commission in the Royal Navy, as you know. I've passed on two promotions so I could stay in the field and not bogged down by regulations and bullshit. We have a country house on the south coast and a townhouse in Belgravia, and as you know I sometimes carry a firearm. I don't smoke, nor do I masturbate on stakeouts." Nick smiled as Stella joined in with a chuckle. "Dianne, my wife, and I have what I would say was a particularly happy home life. She hates the mob I work for, but we have a mutual appreciation of the work each of us does and I think that's a sign of the respect and love we have for each other."

Stella found herself admiring this ageing spy who showed all the intellect and vitality of a much younger man.

37

It was unusual for Nick to open-up about his personal life, but he felt very much at ease with this young, attractive and intelligent lady.

"I started off my naval career as a sailor in the Royal Australian Navy, after my parents moved down under. My father was an engineer, and he was contracted to a mining company. A few years after I joined the navy, they were killed in a road accident in western Queensland. Sometime later I was offered the opportunity of a commission after saving Sir Adrian's life during a brawl in Hong Kong. He was with Naval Intelligence and was getting beaten up in an alleyway in Wan Chai. I was sitting at a coffee stall having a bowl of something unhygienic when I heard a ruckus. Normally I would've been mixing it up with my shipmates. Dave Williamson, as I recall, was occupied with a couple of Wan Chai bargirls at the time, so I headed back to the ship and left him to it, besides Dave never liked sharing." Nick chuckled, "I ran towards the fight and fetched the assailants off. Saved Sir Adrian's life, or Commander Nightingale as he was known at the time." Nick paused. "He asked me if I would be interested in working with him. So here we are thirty-five years or so later, still working together."

"I guess you have some stories to tell?" asked Stella.

"You could say that, but we have Her Majesty's Official Secrets Act of 1939 and 1989 and we also have the Naval Discipline Act of 1957 so forgive me if I don't tell any tales out of school." Nick leaned forward, "mind you I admit to being sorely tempted to write a book one day." Laughing, he

121

accepted the offer of a cup of coffee when the steward approached.

"So, how are you and young Chris getting on? He's a bright lad, I like him." Nick quickly changed the subject.

"Nothing too serious but I like him too," Stella blushed a little and folded her lunch box surreptitiously to cover her embarrassment.

"Good," Nick leant back in the seat again, looking out the window as they passed through Milton Keynes and Bletchley. "Have you ever been to Bletchley Park?"

"The old code breaking centre?"

"Yes, that's right."

"We went there on a university study trip years ago. Loved it," said Stella, "why do you ask?"

"No real reason. I just think that era of espionage was perhaps a more romantic time. Turing was building his code breaking machine, which in effect won us the war, and all we did was persecute the poor devil for being gay. The very people he saved were the ones who turned on him. Our boys and girls worked very closely with Bletchley in those days. Of course, we have Ian Fleming to thank for glamourising the life of an MI6 agent when in fact, life in the shadows is remarkably different."

"So, no tuxedos, casinos and Aston Martin sports cars?"

"I'm afraid not Stella, raincoats, cheap pubs and whatever you can nick from the car-pool."

"I'm sure you've had your moments, Nick?"

"There have been highlights I must admit, but my watershed moment was when my parents got killed and I realised that I never wrote to them while I was away. I only ever spoke to them if, and when, I came home from leave." Nick reflectively gazed out of the window. "After they died, I started a diary and each day I write something as if I'm writing the letters to them that I never did while they were alive."

Stella joined his gaze out of the window, not quite sure what to say next. Instead, they both looked at the passing parade of life rushing past as the train headed to London. It was Stella who eventually broke the silence.

"If it's not too personal a question Nick, are the diaries very detailed or just a few observations of the day?" Stella found herself going into psyche mode. Her subject was a complicated person, and she was genuinely interested both professionally and personally. After all, she thought, I'm working with, and for, this person and there may be a time when her life, or his, could be on the line.

"Quite detailed in places Stella," Nick hesitated, "I know my boss is aware that I keep a diary and it's come up in discreet conversation that it would be advisable if I don't divulge sensitive state and operational details. I'm sure most journalists would give an arm and a leg for some of it but that won't be happening any time soon. I keep them in a safe place."

"I only asked professionally."

"Yes, I know. I find writing quite therapeutic."

"From a clinical perspective it's important to have a relationship with your mind Nick." Stella slipped into evaluation mode. "It can have the same effect as meditation. Writing a journal or a diary requires the application of the analytical, rational left side of the brain. While your left hemisphere is occupied, your right hemisphere, the creative, touchy-feely side, is given the freedom to wander and play. Allowing your creativity to proliferate and expand can be cathartic. It can make a big difference in your daily well-being."

"Well, thank you for that forensic analysis, Stella."

"I was actually quoting from a textbook, but it's true. Are there any juicy bits?"

"Now you're getting personal, doctor," laughed Nick.

38

The train pulled into Euston. Nick and Stella joined with the moving mass as they made their way to the Melton Street exit. Nick stopped to take a call as they passed the local Sainsburys.

"That was my friend in the taxi. Let's grab a coffee. He's picking us up in ten minutes."

They finished their coffee as the black taxi pulled up outside Caffe Nero.

"Allo Guv," Teddy Firkin slid his window down, "Op in, this one's on me."

The two made themselves comfortable in the back seat as Teddy pulled the taxi away from the kerb.

"Have you thought about those new electric taxis Teddy?"

"Yes Commander," replied Teddy, "New electric TX. Smoove as a baby's bum. Fifty-eight fousand quid tho, bit much me finks." Teddy paused briefly as he negotiated a set of traffic lights. "Got some joss on them guns you was after Guv."

"Thanks Teddy, I'll see if I can get you a better deal on those electric jobs."

"Fanks Guv, these diesels don't 'alf make a racket. Listen guv, there's a lot of 'ardware around. I 'erd it comes straight from the armoury, so to speak. Some geezers got the keys to the toy store and they're selling direct. You puts your order in like a bleedin' pizza and then pick it up as per instructions." Teddy paused again as he weaved his way through the traffic.

"So how would someone like me buy some kit Ted?"

"Well that's the tricky bit Guv. You gotta reply to the ad."

"What ad?"

"The ad in the paper."

"What, they're advertising this stuff in the daily paper?" interjected Stella.

"That's right miss, but they's using different lingo. Sort of cryptic if you get my drift."

"Right," replied Nick, "Can you give me an example?"

"Sure can Guv, got a copy of The Daily Mirror right 'ere."

Teddy pulled the taxi up on the left side of Inner Circuit at Regents Park near the Rose Gardens and joined Nick and Stella in the back of the taxi. Pulling down one of the front seats he faced his passengers and opened the paper in the classified ads section.

"'Ere we go, Adult Services," chuckled Teddy as Nick and Stella moved forward in their seats. "Now, we looks down the list until we finds a girl called Sophie. The phone number will connect you to a legit lady but you 'ave to ask for Annie."

"Annie?" asked Nick.

"Yeah. Annie, get your gun."

"You're shitting me."

"I shit you not Guv. I ain't goin' to call 'cos these are prickly geezers, and I don't want no trouble. Then she'll put the call through to the dealer or tell you to fuck off. Sorry Miss Stella."

"Let me get this straight Teddy. If anyone wants to buy an illegal gun in the UK all they have to do is call one of these girls and they put you through to a dealer?"

"That's right, but the phone number and girls name changes right regular but Annie is the go."

"So, hang on, how do you know which girl to call," Nick was starting to show an element of frustration.

"Don't get your nickers in a knot Commander. You got to go underground for the chick's name cos it changes, don't it? Next week it could be Gloria. I dunno," Teddy lifted his eyebrows causing his brow to crease. "You gotta talk to someone in the game, like an Uncle or a fence, can't make it too bleeding obvious or the Old Bill would be down like a shower of shite. Sorry again Miss Stella."

"No offence taken Teddy, this is fascinating," Stella couldn't help smiling at the rapport.

"One word of advice Commander. These are not very nice people. Caution would be required of a very high-order I would fink." Teddy folded up the newspaper and pushed it into Nick's lap. "Where to Guv?"

"Telephone shop Teddy. There's no way I'll be using my own phone, especially considering I'm breaking a number of laws just by soliciting for an illegal firearm, MI6 or not."

The taxi headed back to Euston Station where Nick acquired a 'Pay as you Go' phone. Directed to drive around, Teddy took the cab for an extended tour of the city sights. Stella sat back and enjoyed the view as Nick initiated the phone, thankful that it came with sixty per cent power in the battery.

"Alright Teddy. Shut the fuck up for five minutes please." Nick dialled Sophie.

The number rang a few times and then answered, "Hello, Sophie speaking." Nick suspected this was not her real name.

"Hello Sophie, can I speak to Annie please?"

"She's a popular girl lately, hang on love."

The phone went silent and then started dialling again. After the customary digital tones a gruff voice answered. "Allo." Nick detected a course London accent.

"I'm calling for Annie?" requested Nick.

"What do you want Annie for then?"

"I want some hardware."

"What kind of hardware you after?"

"Glock nine millimetre with a silencer."

"Ang on," was the reply, and then about twenty seconds later, "That'll be two fousand quid with the suppressor."

Nick hesitated for a few seconds, "and what about a rifle?"

126

"What kind?"

"What have you got?"

"Look mate if you don't know what you want fuck off. Iver that or tell me what you want, and I'll tell you if we've got it?"

Nick decided not to press his luck and asked for one of the standard sniper rifles used by the British military.

"Accuracy International with suppressor and scope?"

"Well, you know your stuff," replied the man, "they don't come cheap."

There was another pause as Nick heard the man flip through some pages.

"That'll cost you ten fousand quid."

"How do I pay?".

"I call you back with a 'Bitcoin' account number. When the money's in the account, I call you again with a pickup for the hardware."

"Where will that be,".

"We drop off in the city."

"Where?".

"We tell you when the hardware is available."

"When will that be?"

"Two days for the handgun and seven days for the rifle."

"Can I pay cash and pick it up?"

"Fuck off mate. No-one meets anyone. Are you a copper?"

"No, I'm not a copper but I'll have to think about the price."

The phone went dead.

"Well, I'm not about to fork out ten grand to test the system Teddy," said Nick with a smile.

"Very wise decision Guv if I do say so myself. Them geezers is not to be trusted." Teddy continued through the London traffic, delicately weaving his cab in and out of the congested streets.

"Well, at least we know the black market is alive and well. What next Nick?" Stella redirected her eyes from the passing scenery.

"This is a clumsy way for professionals to acquire firearms, just can't see it," offered Nick as he pushed himself back in the seat. "Can't help thinking that they must have a more reliable and discreet way of getting their hardware. I might have a chat with Sir Adrian."

39

Teddy dropped Nick off at the Vauxhall Building and then, at Stella's request, back across the river, along Millbank, Abingdon St and then dropping her off at the corner of Derby Gate and Parliament St.

"Ah," said Teddy, "off for a bit of nosh Miss Stella."

"Yes Teddy, this detective work is thirsty business," Stella offered a twenty-pound note which was abruptly refused by Teddy.

"No charge Miss, enjoy your lunch." Teddy made the drop and disappeared into the traffic.

Stella stepped into the Red Lion while sending a text to Nick, Chris and DCI Connelly.

'At the Red Lion, late lunch anyone?'

Walking in from the Derby Street entrance Stella made her way down to the Cellar Bar and settled into a padded alcove. The lower bar was quiet in the mid afternoon as she caught the eye of the barman and ordered a gin and tonic. Checking her phone, she noticed that there was no signal and, grabbing her bag, she walked back up the stairs until the signal came back. Chris had texted back to say that he and Nigel were on their way. No reply from Nick which was no surprise considering he was probably meeting with Sir Adrian. Stella made her way back down to the cellar bar and once again made herself comfortable in the alcove. She was on her second drink when Chris and Nigel came down the stairs.

"I'll have a half pint Spencer and get one for yourself." Nigel grabbed a seat opposite Stella while Chris ordered the drinks.

Chris almost fell over one of the chairs in his eagerness to sit in the alcove seat next to Stella. An exchange of knowing eyes was the only visible greeting as Chris took up the vacant space. The drinks came promptly and the three clinked their glasses with a resounding 'cheers'.

"Is Nick coming?" asked Nigel.

"I texted him, but he was meeting with his boss after we dropped him off," replied Stella.

"So how was Manchester?" enquired Chris and Nigel almost simultaneously.

"Bit grisly actually." Stella leaned back into the high backrest. "Looked like another professional hit, no collateral damage once again and just a white van as a suspect's vehicle. The local police seemed to be quite thorough with their procedures."

"They've got a lot brewing up there at the moment," offered Chris, "Street protests by ethnic groups and right-wing militants. It's spread to Liverpool as well. Something else has happened up north, another murder. It came through just as I was leaving." Chris fumbled with his phone. "No signal here."

"Same here," said Nigel as he studied his phone.

"They don't work down here," offered Stella, "mine's the same."

The boys downed their beers in quick time. "I'll have another Spencer, and get one for Stella as well."

"No thanks Chris, two drinks during the day are enough for me."

Chris was at the bar and noticing Nick coming down the stairs, ordered another half pint.

"That was good timing. How is everyone. I suppose Stella has told you about the bikie killing." Nick grabbed the wooden chair next to Nigel opposite the alcove.

"Yes Nick," acknowledged Nigel, "while its quiet in here we might just go over a few things if that's OK with you."

Chris came back with the drinks and was abruptly dispatched by Nigel to the ground floor to check his phone messages.

"Something else has happened Nick," said Nigel, "there's been another incident. Chris is on the street checking his phone, there's no signal down here."

"Yes, I know, up north again." Nick took a long sip of the amber fluid as Chris came back down.

"Don't worry Spencer, we know, Nick just told us."

"Right, no signal down here but clear as soon as you reach the top of the stairs."

"That's right," said Nick, "the cellar here is surrounded by steel re-enforcing and quite a bit of lead as well. OIS used this room during the second world war and somewhere behind these walls is a tunnel that leads down to the old Churchill war rooms. The old chap himself used this very alcove for the occasional port and cigar while being briefed by the agents of the day. They made that leather alcove especially for him."

"Is there anything you don't know?" asked Stella admiringly.

"I'm sure there is Stella, like, for example, that chap in the suit at the bar. Has he been there long?"

"He came down the stairs a couple of minutes after Chris and Nigel arrived," replied Stella.

Nick turned to Nigel, "Don't all turn round for Christ's sake. Do you recognise him, Nigel?"

"I've seen him around the Yard, internals I think, one of Celia's boys." Nigel started getting an uneasy feeling.

"I'll fix this shit." Nick stood up and approached the bar standing a few feet from the suit. "Hello old chum, can I buy you a beer?"

"Thanks all the same but I'm on orange juice."

"On duty I guess, and by the way you keep tapping your earpiece you're not getting a signal down here."

The man shuffled uneasily as Nick moved a little closer. "Your phone won't work down here either but the way you've just fumbled with it in your pocket you've probably tried to discreetly turn the recording function on. So why don't we dispense with the bullshit and put the phone on the counter so I can talk clearly into the device for you."

Back at the alcove the other three could clearly see the deteriorating demeanour of the two men at the bar.

"Oh shit, here goes my pension," mumbled Nigel.

"And my career," muttered Chris under his breath.

The man in the suit placed the smartphone on the bar, very clearly in recording mode. Nick moved even closer and gestured to the barman to move back as he leaned towards the device. There were beads of sweat on the brow of the detective constable, clearly way out of his depth.

"It's like this Celia," Nick started, "If I ever get the notion that I, or any of my colleagues, are being tailed I'll contact the tabloids and tell them about the sordid parties you organise in that Kensington flat with your ginger girlfriend at NCA." Nick paused, "Gee I'm glad we got that sorted," and looking the detective clearly in the eyes, "now fuck off."

Nick turned and walked back to the alcove as the detective gathered up his phone and hurried up the stairs. Nick stopped before sitting down, "I just have to make a call, back in a few moments," as he followed the detective up the stairs.

40

"Well, my pension is gone. I may as well clear my desk this afternoon. I'm history." Nigel put his head in his hands as Stella reached across to comfort him.

"Is Nick always like this. The perfect gentleman one minute and then a totally offensive maniac the next?" Stella was clearly vexed.

Chris was still unable to speak as Nick came bouncing down the stairs apparently full of the joys of spring to be greeted by a look of despair by the three in the alcove.

"What's up with you lot?"

"Nick, are you mad? The whole Yard will be down on these two and you and I may as well start looking for another occupation." Stella was furious.

"Nonsense," replied Nick laughing, "Celia's been on a watch list for a while. She's been constantly undermining the Commissioner who's been too scared and PC to give her a shove. We've had her flat under surveillance for months now and quite frankly she's a security risk together with 'the ginger with big tits' at the NCA and her liberal friends." Nick sat down and took a few gulps of his beer. "Your jobs are safe but hers isn't. She'll get her marching orders tomorrow morning after Sir Adrian and Sir Alex have a few pink gins at the club tonight, discussing her successor. She'll go quietly. Now let's get down to business."

The detective headed out of the Red Lion and turned left into the rear of Old Scotland Yard, hurrying as he called his boss. Outside the Deputy Commissioners office, he tapped on the glass door to her office where she was holding a small meeting. Celia beckoned him in, but he stayed at the door curling his finger requesting she come to him. She opened the door and ordered him in.

"Benson, did you record any conversations?"

"I did Ma'am, but it might be best if I play it to you in private."

"Nonsense," uttered Celia as she turned to the small group, "this is exactly what we've been talking about." She continued, "A total lack of discipline from the top, and we end up with a group of unauthorised detectives and consultants doing their own thing. Now we have a recording of exactly what's been going on behind our backs. Play the recording Benson."

"Ma'am, I really do think that we should play the recording in private." Benson was sweating profusely.

Celia took the phone out of his hand, selected the 'recording app' and pressed play while Benson looked on in horror.

"It's like this Celia, if I ever get the notion that I, or any of my colleagues, are being tailed I'll contact the tabloids and tell them about the sordid parties you organise in that Kensington flat with your ginger girlfriend at NCA. Gee I'm glad we got that sorted, now fuck off."

Celia stood frozen, incapable of movement as she stared into nowhere in disbelief. Benson promptly left the room as the others pushed their chairs away and quickly followed.

41

The discussion continued until the evening crowds came in for after-work drinks whereby the decision was made, having missed lunch, to have dinner where they were and enjoy the atmosphere of the Whitehall social scene. By this time, they had established some key points and, although no closer to identifying the killer or killers, they were firmly of the opinion they were dealing with an organised, resourceful and professional individual or group. The fact that there had been no collateral damage spoke for the discipline and attention to detail. In all probability, if all the ducks were not in a row, the trigger would not be pulled. The victims had been carefully selected based on perceived criteria around corruption, failure of judicial authority and sentencing, sedition, civil unrest, perversion, false narratives, among others. It was unanimously decided that there was indeed a case of vigilantism, perpetrated by a person or persons unknown.

Nick advised that the group was unofficially sanctioned by MI6, however any investigations were to be discreet and not to impede or interfere with current investigations being made by any other authority. They were to work in the shadows, so to speak, with Connelly and Spencer as liaison with the permissions agreed upon between Sir Adrian and Sir Alex who, as of tomorrow would have a new deputy in Cynthia Burrows, fulfilling a role that was seen as being PC for the Woke brigade and someone who was eminently qualified for the role as a loyal and supporting deputy. Sir Adrian had a few personnel within the NCA who would ensure a reliable flow of information firstly to MI6 and thence to Nick and his team.

With a structure now in place and the necessary freedoms of investigation at his fingertips Nick was confident that progress would be made. It was regretful that there would need to be a greater number of murders before any tangible evidence could be gathered and still no guarantee that these murders would be solved. In the meantime, the various police jurisdictions would continue to investigate as if each murder were independent of the others and perceived to be contained within those jurisdictions. For the moment there was a degree of normality in the working routines of Nick's team. Nigel and Chris were given a degree of latitude in their investigations to work independently of other departments, however an incident room would draw unnecessary attention.

Any group meetings would need to be both casual and discreet. Their scope was broad enough that they could stay abreast of current investigations throughout the jurisdictions of the UK and collate the appropriate evidence for consideration by Nick's team. Chris was spending more leisure time with Stella and gave plenty of opportunity for Stella's input in her professional capacity. Nick would touch base on an almost daily basis with meet ups at the Red Lion being a regular event every few days however the pub was getting crowded, and a new venue was needed.

Nick made a call to Teddy Firkin.

"So Teddy, about those new electric taxi vehicles."

"Nice gear Commander but as we said a bit on the pricey side."

"I've got contacts Teddy. I know one of the chaps at Jankel, they do armoured upgrades."

"That's very nice of you skipper, what's the catch?"

"I need a new mobile office, Teddy."

42

Earlier that day

Dressed in a white Arabic thobe with a white ghutra on his head, the man parked the white van at the rear of the Abu Shafi Islamic College in Bradford. The plan was a simple one of offering a Folio of the Blue Quran, recently acquired at auction, to the Sunni Cleric Hakim Mifta. An outspoken opponent of Shia Islam, he held many contentious classes in northern England creating an ever-widening divide between Shia and Sunni communities. With ninety four percent of UKs Islamic communities Sunni and just four percent Shia, friction was frequent and both sides fearful of outside influences exacerbating tensions.

Hakim was quick to entertain a meeting with a fellow cleric with the prospect of the school acquiring an original Blue Quran folio. The man knew that his opportunity was brief and had requested a private meeting. He knew that upon inspection the cleric would soon realise that the folio was in fact a copy and not original.

Carrying a leather shoulder bag the man opened the student entrance door. His disguise was immaculate. The beard was his own and dyed black. The contact lenses and darkened area around his eyes gave him a hollow and sallow gaze. He spoke fluent Levantine Arabic and had spent many years in Syria. His sandals scraped along the floor exhibiting a peasant like shuffle. The school was in recess and devoid of students. A receptionist showed the man to a small prayer room where Hakim was seated on a large Janamaz. With a beckoning wave Hakim welcomed him. The door closed behind the man.

"As-Salam-u-Alaikum"

"As-Salam-u-Alaikum"

The man crouched and opened his bag placing the colourful texts on the mat. Hakim smiled as he touched the texts and then picked one article up and brought it closer to his eyes. Squinting, he reached for a magnifying glass, as the expression on his face turned to a sour grimace. Snarling, he looked up to see the man pointing a gun with a silencer at his forehead. The man pulled the trigger twice and Hakim fell back against the blood-spattered wall.

The man stood up, gathering the false documents and placing the revolver in his shoulder bag. He opened the door and turned back to the body slumped against the wall.

"As-Salam-u-Alaikum"

He closed the door and shuffled past the receptionist as she looked up.

"Salam."

"Salam," replied the man, and then in broken English, "Leave Hakim for a little while. He is in raptures with the nas'azraq."

The riots between the Shia and Sunni Muslims started that evening. Each blaming the other for the murders. Chris got the email and advised DCI Connelly and Nick. They both shrugged, with Nick and Nigel agreeing that there would be little point in inspecting another murder scene. They would wait for the forensic analysis.

43

It was on the Monday following a previous week of data collection and dissemination that Nick made the call. He would be picking up the team members in the new Firkin taxi. Teddy picked up Nick first as directed.

"Hi Teddy, how's the new cab?"

"All shipshape skipper, just off the hoist and ready to rock 'n' roll."

"Excellent, how does she feel?"

"Rides very well even with the extra weight Guv."

"Right let's pick up the crew and I'll brief them when we're all together. I had to call in a few favours to get this job done."

"One thing Boss," Teddy paused and turned around, "please don't ask me how my Firkin kids are in front of the others. I got my pride you know."

"I give you my Firkin oath Teddy, now let's go."

With Connelly as first call, Stella and Chris were the last two pick-ups. Obviously shacked up in Stella's flat and sporting shy grins.

"Climb aboard you two and we'll get started."

It was Stella that immediately noticed the new internal livery.

"This is a nice taxi, Nick?" as she glanced to see Teddy still at the wheel.

"Yes, it is, and the reason I've asked you to go for a ride." Nick paused, "we've added a few new features. Teddy will tell us all about it."

Teddy played with a few switches as the intercom came to life.

"And Teddy, keep it brief and in English please, not that cockney babble."

"Roger that Skipper. Fought I would read off the screen," there was a pause and Teddy commenced his commentary from the media display on the dashboard.

"This vehicle has been modified with a protection cell including roof and under-floor blast protection, in accordance with ERV 2010 and PAS 300 and panels are viable against multi angled attacks. Armoured glass is provided to European Standard VPAM BRV 2009 VR8 and PAS 300. The vehicle has fully certified protection for evading extreme threats at high speeds keeping occupants safe. The wheels are equipped with a run flat system of up to 60km at 75km/h. Defence against IEDs is tested to STANAG 4569 and emergency exit can be made through the armoured escape panel at the rear of the cabin." Teddy paused adjusting his tie as he tried his best to disguise his cockney accent.

"We also have Wi-Fi, multiple phone charging points, fold down tables and gas masks in the space under the seats. Please remain seated during take-off and ensure your seats are upright with fold down table raised. I added that last bit myself."

His last comment caused more than a wry smile from his passengers.

"Even her Majesty would feel safe in here," remarked Connelly.

"Just a precaution I thought, as this is our new mobile office," remarked Nick.

44

With around eleven murders across the UK each week Connelly, Spencer and Wilde were kept busy selecting any that would fit their profiling. They were finally allocated an interview room on the same floor as the new Deputy Commissioner Cynthia Burrows and assured by her of an element of privacy and cooperation while they collated and analysed potential cases. Nick kept a low profile, meeting up each week to be briefed on the profiling and dissemination of information.

The child molestation incidents involving those arrested, as predicted, advanced to bail conditions followed by a media frenzy, as lawyers tackled the publicity with "no comments at this stage and of course my client denies the charges." It had been three weeks since the arrests and two of those accused had committed suicide. One was the cousin of the Queen and the other a member of the government in the house. The murders being examined by Nick's team at the Met during this time were assessed as not being connected with the 'special' cases. It was as if the killer or killers had gone to ground. Nick commented on the fact that it could be that the legal phase of the pornography cases combined with the racial unrest in Manchester was creating enough attention in the media that perhaps this created a hiatus for the killers. It was Nick's view that the team could expect another series of kills in a new phase when the opportunity presented itself.

Stella remarked that the killer or killers considered themselves to be a kind of 'star chamber' where they presented as judge and jury. They had the means and the motive to carry out the murders with almost perceived immunity. It should also not be discounted that there could be a higher entity providing instruction, supply and support.

Connelly and Spencer utilised their contacts within the force and their abilities to obtain specific details of 'crimes of interest' bringing forward pertinent details. The incident board was crowded. There was no pattern developing either geographically or academically.

The three of them became more convinced, as time advanced, that the killer or killers were trained professionals. Nick used the term 'quasi-military' stating they were dealing, more than likely, with a small specialist organisation with inherent training, tactics and subculture. He could not rule out, at least at this stage, that there was a foreign power or entity involved. The victims identified by the investigative group clearly showed that any motive was of a domestic nature.

It was raised during discussion that each of the accused within the child pornography case should be investigated for links to prospective underworld identities however considering that these accused were also regarded as victims of the killers then it was likely that those identified in that case were, in all probability, not linked to the killers in any other way except as victims.

As Nick predicted, it was indeed the calm before the storm.

45

Associate professor Richard Cranston took his usual route to Durham University down Newcastle Road, the A167, from Crossgate Moor. At the intersection of the A690 he slowed his Volkswagen Polo to a stop at the traffic lights. A yellow Honda CB125 pulled up beside the driver window with the rider tapping on the window and pointing down to the front right wheel.

Richard wound down his window as the bike rider pulled out a silenced pistol and fired two shots into his face, spraying the inside of the car with blood. Richard slumped forward onto the wheel sounding the horn as the lights turned green. The Polo crept forward slowly as the yellow Honda sped away across the intersection down Darlington Road, weaving through the traffic before turning left into Potters Bank.

The Volkswagen Polo came to a stop in the middle of the intersection as the surrounding traffic came to a halt. People came out of their cars to see what the problem was. It would be nearly fifteen minutes before a police car arrived, quickly followed by an ambulance. The first officer on the scene moved Richard's body back from the steering wheel and turned the ignition off. The bike rider was already at Wolviston by the time the first officers at the scene had reported the incident as a crime.

46

Oxford, Tuesday 8.30am

Socialist bookshop owner Hector Sommerfield paused at the traffic lights on Heddington Road on the way to his book shop in St Clements Street. His little Renault Kangoo electric van sat quietly behind a small sedan at the lights. A yellow Honda CB125 pulled up alongside the driver's window, tapped and pointed to the driver's side front wheel. Hector wound his window down and the rider pointed a silenced revolver at his head and pulled the trigger twice, drenching the dashboard in blood. Hector fell back in his seat, the van silent and stationary.

The Honda sped off, turning right against a red light and down Marston Road. Initially the cars behind Hector didn't respond until the lights changed but Hector's car remained motionless while several cars beeped their horns. After a full minute of car horns blaring one driver opened his car door and yelled out. With no audible reply he approached the little van with the bloodstained interior. In a shocked state he called for help while dialling triple nine.

The ambulance arrived promptly from the John Radcliffe Hospital close by; however, by the time the police made an appearance, and reported a suspicious death, the Honda bike was passing Lewknor on the M40 and heading towards London.

47

By midday Connelly and Spencer had received the initial details and witness statements. Text messages were sent to Nick and Stella requesting a meet up that afternoon when more details were expected. Stella made her way to the incident room at the Met while Nick advised he would meet them later in the afternoon.

Nick had called Teddy Firkin to have the taxi at his townhouse in Belgravia at 2pm. In the meantime, he would give Age a call even though he knew that Age would have been informed by his people shortly after the early morning incidents. The call would be perfunctory, however from Nick's point of view it was necessary to give Age a 'heads up' that the team was onto it.

At 1.45pm Nick picked up the phone as he reclined on the soft lounge chair in the bay window overlooking the park. The call rang twice before Age picked it up.

"Hi Nick, how's the case going? I heard about the deaths in Durham and Oxford. Any leads?"

"Not yet Age, but London to a brick we're looking at some military experience involved here. Stick's out like dog's balls."

"Well watch out Nick, if they have those kind of connections there could very well be a mole in the system somewhere."

"It's possible, but sooner or later they'll make a mistake. Maybe they've already made it and we haven't seen it yet."

"Keep me posted Nick." The phone call ceased abruptly as a car horn sounded outside the house.

Nick jumped into the waiting taxi as Teddy pulled away, stopping at the intersection.

"Where to Guv?"

"Just drive for the moment Teddy, I need to think."

Something was bothering Nick. Was it his phone call to Age? The abrupt ending to the phone call? No, that often happened. When Age had finished what he wanted to say he would often just hang up.

Teddy was waiting at the lights when a motorbike pulled up alongside the taxi. Without any warning the rider fired several shots into the windows on the right-hand side all of which left small holes that penetrated partly through the armoured glass as the material around the indentation sent out a complex spider's web of cracks and fissures. None penetrated to the inside layer and both Nick and Teddy remained unharmed.

The bike rider sped off turning right at the intersection, disappearing into a laneway into who knows where. Teddy was a little stunned. Nick had drawn his Elite handgun and was angry more than anything else.

"Are you ok Teddy?"

"I'm fine Guv, shaken but not stirred. No chance of me following him through this traffic."

"Let's get this taxi off the road quick as you can. I don't want a nosy journalist or someone with a smartphone loading a picture up on social media. I know," remarked Nick, "do a U turn and drive into the mews at the back of my house. I have a garage there. We'll get the taxi picked up and sent to Jankel for repairs."

Teddy turned left and around two blocks and then into the mews where Nick operated the garage door with his remote. The taxi drove straight in. "My first time here Guv, geez you got a good setup here."

Over the years Nick had acquired three garages on the ground level and rented out the two-story flats above. There

146

was a cellar under each garage floor, so Nick was able to put a ramp down in one garage giving access to a massive extended under-street area through to the back garden of his house and into his own cellar. This created a large garage for Nick and Dianne to store their city cars as well as a few collectables. A 1967 Austin Healey convertible 3000 Mk3 with a champagne silver metallic duco, a 2019 Mercedes AMG GT, Dianne's Lexus RX 350 Sport, a 1959 Jaguar XK150 drop head coupe in British racing green and tidy little 1968 Morgan Plus 8 were immediately noticeable as Teddy parked his taxi.

"Cor, Mr 'ood, you got some nice motors down 'ere. Where's the DB5?"

"Not everyone at MI6 drives an Aston Martin Teddy."

"Overrated I reckon," remarked Firkin, "mind you, still some nice roadsters Commander."

"Yes, keep quiet about it, Teddy, don't want the world to know."

"Of course, Guv. Mum's the word."

Nick was on the phone to Jankel and assured a covered breakdown vehicle would be on its way shortly. He then phoned Age whose phone went to message. *"Don't leave a message this line is not secure."* That was Nick's queue to hang up. Age would know who called so Nick could expect a call sometime soon.

They waited for the Jankel vehicle, an unmarked Pantech, to back into the mews and drop the ramp whereby Teddy drove the taxi into the back, the rear ramp automatically raised and closed the back off as the truck departed with Teddy inside, still at the wheel. *He'll be fine*, Nick said to himself as he watched the vehicle turn into the street.

Age called back, "What's up Nick?"

"We just got shot up by a gunman on a motorbike," replied Nick.

"You must be getting close Nick. How's Dianne? Is she safe?"

"I'm just about to call her rooms and might be best if I get her to a safe house."

"Do you need a hand with that?"

"No thanks Age. I'll look after it. I'll call you back after I've met with the team."

"Is your taxi driver, OK?"

Instinctively Nick fired back, "How did you know I was in a taxi, Age?"

"I assumed you were with Teddy, Nick, you don't drive around London much, if you can help it."

"True, sorry."

"That's OK. Get back to your team and get this killer off the street."

48

Nick called Nigel and told him to have the team together in the meeting room as soon as he could that afternoon. He quickly followed up with a call to Dianne however her phone was engaged. Not wishing to wait, he picked up the keys to Dianne's Lexus from the key safe on the garage wall at the same time calling her receptionist. Dianne had left the rooms and didn't leave a message. So unusual for Dianne. Harley Street was fifteen minutes away if the traffic was normal. *What the hell was normal in London*, Nick thought. *I hate driving in London.* He would head to her rooms in any case and go from there. *Where could she have gone without telling her receptionist. Maybe a house call to a patient,* he said to himself.

Nick composed himself as he was starting to speculate; something he told himself never to do. Stick to the facts. At this point in time there was nothing unusual about a doctor leaving the rooms and making a call on a patient. She took a taxi to work so that means she may have caught a taxi to a patient. *Ring Teddy. He could tap into his network.* He passed Wellington Arch towards Park Lane and called Teddy.

"Teddy it's Nick, any chance you could check the taxi network to see if Dianne took a cab from Harley Street in the past hour?"

"Leave it with me Commander."

Nick continually pressed her button on his mobile. "Pick up, pick up."

The phone went to message. *"Not available right now, leave a number and I'll call you back."*

"It's me, Nick, call me as soon as you can."

The traffic in Park Lane was moving. *Thank God,* he thought. Turning right into Brook Street he weaved through the traffic, tooting his horn every now and then. Left into Duke Street and still Dianne's phone goes to message. Right into Wigmore Street heading towards Cavendish Square Gardens.

"Fuck," yelled Nick, "Fucking Harley Street is one way," as he swung into Wimpole Street."

Thankfully, Dianne's rooms were in the south end of Harley Street. He swung right into Queen-Anne Street and then right again into Harley Street. Turning the Lexus in front of a delivery truck he pulled into a vacant doctor space thanking the fact that Dianne kept her permit fastened to her windscreen and her emergency permit hanging from her rear-view mirror. No sooner had he got out of the vehicle than he caught a glimpse of Dianne walking up from Cavendish Square with a shopping bag.

"Well, this is a pleasant surprise, are you taking me out for coffee?" questioned Dianne as she moved forward to kiss Nick on his cheek. Then she noticed the Lexus, "and you've brought my car...hoping to get a free parking space, were you?"

"More important than that sweetheart. I needed a car that I could park anywhere just in case."

"Just in case of what."

"I don't have time to talk Dianne, we need to go now."

"I have to get my briefcase Nick, what's the matter? What's happened?"

"Well, get your case and I'll tell you in the car. We need to get moving quickly. Where were you?"

Alarmed, Dianne ran up the stairs turning back to answer, "I just ducked out to buy some underwear." She pushed open the door and disappeared.

Nick's phone rang. "Teddy here guv, no cab calls for Dianne."

"I've found her Teddy, thanks anyway."

"Not a problem Commander, just pick up the dog and bone and I'll be there," Teddy paused wondering what was going on "wherever that is." And hung up.

Nick was on the phone as Dianne opened the rear door and threw her bags on the back seat. Opening the passenger door, she climbed in and fastened her seat belt.

"Sexy nickers Nick."

"What?" asked Nick as he pushed the phone into the pocket in the console.

"I was buying some sexy underwear. You know the type you like ripping off my body." Dianne adjusted her clothing. "Now, are you going to tell me what's going on?"

49

Nick pulled into the parking entrance to New Scotland Yard.

"Commander Hood and Dr Hood, DCI Connelly is expecting us."

"Yes sir, we've just been informed. Please park in the area to the right sir."

Nick and Dianne were greeted by Nigel in the foyer and escorted to the lift. As they entered the lift Nigel touched his lips with the index finger of his right hand. The three were silent as the lift made its way to the level where the meeting room was located.

They entered the room where Chris and Stella were seated and within a few moments the new Deputy Commissioner Cynthia Burrows arrived.

"Commander Hood, good to see you again. It's been a few years."

"Indeed, it has Cynthia," Nick paused and gestured towards Dianne, "my wife Dr Dianne Hood."

Cynthia extended her hand. "Pleased to meet you Dr Hood."

"Please, Dianne."

"You won't have heard yet, but our patrol cars have answered a few house breaking calls in the past few hours." She turned to face Stella and Spencer. "your flats have been broken into, bit of a mess I'm afraid." Turning to DCI Connelly. "You too DCI."

"And us?" asked Nick.

"Yes and no, Commander, one of your neighbours saw a man break into an upper-level window from the roof and called the police."

"He would have got a surprise," said Nick.

"He did, so the neighbour said. Came out of that window a lot quicker than when he went in. Climbed onto the roof and bolted. Who knows where?"

"These were just warnings," said Nick.

"Yes," agreed Cynthia, "warnings indeed. If they wanted to, you'd be dead, of that, I'm sure."

"By the way Commander, what was in that room?" asked Cynthia.

"A friend of mine is into special effects. Works in the film industry and asked me to look after a few props while he took a sabbatical overseas."

"What were they Nick," asked Stella.

"I would think the motion sensor on the large spider activated as he came through the window."

"That would do it for me," laughed Nigel.

"We've posted uniforms on your residences for the time being," Cynthia turned to the others, "Dr Wilde, Connelly, Spencer. Please, if you all come with me." Cynthia walked towards the elevator. "If any of you speak about what I am about to show you," she paused, "I'll have you locked up, I assure you." She spoke directly to Connelly and Spencer. "You can come back and collect your evidence later on."

50

The elevator descended to the lower basement of the two underground levels. Cynthia pulled a key out of her pocket, placed the key in the lock and turned it to the left whereby another level appeared on the digital readout, and she pressed down.

"I had no idea there was a third level," stated Nigel.

"Not many people do," offered Cynthia. "The third level was always here but only as a maintenance level with some pumps in case of flooding from the river."

Cynthia led the team into the pump room towards a steel door at the southern end of the basement. Once there she produced another key and opened the padlock revealing a dark passageway. She flicked an old brass light switch just inside the door and the full length of the passageway was revealed. They walked for what Nick estimated to be about fifty metres until they arrived at a lift standing in an empty square room of about twenty metres by twenty metres. Dimly lit by antiquated incandescent globes, the group stood close to what appeared to be an equally antiquated elevator. A dark stone stairway to the right of the lift well, led up into the building above. Three steel doors, one on each wall, secured with large brass padlocks added to the mystery.

"This is all part of a network of tunnels hardly used since the second world war. Sixty-five years ago there were soldiers guarding every entrance and doorway down here." Cynthia turned to Nick, "I'm surprised you didn't know about this Nick."

"I don't know everything Cynthia." remarked Nick.

Dianne laughed. "Well, that's a first."

Once again Cynthia produced a key and the lights on the lift indicator panel came to life revealing three red basement floor levels and five numerical orange indicator lights. They entered the lift and Cynthia pressed a green button on the internal panel and the motors pulsed into life. She pushed the large brass manual lever forward and the lift slowly rose. Nick noted that it was like being in a contraption out of a Jules Verne novel.

The lift stopped at level 5 and the group stepped out into a foyer with a passageway on the left and right and small windows overlooking the Thames.

Cynthia explained. "When Scotland Yard vacated these buildings and moved to 10 Broadway, they were handed over to the British Parliament for their use as extra office space. However, the proviso was that we, the Metropolitan Police, would maintain a presence in the north corner of the building in the three upper dorm levels within the roof structure and on level four we would have the north-east corner quadrant. That area has been closed off to the rest of the building and we retained the use of this elevator. I'm not going to go into detail about why and by whom. Suffice to say that we have a number of ensuited bedrooms on the dorm levels, five, six and seven with meeting rooms and offices on the fourth level." Cynthia paused. "The Commissioner and I are the only ones who know about this. My predecessor Celia was never given any knowledge of this area and it has only been used on a small number of specific occasions where absolute secrecy was assured."

Cynthia opened a few doors on level 5 revealing the bedrooms. "For the next few days, at least, you'll be staying here. You're free to go about your business of course but as soon as you bring your personal possessions in, and the material from the meeting room, you will only use a single door at the rear of the building which leads to steps taking you down to the lower level where we entered the lift."

Cynthia walked them back to the lift where they travelled down one floor to the office spaces.

"You old chaps will like this," as she opened the door to the office on the corner of the building. It was a bright room with a rounded bay window area with a marvellous view down the Thames and across the existing New Scotland Yard. There were no blinds on the windows which made Nick comment.

"Not very secret if anyone wanted to look in from outside."

"The inside of the windows in this corner of the building are coated with a film that allows you to look out but not look in. The only proviso is to make sure you pull the blinds across the windows when it gets dark. That goes for all the windows." Cynthia turned to walk out. "You'll hear noises, as parts of this building are being renovated by a contractor so if a bit of light shows, anyone looking up will think there are workmen up here. There's a small kitchenette next door."

Nigel Connelly finally spoke. "I like the blackboard Ma'am, even got a duster and box of chalk."

"I thought you'd like that Inspector. You might have to show DS Spencer how to use it though."

They walked towards the lift where Cynthia gave Connelly a bunch of keys. "I'll leave these with you DI. You might need to make a few copies for your team."

"It may be a silly question Ma'am," asked Nigel, "but why didn't we use the bridge between the two buildings?".

"Not really a silly question DI, we just don't want anyone else to know that you're in this building. More for your benefit, I think. I want you to access this building from Parliament Street. Bring your cars in through the tradesman's entrance and park at the rear of the building. There are so many tradesmen and public servants around you won't be noticed." Reaching Into her pocket she pulled out ID cards for Stella and Nick. "These will get you past any curious security officers. Connelly and Spencer will use their own. Use only the entrance door at the northwest corner in the laneway to come and go. Now is that clear?"

"Very," in unison with nodding heads.

Nigel nodded as Chris and Stella looked at each other. *Trying to work out their sleeping arrangements,* thought Nick.

"I have arranged cars to take you to your residences to collect your personal effects. Please be quick and don't talk to anyone, the drivers or neighbours if possible. If you get a nosy neighbour just tell them, you decided on a short holiday."

"How long will we be here for?" asked Dianne. "I have patients to look after."

"Perhaps you can get a colleague to help out, only for a week, perhaps two at max." Cynthia turned to Nick.

"What do you think Commander. Will you have this wrapped up shortly?"

"Let's hope so Cynthia." Nick gave Dianne a wry smile.

"Not good enough Nick," exclaimed Dianne, "I can't just walk out, I've got hospital rounds this evening."

"Perhaps if your husband accompanied you Dianne," offered Cynthia. "Anyway, you work it out, but someone has your number," she glanced around, "all of you."

Cynthia entered the lift and turned, "Connelly, Spencer, you two report directly to me now. Assistant Commissioner Larkin and Commander McIntyre are no longer involved. Commander Hood, please give me a call if you feel the need. Dr Wilde, Dr Hood, good to meet you both. I'm sure we'll meet again soon." She started to close the steel mesh elevator doors. "Oh, by the way, if there are any new murders in our jurisdiction, we'll deal with them as we normally would, however we'll keep Connelly and Spencer informed in case any fit the model you're working with. Good day to you all."

51

Connelly gave Spencer the job of copying the keys while they made their way to the waiting squad cars to take them to their recently defiled accommodation. Nick locked the upper window and reset the spider's sensor however was confident that their regular alarm system would be more than capable of dealing with any further intrusion.

By six pm Connelly, Spencer and Wilde were back in their new accommodation after setting up the corner incident room. Nick accompanied Dianne on her rounds, staying an acceptable distance but remaining visible as he enjoyed some chatter and banter with the nursing staff. This would have been the first time most of them had seen, known or even heard that Dr Dianne Hood had a partner. Such was a life usually spent in the shadows, and now he was security detail for his wife. He enjoyed that thought.

During the rounds at the hospital, it was decided by Dianne that she would occupy one of the rooms at St Thomas's during the day. Nick would take her to work and bring her home ensuring that a constable was on duty during the day.

Chris Spencer and Stella Wilde had adjoining rooms to the south on level five. There was no surprise there. Connelly had a room on level six above the incident room with Nick and Dianne in a family sized room on level 5 immediately to the left of the elevator. Nick said he would feel more secure sleeping where he could hear the elevator if it was engaged.

All of them commented on the fact that the only access other than the elevator were the stairs around the lift well. However, there was a locked door on level three, closing off the stairwell. Nick noticed that under each window was a ring and cleat on the inside where an escape rope could be secured for escape purposes but no ropes. He promised to acquire the required rope the next day much to the satisfaction of the others.   It was remarked that many old buildings under renovation had been known to catch fire due to carelessness.

Spencer and Stella volunteered to organise breakfast from one of the cafés close by for themselves and Nigel, with Stella abstaining apart from herbal tea. Nick and Dianne said they would catch something enroute as neither of them were heavy breakfasters.

52

On his way back from St Thomas's on the first morning, Nick fulfilled his promise and returned with coils of manila rope which he said were less flammable than nylon. The first few hours were spent tying a series of knots in each rope with Nick ensuring that the fall on each rope was at least 100 feet.

"It may not have been absolutely necessary, but I feel better knowing the rope touches the ground, Nick."

"Better to have them than not Stella, considering no-one knows we're here." Nick tied the final knot and made sure there was a coil under each window. "Now let's get back to work."

Chris had sorted the reports and had each group and demographic in stacks on the table. He had correlated the reports on his laptop into a matrix with dates in the left vertical column and numerous columns to the right with summaries at the base of each vertical column.

"This all looks damn complicated Spencer," quipped Nigel.

"I see where he's coming from," remarked Stella, "it's important to get as much information as possible on the one chart."

"Well indulge me a little," requested Nigel, "could we put some information on the board. I prefer to see a bigger picture."

"I tell you what," said Chris, "I'll do some charts looking at some specific information and see where that takes us."

"Bravo," said Nick, "fire away."

Chris drew a semicircle with a flat line underneath. He then drew a vertical line in the centre from the middle of the flat line.

"I see," remarked Nick, "like half of a compass rose."

"Exactly," remarked Chris, "Now if we call this a political analysis of the victims, I will call the right side of the vertical line 'conservative' and left of the vertical line 'left/democrat'. The further left or right we go in either direction indicates the level of radical position. If we go below the flat line on either side, we go into what I'd call the anarchy zone."

Chris proceeded to draw a few markers to explain. "Let's take the biker from Manchester. His profile, and thanks to Stella for fine tuning the analysis, would border on anarchy with his far-right perspective. He was anti-Semitic, anti-Islam, a border case of neo-Nazi fascism, worshipped Hitler and you know the rest so we would put him just below the line on the right."

Chris then referred to the murdered current affairs producer who was heavily criticised on social media, as well as by conservative broadcasters, of producing extremely left biased commentary. Always targeting conservative politicians and not once in the life of the programs, despite many indiscretions by labour politicians, never reported on any of the incidents. Chris marked him about five degrees above the line in the left quadrant.

"Do you see where I'm going with this?"

"Continue," said Nick.

By the time Chris had marked fifteen on the chart there were roughly an even number on each side of the vertical line however none of them were within forty-five degrees of the vertical. Chris stepped back with the others as they studied the blackboard.

Nick was the first to speak. "Stella, care to say something?"

"The victims that Chris has highlighted had extreme rather than profound or substantial political views."

"I'd go along with that," commented Nick, "Nigel what say you?"

"I agree with Stella. These people did not have moderate political views. Quite the opposite and some of them engaged in radical or extreme behaviour."

Chris interjected, "and this is just one of the behavioural charts."

"I know this is the scientist coming out in me, but Chris is really onto something here. Behavioural science, by definition, is any of various disciplines dealing with the subject of human action. Fields such as sociology, social and cultural anthropology, psychology as well as behavioural aspects of biology, economics, geography, law, psychiatry and political science. Someone could be engaging in a form of social engineering to kill the prominent exponents in a particular field, to influence others, through fear, to disengage or cease and desist."

"Too much for an old copper," said Nigel.

"Not so Nigel," commented Nick, "you do this daily, but you don't realise you're doing it. You make observations, you make assessments, use your instincts, your gut feelings and then you analyse. You may not be scientific about it, but you do arrive at the same conclusions."

"We do?"

"Yes mate, you do," turning to Chris, "is that correct Chris?"

"Yes, I would say it is. Nigel calls it old fashioned police work, but it really is the same, just a different way of going about it. Today the language is different, and the techniques are given labels instead of a more mechanical approach."

"That's why people like me get involved. We assist with a more detailed perspective on the characteristics and foibles of both victims and perpetrators," offered Stella.

"I'm getting hungry," piped Nigel.

"And I have to pick up Dianne," remarked Nick. "You guys go for it. I'll take Dianne out for a bite before we come back. Won't be late."

53

The analysis continued the following day.

"It looks to me like the assassin is trimming the edges," commented Nick, "moderates aren't targeted, just the radicals on the fringes."

"And no collateral damage," offered Stella.

"Exactly Stella, if this was a terrorist there'd be mass casualties."

Nigel's phone rang. He made no comment during the call, finishing with "Thanks Kevin."

"That was your Constable Constable from Manchester. A report will be coming down the line, but he thought he would give us a heads up." Nigel stood up to face the group. "Another bikie member was gunned down two days ago. He apologised for the delay in telling us, been a bit busy up there. Apparently after the initial murder of the club president they had an election and elected a new president." Nigel paused. "He had his head blown off by a shotgun at short range. Not only that but it was during a drug delivery and the drug courier also got his head taken off. A few of the members interviewed by the police during the night have said the club is disbanding and have admitted to drug trafficking and dobbed in the local drug kingpin who's just been arrested. Full report will be here later today."

Nick stood up. "Well, apart from sending the bikies a clear message, that's an interesting development."

"Why so?" asked Stella.

Nick continued. "Well, for a start our assassin would be saying mission accomplished. Bikie gang disbanded, drug operation shut down, group no longer instigating Islamic hatred but of most interest is if the assassin was in Manchester two days ago blowing the heads off bikies and drug pedlars, who was breaking into our apartments."

"Someone else?"

"Exactly Chris, which means there's more than one person involved. It also means that someone's in charge and that someone is giving the orders."

"This was a big mistake," observed Stella.

"Damn right," said Nick, turning to Nigel and Chris, "is there any chance you can get onto your communications people and see if they can detect any unusual mobile traffic that day and evening between London and Manchester? Long shot I know. Also check the traffic cams for white Transit vans and yellow Honda 125s in the vicinities."

"I'll contact the Deputy Commissioner," said Nigel, "I'm sure she can get the approvals going."

"It could be that before and after our flats were broken into the culprits reported in." remarked Stella as Nigel made the call to Cynthia. Chris was also on the phone to his tech mates to ascertain what possible GPS info could be attained through existing 'side gates'.

"There has to be some rumbling on the streets Stella, I'll give Teddy a call and see if he can find out from his sources." Nick made his call as Stella started sifting through the stacks of reports and other files on the table to see if anything had been missed.

54

Teddy took the call while he was checking out the repair of his taxi at the Jankel workshop.

"Allo Guv, just finking about you."

Nick briefed Teddy about the break-ins and the recent activity in Manchester. "If you hear anything let me know."

"Right, you are Guv, by the way I did get some goss the uvver day. Some geezer got ruffed up in the East End. 'E was making a delivery and 'e got curious about what was in the crates as they was very 'eavy. Anyway, 'e dropped one and says it was guns and the uvver guy came out and smacked him around. Says, if he says anyfink it's over red rover. 'E told me 'e was disappearing for a while."

"Thanks Teddy, that's interesting. Any idea exactly where this happened?"

"Leave it wiv me."

Chris looked up from his laptop. "Commander Hood, you do know how many white transit vans and how many yellow Honda 125s there are on the roads?"

"Not exactly Chris but I'm sure you're going to tell me."

"Well, "said Chris, "there are over nine hundred thousand Ford Transits registered with the majority being white."

"And yellow Hondas?"

"Can't tell you yellow exactly but in the last three years over one hundred and seventy-five thousand Honda 125ccs have been registered."

"And given the MO of our killer, or killers, they change the number plates and maybe even the colour as well." Nick sighed, "and the bikes were probably stolen anyway." Nick sat down and placed his head in his hands. Dropping his hands, he raised his head, "we're missing something."

Nick turned to Chris. "Chris, you and Nigel do your thing over at the Met. Stella and I will keep going here and see what we've missed."

Nick and Stella moved to the main table as Nigel and Chris walked over to the Met building, close by.

"Stella, you first. Just rattle off what you know." Turning to look around the room he suddenly stood up and walked into the small kitchenette. "Fuck, there's no coffee machine. I'll be back."

Nick returned an hour later with a tidy espresso machine, a carton of milk, ground coffee and sugar. A few moments later he was sipping on a coffee while Stella was steeping a camomile with wild- flowers infusion.

"That's better," Nick savoured the rich foaming crema, "got to get those fucking grey cells working. Where were we Stella?"

"I'm about to put forward my ideas."

"Fire away."

Stella walked over to the chalk board. Half turning to Nick she started writing. "Firstly, in my opinion, we have military or military experience. Then we have more than one person involved, probably three, four or even more, so four plus. In terms of politics neither left nor right, probably apolitical," smiling at Nick, "or simply don't give a fuck. Not racially motivated attacks but possibly to create racial tensions. Very targeted with no collateral damage. Not terrorism related in any way. Possibly ethically compromised or with some twisted or pervasive ideology. Cold, calculated, devoid of emotion."

Stella turned away from the board. "We also have to consider that the perpetrators are paid mercenaries and, in my view, ex-military or ex-police".

"What about serving military or police?"

"I would think not Nick. I doubt if someone in regular employment in those regimes could be flexible enough to engage in the travel, planning and execution of the crimes."

"Unless an entity, government or private operator was employing them do the work."

"Nick, you can't seriously consider that a government entity would be using its own employees to commit these crimes?"

"Well, if that was a question Stella, and I think it was, I'm not going to rule anything out at this stage." Nick continued, "if we're close, or they think we're close, it means they too are close. It could be a group of police on a vendetta. I wouldn't rule it out. Look at the state of the judicial system." Nick stood up and raised his arms, "the cops arrest people, they have proof, evidence, witnesses and the fuckers get off with a light sentence or some dickhead lawyer gets them a non-custodial sentence and they're back on the streets. A fucking good reason to blow their fucking heads off if you ask me."

"I wish you'd be more direct Nick. You know," she smiled, "come straight to the point."

They laughed in unison.

"It would be funny if it wasn't so fucking serious, Stella. The system is so fucked up with political correctness, wokeism, whatever the fuck that really is, and pandering to these minority wankers and loopy do-gooders." Nick grabbed his cup and gulped down the last of his coffee. Looking at his empty cup, "you know that's not a bad cup of coffee."

Nick glanced at the board and Stella's list.

"I think you're spot on with most of that."

"Most of it," said Stella with indignation.

"Well, all of it actually. I would have written down the same, but I reckon we can add to it."

"How so?"

"I don't have a fucking clue." Nick grabbed his cup and headed to the kitchen. "Maybe some more caffeine will help."

Stella was still looking at the board when Nick returned with the steaming brew.

"Any ideas?"

"We said it before Nick. A star chamber. Judge, jury and executioner. Decisions made. Sentence proclaimed. Execution carried out. No emotion, no hesitation, no remorse."

"A vigilante." Nick sipped his coffee.

"Plural Nick. There's an 's' after that."

"Correct." Nick paused as he took another sip. "You know if it was just one person, we'd have less chance of catching him or her. If he, or she, was professional, careful, didn't get excited or over-confidant, did everything right, as say a trained sniper or insurgent, then with the resources available to the authorities he, or she, could remain incessantly at large."

"But, let's call it a 'he', and he is not a lone assassin is he Nick?"

"No Stella, and that's the weakness." Nick finished his coffee satisfied that the caffeine was doing its job. "Because he is not a sole operator, he needs communication, he needs intel, he needs instructions, he needs transport."

"You're onto something, aren't you?"

"Yes, Stella, I think we've narrowed our assassin, or assassins, down from 4.7 billion to 47 million."

"How do you work that out?"

"Well as of today, globally, we have around 4.7 billion adults aged between 15 and 65. Statistically around 1% of the population have served or are serving in the military. So, during the last few minutes we have eliminated 99% of our suspect list." Nick smirked, "I think that's quite an achievement, don't you?"

Stella stood there not sure whether to laugh and wondering if Nick was serious.

"Don't worry Stella, I've got this. When Chris comes back, we get him working on eliminations." Nick looked at his watch. "I've got to head off to pick up Dianne."

"Well, I can help Chris with the stats in the meantime."

"Yes, you can Stella, splendid. I'll contact my office and see if we can get a list of military and ex-military personnel who may have the skill set to do this kind of work. The mob we are after may not be British ex or serving military, they could be foreign nationals which will make it extremely difficult but, as I said, we work on a process of elimination and see what we end up with."

Stella called to Nick as he walked to the elevator. "How about we all go to the Red Lion for dinner tonight."

"Sounds good, can't stay cooped up in this place, the foods crap. I'll see you there."

55

By the time Nick and Dianne arrived the others had secured their space in the lower bar. Stella and Chris were cosying up in Churchill's recess with Nigel, relaxing with a pint of Fullers which he insists contains enough vitamins and minerals to keep him healthy. Nick ordered drinks from the bar while Dianne occupied one of the vacant chairs around the table.

"No talking shop tonight," offered Nigel with the others nodding in approval.

"I'm quite ok with that as well," commented Dianne, "I'm sure you don't need an elucidation of my day in the theatre."

"I don't know," asked Chris smiling, "what show did you see?"

That's where the laughter started and at ten o'clock, they made their way through Derby Gate, past pallets of building materials, to their entrance at the back of the North Norman Shaw Building. They were all quiet in the elevator and it was Nick who broke the silence. "I'll do breakfast after I drop Dianne off in the morning."

"Suits me," said Nigel and the others nodded.

When Nick returned with bags of takeaway breakfast Stella had the coffees ready to go after mastering the new coffee machine. A quantity of hash browns with egg and bacon muffins were handed around. Stella frowned until Nick produced a gluten free, wholemeal blueberry muffin and proudly placed it in front of her. "Well thank you Nick. You do listen after all."

"Took me a while Stella, but the herbal teas were a bit of a giveaway. I know you don't get hungry until lunchtime, but I was beginning to think you didn't eat at all."

"I do eat quite a lot but not this crap," she quipped with a wry smile, "and I miss my pole exercise."

"We should be in an old fire station," offered Chris, "but I don't think poles were quite the fashion at Scotland Yard."

Nigel's phone rang as he struggled to answer with a mouth full of muffin. The expression on Nigel's face spoke volumes as he half swallowed, half spat out what was in his mouth.

"Yes, got that, yes I will, yes ma'am, we'll get there right away."

The team looked up at Nigel's face.

"What's happened?" asked Nick.

"There's been a double murder. Celia Graham and her girlfriend. The deputy commissioner has asked that Chris and I attend the scene. Sorry, she said it was a jurisdiction thing." Nigel paused. "Celia's girlfriend worked for the NCA, and they're taking over. Bit of a bunfight going on apparently."

Nick's phone rang. He just listened. His only words were "Right," as he hung up.

"That was my boss. Celia's girlfriend who worked for the NCA was our contact, she was keeping MI6 informed on some cases including the murders of the Judge and Bishop. I'm sorry now I called her 'big-tits'. I didn't know she was one of ours."

"So, were they both targets or was one the target and the other by association?", asked Stella.

"My money is on our girl in the NCA," suggested Nick, "Celia was on extended leave and was never really close to any of the current investigations as I could see."

"So, they targeted," Chris jumped in, "sorry, what's her name, the girl from NCA?"

"Her name was Victoria James," mentioned Nigel, "The DC just told me."

Chris continued, "So, they targeted Victoria James and Celia got in the way."

"More than that," uttered Nigel, "The DC said they put up quite a fight. Spencer, we've to get over there right away."

Nick was back on the phone to Age.

"Can you get us in over there, Age?" was all that could be heard of the brief conversation.

"Age is going to call me back." Nick gazed out of the corner window as Nigel and Chris headed for the lift. "There's that fucking reporter with the weird hair. She's looking up here."

Stella joined Nick at the window. "Well, she can't see us, the window's shielded."

"No, she can't but she may have seen the lights on," turning to Stella, "did you see her at the pub last night?"

"No, but it was pretty crowded."

"I wonder if she saw us going into this building last night?"

"She could have," replied Stella, "if she was tailing us."

"We might pull her in later," Nick paused, "give her a fright."

"Could we use her?" asked Stella.

"Use her, how?" replied Nick.

"I don't know, but it would help if we knew what she was up to and maybe we could just feed her some stuff. She might even be able to do some groundwork for us."

"Yes, you're right Stella. It would be good if we could get some benefit from a journalist instead of the bullshit and tripe they usually write."

"She's obviously a smart girl, despite her dishevelled appearance which probably works in her favour when she's scratching around." Stella walked over to the coffee machine. "Another cup Nick?"

Stella took his silence as a yes, as Nick continued to look at the girl in the courtyard below.

"You know I'm looking at you, don't you," muttered Nick.

"How would you like to go down and have a chat with her Stella?"

"Yes, OK."

"I think the 'female to female' approach may be better."

"Much better than the Nicholas Hood to female approach I'm sure," laughed Stella.

56

Nick accepted the espresso cappuccino from Stella as he returned to the window observing the journalist now sitting on a bench beside the car park entrance, smoking and making notes. He heard the elevator descend and waited. Within a few minutes he saw Stella walking down the side lane and across the front of the Met building towards the girl on the bench.

"Coffee?" Stella reached forward holding a takeaway cappuccino.

The girl looked up, taking a draw from her cigarette before stamping it out on the ground.

"Thank you, don't mind if I do."

She took the cup from Stella and looked up at the corner window.

"You got a coffee machine up there as well?"

"Yes, we have. Can I sit down."

"Go for it," as she shuffled across making plenty of room for Stella.

"Are you working for Commander Hood?"

"No, I'm a consultant with the Met."

"What sort of consultant?"

"I tell you what," offered Stella, "How about quid pro quo?"

"You've been watching Silence of the Lambs, have you?"

"Not for a while and I'm pretty well a vegetarian and don't fancy chopped liver."

"Touché."

They both smiled.

"I know you're working on these murders."

"I'm Stella, Stella Wilde."

"Emily, Emily Chancer."

"Well," said Stella, "I'm glad we got that out of the way now let's get down to business shall we and no bullshit please."

"Oooo, you're a bit touchy."

"No, I just don't like having my time wasted Emily. You want a story, and I can give you more than the media department of the Met."

"And?"

"And I want to know what you know at the moment, and don't hold back or I walk away."

"So, was that a question or a statement?"

Stella didn't answer the question. "Do you have a recording device?"

"Just my phone."

"Are you recording now?"

Emily hesitated. "Maybe."

"What is it with you fucking journalists. Do you want a story or not?" Stella surprised herself with her voracity. *Too much time with Nick,* she thought.

"All right, all right," Emily lurched to her right a little, surprised at Stella's sudden change in demeanour. "If it's OK with you I'll record our conversation."

"That's better Emily, now where are you with your story so far."

Emily relaxed a little and lit another cigarette, gulping down half of the coffee.

"I know the murders of the Judge and the Bishop are connected. I know the judge let the bishop off and there are plenty of people pissed off about it including the police." Emily took another drag. "The arrests of the suspects in the child pornography sting I reckon are also connected but the police won't comment on where they found the evidence."

"They found the judge's computer, videos and DVDs at the judge's house," commented Stella.

"I knew it," remarked Emily.

"You can quote an unnamed source Emily. Say anything about me and you'll spend the rest of your life in a suburban rag."

"The Commander has already warned me Stella."

"More."

"I think the Manchester murders are connected as well."

"You're fishing and you can do better than that."

"The murder in Durham and the murder in Oxford are connected."

"Why do you say that?"

"They were both active with Antifa. Every time there's a major protest those two are, or were, always involved. I heard that they were the bagmen for the paid protestors. Got no proof but that was the word. They recruited through the universities. Students need money so they pay the radicals and some ringleaders to get the numbers up. They also pay a few extra pounds to get some violence, you know smash windows and stir things up."

"Do you know where they got the money from to pay the protesters?"

"How about something from you first."

"There's been two murders last night."

"Kensington?"

"Yes, how did you know?"

"It's all over Twitter Stella, Duh!"

"One of them was a copper."

"Who was the other one?" asked Emily.

"Can't say. More." Stella glanced up at the window.

"He's looking, isn't he?"

"Who?"

"Commander Hood."

"What about the bag money Emily, where's it coming from?"

"Got no proof but there's a toff involved, pollie I think."

"Left, or right?" asked Stella.

"What do you think?"

"I'm thinking left."

"Sounds like a conservative comment," uttered Emily.

"That touched a nerve. Do you protest Emily?"

"I'm a journalist, I report."

"I don't like either side, particularly, Emily." Stella stood up, "But there are good people on both sides of the House. "For once I'd like to meet a journalist who was straight down the middle. Not many of those around."

"I'm not biased either and my paper is broadly conservative anyway. I like to think I'm keeping my side honest." Emily stood up and offered her hand. "I like you."

Stella shook her hand. "Stick around Emily but don't get in our way. If you've got some information for me, sit on this bench and I'll come down. If not stay away and don't follow us again." Stella turned to walk away and stopped. "One more bit of information Emily but you'll have to work with it. Look at the victim data, do some research. Nothing that you can't find out legally."

"Which victims?"

"All of them."

"What do you mean all of them?"

"Exactly what I said."

"You're not making it easy."

"You're a smart girl Emily, I'm sure you'll work it out but not by sitting around here."

57

Nick smiled as he watched the ladies on the bench. His phone rang.

"Nick, its Age. I can get you over there but not until after the dust has settled. With three agencies involved it's getting messy. Your friends Connelly and Spencer will have access to the forensic images. Cynthia assures me they'll have full access to the reports when they come in. They were tortured Nick. This looks like it was personal."

"That would be another mistake."

"Yes, it would Nick. I can get you over there once the forensic team have left but that will take another 24 hours I would think. It was a bad crime scene; the apartment is a total shambles. It must have been one hell of a fight. Apparently, the neighbours weren't that concerned as they often have parties. They said the noise was louder than usual."

Stella arrived back while Nick was on the phone. Helping herself to another herbal tea she waited by the window until he had finished.

"How did you go?"

"Good Nick, she's a smart girl. I gave her a few crumbs. Interestingly she told me that the Durham and Oxford murders were not only Antifa members, but she thinks they were involved in the financial side."

"Well, Chris identified they were radically inclined, committed socialists I think he said. We'll get him onto that. Perhaps they were on a watchlist somewhere." Nick sat down as Stella moved away from the window.

"She said, quote 'a toff maybe a pollie' unquote, could be supplying some finance to the organisation."

Nick frowned, "Interesting. Good work Stella. Let's have some lunch."

"Let's go healthy this time, my shout."

Connelly and Spencer returned mid-afternoon from the Kensington Apartment. Nigel had requested images which were starting to arrive on Spencer's laptop.

"It was fucking terrible," remarked Nigel, "I've been a copper for just over forty years, and I've never seen a murder scene quite like that. Not since that job I was on with you, all those years ago. Remember? Celia was not one of my favourite people, but no-one deserved to be killed like that."

Nick nodded recalling grisly scenes from the past. "Yes, I remember all too well."

Chris was looking rather pale but persevered with downloading the images. Stella laid a reassuring hand on his shoulder while he struggled with the images. Even she found herself turning away from some of them.

"I don't get it," said Nick, "we've had all of these clean almost clinical kills with one or two bullets and now this egregious rage."

"How do we know it's the same killers?" asked Stella.

"Well, I guess we don't, do we. We're just assuming," said Chris looking up from the screen for a moment and taking a deep breath."

It was Nick who took the lead. "I think we assume it's the same killers. The way in which they carried out the attack was needlessly violent and, probably for the first time, their victims fought back, and they got pissed. They almost got a thrashing by two females, and they were angry, very fucking angry and when you get angry you make mistakes. I give you London to a brick their DNA is all over that place."

"I agree." Nigel had just returned from splashing some water on his face and was drying off with a towel as he came back from the kitchenette. "Whoever it was would have got knocked around pretty bad. I have no doubt they had gloves on, but everyone bleeds if they get hit hard enough. Actually, I'm surprised they didn't torch the place."

"If they did that, we wouldn't be able to see the crime scene. It would have been a charred mess." Nick paced around excitedly. "They wanted us to see the crime scene. They wanted us to see what retribution looks like. They wanted us to see that those poor women suffered pain and torture."

Stella moved away from Chris's side. "They must feel empowered Nick, as if they're a protected species."

"Damn right Stella. They do feel protected. They feel they're beyond the law because there's someone, somewhere who has told them they are."

Nick stopped pacing. "Nigel, how soon before the DNA is available?"

"There's a huge amount to be collected Nick. Some of it will be at the lab already but it can take up to seventy-two hours depending on the type of material they're testing."

"Blood?"

"Well, there was lots of it. Their throats were cut, and they were shot in the back of the head, plenty of blood from the neck wounds, so cut first then shot. That bit was very much in anger. Symbolical perhaps." Nigel paused, "There were blood spatters up the walls but that was from the fight, I think. Someone had a knife, could have been the attackers or maybe one, or both girls. Looks like they were preparing dinner when they answered the door. No break in, they must have opened the door to the attackers."

"Was there a peephole in the door?"

"Yes, there was," replied Chris. "It's possible that one of the girls recognised them or knew one of them. Or it could be that one or both were in police uniform."

"That could mean that the killers could work for the NCA or the Met," commented Nigel, "surely not."

"We need to keep an open mind on this," remarked Stella, "there could be any number of scenarios to consider. They could have had a key or even picked the lock, so let's not jump to conclusions."

"I need to get into that crime scene as soon as possible, in fact the four of us, together," Nick uttered in frustration, "and we need that DNA and forensic report now."

"I'll get an interim forensic report copy as soon as it's ready, the DC will see to that, but it'll be a few days before a complete analysis is ready."

"I'll call Sir Adrian and see if he can pull any strings and bypass this territorial bullshit."

Nick was on the phone while the others looked through the images.

"Right," Nick sat down in front of the group, "We're going in early tomorrow morning. Age will be with us."

"How would Dianne be Nick, about going with us. She might be able to offer some clinical observations?" asked Stella.

"I'll check with her at the hospital. Might be a good idea to stay home this evening and stay tuned to the reports as they come in. I'd better head over now and pick her up."

Stella stood up and tapped Chris on the shoulder. "You and I are on dinner tonight, real food guys."

58

Dianne had just finished rounds when Nick called in.

"Bad day?" Dianne could see the strain in Nick's face.

"You've got no idea."

"Oh, I think I might," Dianne gave him a peck on the cheek, "I've seen that look before."

Dianne grabbed her bag from her temporary office and bade a good night to the duty constable as she grabbed Nick's hand. "Good night constable, and thanks."

"Pleasure Dr Hood, have a good night."

"I hope so," although she was not quite sure about that.

The traffic was congested, but the slow pace gave them time to talk.

"So?"

"So," Nick looked to his left and met her gaze, "two officers down, bad crime scene, still no real leads, just supposition and we're off to the crime scene early in the morning."

"What time?"

"Age will meet us there at six o'clock."

"Need some company?"

"Are you sure, it'll be pretty disturbing."

"I'm not exactly a shrinking violet Nick and a clinical opinion may help."

"I was hoping you'd say yes."

"Well, the answer is yes. I can also attend the autopsies if you can get permission for me. Or at least speak with the medical examiner."

"I'll give Age a call when we get to our digs."

"Why not now?"

Nick activated his Bluetooth. "Siri, call Age."

"Calling Age."

"Yes Nick, what's up."

"Can we bring Dianne tomorrow morning as our medical specialist?"

"Can't see why not. We've got to get dressed in PPEs as they haven't finished yet, so we tread carefully, and Nick, "Age paused, "don't upset anyone."

"Wouldn't dream of it, Age, will you have the PPEs there for us?"

"Yes, plenty of spares for Dianne as well. There's a tent around the entrance to the flats. The other apartment owners have been relocated until the CSIs have finished."

"What's happening with the autopsies?"

"They're starting at midday at the Coroner's Court lab. Why?"

"We'd like Dianne to observe so we can get a heads-up as soon as it's over."

"OK, I'll get it organised. Make it five-thirty tomorrow morning Nick, it's going to get crowded, and we need to get in and out as soon as we can."

Despite grumbling from Nigel concerning the lack of carbohydrates and animal fat, the evening meal of antipasto, Greek salad, souvlaki and baklava was received very well. The acquisition of the coffee machine was agreed as the best tactical decision of the week and toasted with a crisp Semillon Sauvignon Blanc. Nigel lamented the lack of a robust stout but agreed that white wine suited the menu on this occasion.

59

It was still dark in London the next morning as a light drizzle created a translucent mist in the labyrinth of streets, alleyways and narrow brick corridors of the inner suburbs. A white tent had been erected outside the apartment building and fifty metres in each direction the blue and white tape indicated the exclusion zone. Squad cars and armed police patrolled the street, alert to any untoward presence as Dianne's Lexus pulled up with Nick at the wheel. The five occupants alighted the vehicle parked in the middle of the road in full view of the attending officers. Age had previously arrived and was already in white disposable coveralls.

"Follow me," Sir Adrian walked ahead into the entrance tent. They were required to sign in before slipping the overalls, facemasks and shoe coverings on, and were escorted to the apartment on the second floor.

As anticipated, there were no signs of forced entry. The images they had seen did nothing to disguise their horror as they entered the apartment. They smelt the iron from the blood everywhere, it was a metallic odour that stung the nostrils and permeated the air. Chris had his iPad with him and was able to clearly show the position of the bodies, where they lay after death.

It was difficult to find a space on the floor that didn't have a trace of blood. Each member of the group delicately placed their feet as best they could but were assured by an attending officer that the floor samples had been taken and there would be no forensic issues with moving around.

Nick and Age led the group into the kitchen where it was their belief that the attacks had started. Nick looked around for security installations. "Strange, the only sensors visible are domestic motion type. One in the corner of the passageway, one in the kitchen. I would have thought Celia would have had something more sophisticated."

A smoke alarm was just inside the entrance door and one in the passageway at the far end. There was also an alarm control panel just inside the door which was, of course, now disabled.

Chris, holding his laptop, commented on his emails. "The report here says that there were no laptops, smartphones or computers in the apartment." A comment that caused raised eyebrows.

The group stood around the kitchen island bench. It was a modern kitchen, recently remodelled, indicated by the design of the tap wear and the stone benchtops. The cupboards were an off-white glossy two pack design with large drawers and generous benches around the walls. The European oven, cooktop and dishwasher were like new, and it was Nick's guess that the renovation of the apartment was quite recent.

The hallstand in the passageway was devoid of any items of apparel. No handbags, scarves, hats or coats. Chris noted Nick's interest and mentioned their absence.

"Says here that items of apparel, clothing and handbags have been sent for forensic analysis."

The tops of the wall cupboards contained a range of items both decorative and functional. Containers, small sculptures and some utensils, among others. Nick noticed the knife block and magnetic knife board on the wall with a few of the knives missing.

"The missing knives on the rack have been sent for forensic Chris?" questioned Nick. "Have they all been accounted for? I can see seven spaces in the block and on the wall board."

"Can't tell you Commander, the report is far from complete. It is just noted that items from the kitchen taken for examination. It also says that a number of bloodstained knives were found at various locations, and we have images of those knives where they were found."

Stella found herself feeling a little nauseous and requested she get some fresh air while Dianne was carefully studying the blood patterns on the walls and furniture.

"There's quite a bit of arterial blood spray on the walls. One, or both, had some serious wounds."

"Maybe the attackers as well. The girls put up quite a fight," commented Sir Adrian.

"Indulge me a little here," commented Nick, "let's say the girls were in the kitchen preparing a meal and somehow the attacker or attackers came in through the front door with a key or a lock opening device."

The group nodded.

"Then knowing how these attackers operate, assuming these are the perpetrators of the other murders, why didn't they just fire off a few rounds and shoot the girls where they stood. Why engage in a knife fight. Very risky in my view. After all, both girls have been trained in self-defence and the use of weapons including knives."

"Good point Nick," offered Nigel, "maybe they didn't hear them. Were they playing music perhaps?"

"They may also have been talking over the music," commented Dianne, "also they were in a relationship perhaps they were having a cuddle."

"Or something a little more intimate," commented Nick.

"Careful Nick," remarked Dianne.

"Just being realistic Di. Whatever they were doing, they were distracted from any noises from the intruders."

"I think we can accept that, Nick." Dianne wandered off down the passageway avoiding the pools of blood now drying on the carpet.

"Where would the music come from?" asked Nick.

"Could have been from a phone, iPad or laptop computer," offered Chris, "maybe their TV wherever that is. They might even have a wireless speaker somewhere like an Apple or Sonos. Plenty on the market."

Nick looked around. "Chris, could you check out the cupboard tops, maybe the corner."

Chris grabbed a chair and stood on the kitchen bench which gave him a good view of the cupboard tops. "Are you psychic Commander. There's an Apple Homepod in the corner."

"What the fuck is an Apple Homepod?" commented Nigel.

Chris reached forward and passed it to Nick as he climbed down. "It's basically a smart speaker system Guv. It doesn't need a host device like a computer or smartphone. My guess is there could be other speakers around the apartment."

"So, what's so special about these gadgets?" asked Nigel.

Nick jumped in, "well for a start, and correct me if I'm wrong Chris, they operate by voice commands, like music, lights, heat, cooling etc."

"Correct Commander," in this case ask Siri a question or give her a command and however it is programmed with a variety of Apps, then she activates certain functions."

"Who the fuck is Siri?" asks Nigel.

"Siri, my friends, is our silent or not so silent witness." Nick smiled as he placed Siri in the middle of the bench.

"Not so fast Commander," interjected Chris, "I would suggest that Siri is programmed to one or both of the voices of our deceased ladies." Chris paused and then spoke to the device, "Good morning, Siri."

There was no reply.

"As I thought," continued Chris, "the voice activation will only recognise the voices of the ones who have programmed it and any messages, recordings, phone calls made through this device will be encrypted; even Apple can't decode them. Pretty foolproof."

"Buggar," uttered Nigel.

Sir Adrian spoke. "Victoria has a daughter. She's fourteen years old and lives with her father Sebastian, in Nottingham. She often comes down here during school holidays for a week or two. My guess is that she has voice access to this Apple system. I doubt that a fourteen-year-old girl could live in the vicinity of Siri without utilising its service."

"I agree sir," offered Chris hesitating, "sorry for interrupting. Kids use these devices like its second nature to them. If she stayed here, she'd be using it. Her mum would have given her initial voice access I'm sure, especially if she spent time in the apartment alone."

"She wouldn't have been here two nights ago?" asked Nigel.

"No," replied Sir Adrian, "there are no school holidays at the moment."

"What does her father do?" asked Nick.

"He's a software designer so I wouldn't be surprised if his daughter was also pretty up with it all," commented Sir Adrian. "We'll need to offer them some protection in case this incident spills over. Leave that with me."

"What about getting her to help with accessing the information on the Apple device," asked Nick.

"I'll get that organised Nick," offered Age, "but first we need to get them to a safe space and a social worker on the job as well. I'm not sure how badly the girl is going to take this."

Stella came back into the room at the end of the conversation, "I'll be happy to help with the girl. What's her name?"

"Felicity, Stella," Sir Adrian showing a little emotion as he grimaced at the scene. "Her mum was one of ours. The bastards."

Nick continued with his summation. "Right, so why not kill them outright." Pausing as he looked around. "Did they want a fight? Did they interrupt something that made them act in this way? Did they need to get some information before they killed them? I think it might have been a bit of all three."

Nick gathered the group around.

"The girls were here. One of them probably already had a knife in her hand or at least close by. The music was playing. They were engaged in some behaviour that took their attention away from the intrusion. They suddenly became aware they were under some threat, and they responded by grabbing weapons, in this case it was kitchen knives. Did either of them have a gun in their possession somewhere in the apartment? Perhaps they did and they tried to fight their way to one of the other rooms. How am I doing?"

"Keep going," said Sir Adrian.

"OK, so the fight started. The girls ignored the fact they had guns, or the intruders put their guns away and drew knives, probably Fairburn-Sykes type. The girls lashed out, kitchen knives no match for F-S, especially in the hands of specialists, perhaps one trying to protect the other who may have been trying to get to a gun, if they had one. Or they both engaged with each intruder. Knife fights get bloody. Slashing and lunging. It all happens very quickly. The girls would have come out of the kitchen to avoid being backed in, and both girls and intruders had scored injuries on each other. The slashing and stabbing continued but the intruders probably better protected, maybe with combat clothing. The girls, by the looks of the images, were only wearing light casual clothes offering no protection."

The group nodded.

"Within a minute or two, after a lot of furniture was knocked over and covered in blood, one or two received serious arterial wounds. My guess the girls got some serious slash wounds and were bleeding heavily and maybe knocked unconscious or overpowered. They get their hands tied with cable ties as in the photographs, kneeled down, questioned and then have their throats cut and a gunshot to the back of the head."

"In the absence of anything to the contrary, that would be pretty accurate Nick," Nigel put his notebook away.

"I would say, almost categorically that there'll be DNA here from both intruders and victims," offered Dianne, "I would also say that, in all probability, the intruders sustained some significant injuries, and that would have made them angry."

"And angry people make mistakes," commented Stella.

"And that's why we'll get these bastards," uttered Nick emphatically.

60

Dianne phoned from the Coroners Morgue. "There's not much that can be added Nick. The scenario you envisaged was about right. Numerous knife wounds, severe blood loss. Poor girls. The report will be distributed in a few days."

An air of sadness pervaded the room as Nick hung his phone up.

Sir Adrian phoned to say that Felicity and her father were in a safe house in Newark and being looked after by the 'landlady', a Mrs Wilkinson, who Sir Adrian said was more than capable of dealing with any issues. They've both been informed of the incident and that Felicity's mother is deceased. The father had been informed that Felicity would be required to open the voice activated device and gave his assurance that they would both co-operate as required. Sir Adrian remarked that Felicity was quite composed when advised.

"Was my mother a spy?" she asked.

Sir Adrian gave a tactful reply. "Your mother was very important to our organisation Felicity, and you should feel very proud of her. I'm so sorry for your loss."

The team was sitting around their incident room when Chris received the DNA results.

"You're not going to believe this Commander."

"Why's that, Chris?"

"The DNA of Celia and Victoria was obvious and clear. The locations of the samples were as expected and found on the kitchen knives. The DNA of the intruders clearly showed them as male, one of 85% German origin, the other 25% German and

60% Czechoslovakian. However these results are indicative only."

"Nigel, can we suggest a search of the Police DNA register just in case there's a record?" asked Nick.

"I can only try." Nigel made the call.

"We need to get that Homepod recording as soon as possible," uttered Nick. "When will the murder scene be cleaned?"

"The cleaners are in there now," replied Nigel, "I reckon we could get the daughter down tomorrow. She only has to be there to unlock the device I would think."

"Right let's get that organised Nigel." Nick turned to Chris and Stella. "Stella, I want you up at Newark tonight to escort the daughter down here in the morning."

"Felicity."

Nick turned to Stella, "What?"

"The daughter's name is Felicity,"

"Right, sorry. And Chris, I want you on site to record the conversation."

Chris nodded and smiled at Stella.

"She shouldn't be there when the recording plays," observed Stella.

"Of course. Will you look after her and get her out as soon as we get access?"

"Yes, her father will need to travel with her. I'll get him to wait in the car."

"Right, we're all set for tomorrow then." Nick sat down and gazed at the mounds of evidence and material building up on the table. He turned to Chris. "Have you got all of this on your laptop?"

"I think so, most of it anyway. Anything that comes to Chief Inspector Connelly, comes to me as well."

"Good, just in case we have to move again, quickly."

Nigel enquired, "and what makes you say that, Nick?"

"Just making sure we're prepared Nigel."

"Is that one of your hunches again?"

"You could say that. I'm getting Dianne to stay at the hospital. More secure there I think, and it keeps her at a distance from us."

"So, Nick," commented Stella, "are you saying that we're not safe here?"

"Not exactly Stella," Nick placed his hands on the table, "what I am saying is that these people seem very well resourced, capable and dangerous. There has to be someone behind this in authority of some kind."

"Like what?" asked Nigel, "police, government, NCA, MI5 or 6 even?"

"I'm not going to rule anything out Nigel."

"That means we're not safe anywhere," objected Stella.

"You're about right Stella, I think we need to get some hardware."

"Nick, the Commissioner won't wear that," stated Nigel, "he'll opt for a SWAT team before we can carry iron."

"Well, we do it ourselves. Myself, you and Chris. Just sidearms for personal protection. I'll get a couple of Glocks for you."

"What about me?" asked Stella, "I'm a big girl."

"Have you done any small arms training?" asked Nick.

"Yes, I have, only a few hours. Sir Adrian insisted before he assigned me," commented Stella, "I was actually a pretty good shot."

"It's a lot different actually shooting at someone Stella," protested Nick.

"Well how many people have you shot at Chris, or you Nigel?"

Nick threw his hands in the air. "Point taken, 3 fucking Glocks then."

"And a couple of clips," remarked Stella.

"And a couple of clips."

61

Chris and Stella brought Felicity and her father Sebastian to the Kensington flat. London did not disappoint. Wind, sleet and a somewhat depressing ambience. The road closures were still in situ as were the tent and uniforms on point. Sir Adrian insisted he be present and, as he informed Nick and Inspector Connelly, he would be the most senior officer in attendance in case others were to intercede during the interview or the playing back of the Homepod.

Nick, Nigel and Sir Adrian were inside the tent when Chris and Stella escorted Felicity and Sebastian from the car. Sebastian was told to wait with the attending officer and was assured in the car ride from Nottingham that Stella, in her capacity as a psychologist, would ensure that any duress imposed upon Felicity would be managed and kept to a minimum. In Stella's view Felicity presented as a very competent witness and exhibited a demeanour that exceeded her fourteen years. During the ride from Nottingham Stella explained what had taken place, without the gory details of the actual wounds inflicted, in effect breaking the ice with Felicity. Both father and daughter were surprisingly composed during the explanations and even asked a few questions. Felicity explained that she was a frequent user of the Homepod and was often in the apartment by herself while her mother was at work.

It was a relief for all concerned that the apartment had been cleaned of blood residues on the walls, furniture and carpet. The cleaners explained that some items that had been difficult to clean had been placed in a bedroom out of sight. Sir

Adrian asked the cleaning team to take a break while the interview took place, leaving an officer at the door and Nick's team within the apartment.

Stella took the lead. "Felicity, do you know the locations of the Homepod system?"

"Yes, there's one on top of the kitchen cupboards and smaller ones in the other rooms."

"Can you activate it for us please."

Felicity turned to face the unit in the kitchen. "Hello Siri."

"Hello Felicity."

Felicity continued with the words agreed with Stella. "Is there a recording from the 13th of June Siri."

"Yes, Victoria requested a voice recording at seven fifteen."

"Can you replay that recording please."

Chris was recording the conversation on his laptop.

"Playing now."

Stella grabbed Felicities arm and as agreed assisted her out of the apartment.

"Who the fuck are you?" shouted Victoria,

"Kill them both." A female's voice with an accent.

Felicity froze and turned around as she was taken towards the door. "That's Auntie Helga."

"Can you ask Siri to pause?" asked Stella calmly.

"Siri pause," commanded Felicity.

The recording paused as everyone in the room stood silently as Stella faced the girl.

"Who is Auntie Helga, Felicity?"

"She's a friend of Auntie Celia. She lives in Brussels."

"I have to take you out of the room now Felicity," Stella put her arm around Felicities shoulders, "Can you start the recording again as we leave the room."

The two made their way to the front door of the apartment. "Siri Play."

Chris nodded as the recording played again.

"Helga, you fucking bitch."

The recording revealed the pushing of furniture and some clatter in the kitchen. Screams and grunts as the sound of scuffles prevailed. It was Victoria's voice that was most prolific with Celia also making quick observations.

"Two males, combat clothing."

"European origin."

"One point eight metres, Caucasian."

"Commando knives, Glocks."

Some of the words were screamed as Nick and the team listened in amazement.

Sir Adrian muttered. "Those brave women were giving us clues."

"Tattoos. Blue eyes."

There was more scuffling and screams, then male voices.

"You English bitches, you cut me and so I'll cut you."

"Tie them up." Helga's voice.

More screams and grunts.

"They are bleeding too much."

"Don't worry they'll be dead soon."

It was Helga's voice that spoke calmly. "You could have avoided this. Now tell me who your agent is at the EU?"

"Go to hell."

"I will ask you once more Victoria."

"You can get fucked Helga."

"Cut the other one's throat so she can watch her die."

There was a scream and silence.

"Celia, no."

"She's dead now. Who is your agent in Brussels?"

"You'll die Helga; they'll get you."

"Your Siri will not help you. We'll take your devices. It was a stupid thing to do."

One of the men spoke. "Ich blute stark."

The other also spoke. "Ich auch, die hundinnen."

Helga spoke. "Schneide ihr die verdammte kehle durch."

There were more sounds of shuffling furniture.

"Nehmen sie die smartphones und laptops und fick auch Siri."

Then there was silence. It was Chris who spoke first.

"I reckon Siri would have stopped recording at some stage, but I wouldn't know how long the recording function will go for."

"Did you get a clear recording Chris?" asked Nick.

"Yes, but my German's not that good but I can guess."

"Maybe someone can fill me in?" asked Nigel.

Sir Adrian answered. "The two men said they were bleeding, then Helga told them to cut her throat and collect the smartphones and laptop."

Chris observed, "I think Helga thought that any recording was being activated on a smartphone or laptop. By now she may think that the recording App didn't activate."

"Right," said Nick, "Let's see if we can pick up this Helga bitch. She must be easy to find through customs. Maybe she's one of Celia's party friends in which case we should have some video surveillance."

Nigel made the call while the others gathered their items and made their way down to the street. Felicity and Sebastian were waiting in the tent with Stella offering what comfort she could. Despite the ordeal both the girl and her father were remarkably stoic. Chris remained at the tent as Stella steered them to the squad car.

"I'll stay with you on the drive back home," said Stella as she opened the front passenger door, waving to Chris and Nick. Once belted up the constable pulled away for the two and a half-hour drive back to Newark.

Nigel told Nick he'd go back to the Met and see what surveillance video there was while Sir Adrian just nodded and made his way to his patient driver in the Land Rover Sentinel.

Nick motioned to Chris to go with him back to their operation rooms at the old Yard.

62

Once back at the old Yard Nick made some calls to get access to the surveillance videos of Celia Graham's parties which were currently with MI5. Having secured their release, he turned to Chris who was listening to the recording from Celia's apartment.

"I'm heading off to the hospital and check-in with Dianne. I'll be late I expect. Dianne will be staying over there tonight."

"OK Boss, I'll stay here and wait for Stella and Nigel."

Dianne and Nick were having a light evening snack at the hospital café when Nick's phone rang. His face was grey as he nodded to the conversation on the phone. Without saying anything he hung the phone up with reddened eyes.

"That was Chris. There's been a car accident on the A1 near Grantham. It's the police car that Stella and the father and daughter were in. They collided with a truck that left the scene. They're on their way to QMC in Nottingham, one fatality, three in a serious condition."

"Oh, my goodness Nick, we have to go up there."

"Right. Chris says he's on his way there now and Nigel will hold the fort down here."

The rain was still pouring down as they travelled up the M1. They avoided the A1 in case the traffic was affected by the accident. The time difference would be much the same in any case, it all depended on the traffic, which could be frequently heavy. Dianne's permit once again got them a prime spot close to the hospital as they made a dash in the rain from the on-call car parking area outside the main entrance, above emergency.

Dianne flashed her medical ID which gave them access to the emergency desk. The only advice they could get was that three persons were being treated with one in theatre. Dianne decided to go to the ramp and speak with the ambulance drivers. She needed to know more details. Fortunately, the ambulance that brought two of them was still at the ramp tidying up the equipment. With an element of relief but also sorrow, it was the police driver of the vehicle that was deceased. The paramedic advised that it appeared the driver of the truck had crossed lanes and pushed the squad car into a steel barrier. After the accident it had headed away from the scene down a side road.

Dianne returned to Nick at the emergency desk awaiting a report from one of the doctors. Chris came out of the emergency ward in tears.

"Stella's in theatre right now with head and internal injuries. Felicity and Sebastian both have broken bones but nothing complicated or life threatening. A few cuts and bruises and extremely lucky to be alive. They let me in for a few minutes, but they're under sedation now."

"This has to be related," said Nick, "It can't be coincidental."

"I think we have to go in that direction Nick. How much reach do these people have?" asked Dianne.

"I'm going to talk to Sir Adrian as soon as I get back. I've had enough of this shit. How's Stella?"

"They aren't sure. She came in unconscious, so it's been difficult to diagnose exactly." Chris was having a hard time holding it together. "Someone said there was internal bleeding but that's all I know."

"Dianne, you and Chris stay here. I'm heading back to London."

"What are you going to do?" asked Dianne.

"What I do best."

63

The drive back to London was therapeutic. He needed time to think this through. So far, his team had used standard investigative procedures with a little subterfuge. They had probably taken conventional procedures as far as they could go. It was time to bend the rules. It was time to talk to Age.

The world seemed to be resting on his shoulders as Age sat at his desk. A lonely figure at the top of his game. He could call in whatever legal resources were available to him. There were other assets available, although sitting very uncomfortably in places he would prefer not to access. It was an unenviable task to sit between the British Government and the world community, knowing that whatever direction is taken neither would ever know the whole story let alone the truth, nor should they. It was a known fact that once words are spoken, written or transmitted that control is then lost to the receiver. From there it's like a virus that passes and mutates and eventually bears little resemblance to its original form. Keeping an issue inhouse is an absurdity, a nonsense, it's an impossibility. A paradox.

These were not just murders that were being committed. He had known that for some time now. The killings were targeted, that was obvious. The motives were somewhat more complicated than anyone could imagine. The Met had lost one of its own and one of his team lay injured. Witnesses were also in hospital, and it was time to turn the tables, and to hell with the politics. Jurisdictions were being overstepped and the lines of demarcation were becoming blurred. He felt compromised by his responsibility to the crown and his own private sense of duty. He was indeed conflicted.

Sir Adrian's intercom broke his troubled silence.

"Commander Hood, Sir."

"Send him in."

Nick strode in to find Sir Adrian sitting at his desk with his head in his hands. Age looked up with a furrowed brow and red eyes.

"What a fucking mess Nick. It should never have got this far."

"I agree Age, time to take the gloves off."

"It would seem that convention's not going to get us onto the front foot Nick, and I have a minister breathing down my neck to boot."

"I need to find this Helga woman," Nick put his hands onto the desk as Age leaned back.

"If I allow you off the leash, I can't give you any official support. You'll be on your own, you understand that?"

"I've been there before Age."

"Then this conversation never happened. She works for the European Commission. Helga Vormelker." Age flicked a file across the desk.

"Do we know where she is at the moment?"

"She flew by private jet from Gatwick to Luchthaven Zaventum during the night following the Kensington murder. Careful Nick, she has diplomatic immunity."

"And I guess I don't have that?"

"No, you don't. Officially you don't work for the British Government and now we're into Brexit the pricks delight in making us uncomfortable whenever they can."

"Any assistance?"

"Take the Eurostar and I'll have someone contact you when you arrive."

64

Nick boarded one of the frequent morning Eurostars at St Pancras, thankful to be in Business Premier class and able to walk into the station within ten minutes of departure. The Friday morning train would give him enough time to locate Helga, do his business and be back on the train later that evening. With memories of the domestic Virgin train fresh in his mind, he was thankful to get the Premier Business class refreshments and the ambience of a carriage with a lounge and only a few business travellers. The two-hour journey in the new E320 would give him time to review his case before he meets his contact at the Brussels Midi Pullman Bar.

Following a brief exchange, the two moved to the station carpark where Nick was given a black leather shoulder bag and the keys to a Fiat 500, easy to park and inconspicuous. Checking the bag Nick found a smartphone, spare car key and a P229 with .357 SIG ammunition, silencer and extra clip. Nick's favourite choice and very lethal.

Nick drove past the Commission Buildings where Helga worked and then to her apartment building at Ville de Bruxelles on Avenue Roosevelt. Her apartment was on the first floor with no facing buildings. Parking the car across the road Nick waited opposite the entrance for someone to exit or enter the building. His alternative was to wait until dark and climb the corner balconies however his first preference was to use the main entrance and bypass the first stage security door. Once inside he would take the stairs to the first-floor apartment, unlock the door, disable any security and wait.

As fortune would have it, contract cleaners were on site and as one of them came out of the building Nick was able to slip in. Once inside the entrance hall he made his way to the stairs and put on a pair of leather gloves. Surprisingly, he did not see any security cameras. *A safe neighbourhood* he thought. Once on the first floor, he made his way to apartment three and was pleased to see a manual lock. He would pick that with ease.

The apartment was spacious, with modern furnishings and a curved mezzanine. There was a simple security system which he was able to disable quickly before climbing the stairs to the master bedroom. Once in the master suite he placed his bag in the walk-in robe timing himself from the entrance door to the robe. The amount of black leather apparel, chains, handcuffs and a Nemeth stock whip hanging from a hook did not go unnoticed. *Just what every modern German girl needs*, thought Nick.

He assessed that fifteen-seconds would give him plenty of time to go back, reset the alarm system and get back into the robe before the system reactivated. It was Nick's guess that Helga would deactivate the system as soon as she arrived home later that afternoon. Once Helga arrived, he knew he would then be free to move around as she settled into her usual routine. He was hoping that she would be alone. He had no doubt that she would have a weapon or two in the apartment, but he did not wish to rummage around in case she noticed any misplacement. He would however make a cursory inspection of the bedside tables just in case a weapon was close by. He was cursing the deep pile carpet, concerned that he may have left noticeable footprints.

65

At five-thirty he heard the door open. Helga turned the main lights on, switched off the security system and kicked off her high heeled shoes. Throwing her bag and coat onto the couch she went into the kitchen, opened the refrigerator and poured herself a glass of white wine and took a large gulp. Placing the glass on the bench she picked up her shoes and made her way up the stairs to the bedroom.

Nick had taken up his position in a small tub chair against the window and to the far right, on the opposite side of the room to the walk-in robe. Helga walked in without noticing the person in the room, throwing her shoes into the robe. She turned to face the window and gasped as Nick sat there with the Sig Sauer pointed at her. He waved the gun to his left toward the bed.

"Sit down Helga, we're going to have a chat."

"Who are you?"

"That really doesn't matter Helga, sit down."

Helga complied, with contempt building inside.

"You and your friends killed two of my associates in London a few days ago."

"I have no idea what you're talking about."

"Not only did you kill them, but you tortured them as well."

Helga lunged for the bedside table and pulled out a small handgun and pulled the trigger twice, but nothing happened. Nick threw six bullets on the floor.

"Now we're going to talk Helga, and no lies please."

"Go to hell."

"I had an idea you'd say that Helga, but I have a feeling hell is where you're going."

She opened her mouth to shout an expletive, but Nick shot her in her left shoulder. She flew back onto the bed clutching her arm. He could see she was containing the pain as the blood seeped out of the wound.

"Try screaming and it's all over. That bullet passed straight through Helga and didn't damage anything of consequence. Perhaps I should cut your throat like you did with Celia and Victoria and watch you gurgle away your last few minutes on this earth."

Nick took a knife out of his pocket and opened the blade.

"If I use this it will hurt Helga. I'll make sure of it. Now tell me who gave you the orders to kill our officers and what are the names of the two Germans with you in London."

"How did you know they were Germans?"

"Well, the girls did a good job getting a few cuts in during the struggle. Pity they didn't stick one into you. DNA Helga, and of course Siri helped us as well."

"Go on, get on with it. I'll say nothing."

"Let's not forget your truck driver who tried to kill the witnesses and one of my team."

"You will all die. You have no idea what is being planned."

"Well, I'm hoping you'll tell us Helga."

"Hope all you want. You'll get nothing from me."

Nick fired off another shot that shattered her right kneecap and broke her leg. Blood spurted out but settled into a slow bleed.

"You'll be in a bit of pain now, but I don't need to tell you that. This will keep going until you talk. I will keep you conscious and alive and in a lot of pain. Left leg next."

"Hans and Volka."

"That sounds like a drink Helga, give me more."

"I only know them as Hans and Volka."

Nick stood up and moved closer to Helga and held the gun against her left kneecap.

"This next shot will put you in a wheelchair for life Helga."

"They don't work for me."

"Who do they work for Helga. Remember we heard you say, *'Kill them both'* so don't push me too far."

"Are you going to kill me?"

"I haven't made up my mind, more information please."

"That's all I know."

"Wrong answer Helga." Nick stabbed her left foot with the knife.

"You're going to walk with a limp Helga." Nick wiped the knife on her skirt.

"He runs a para-military group, I don't meet him. He calls me."

"Do you have his number?"

"In my bag, my mobile phone, the call log has the number."

"Is that all?"

"That's all I know."

"Are you planning any more murders in Britain?"

"No."

"I don't believe you. Where are Hans and Volka?"

"I don't know."

"Are they still in Britain?"

"I don't know."

"I'm getting bored with your answers Helga."

"I only know my orders. They get their own orders."

"So, there will be more murders?"

"I don't know."

"What's the bigger picture Helga? I could let you live."

"It's about disruption and your corrupt conservative government."

"Is this about Brexit and UK leaving the European Union?"

"Work it out for yourself, you pig."

Nick pointed the gun at Helga's forehead.

"I told you what I know. You said you could let me live."

"I lied." Nick pulled the trigger.

66

The bed and the surrounding carpet were covered in blood. Nick was careful to avoid stepping onto any spatters as he reached into the robe to retrieve his bag. He put the bullets back in Helga's gun and placed it back in the bedside drawer. He took off her watch and rings and emptied her jewellery case onto the floor. Downstairs, he searched Helga's bag and put her phone in his pocket. He opened some of the drawers and cupboards, ruffling up the contents and throwing items on the floor. It gave the appearance of a robbery gone wrong or at least pointed in that direction.

Nick's contact was waiting at the station where he parked the car leaving the bag and its contents on the seat. He retained Helga's phone and walked towards the Pullman Hotel bar for a stiff whisky before boarding the last Eurostar back to London. Helga's body would not be discovered, he thought, until Monday or Tuesday when she failed to turn up for work.

Nick checked his phone for the first time in twelve hours as he relaxed in his business premier class seat. Three messages from Dianne, two from Nigel, one from Chris and one from Age. He decided to start at the top, in order of importance.

"Hi Dianne, it's me."

"Where have you been?"

"Can't say, quick trip, nothing to worry about."

"I wanted to give you an update on Stella."

"How is she?"

"Do you want the full clinical assessment or plain language?"

"Plain language I think would be best."

"Well, she's fine. No need to operate. She's got a lacerated liver, only mild and it should repair itself. She'll stay in hospital for a couple of days for observation, but she'll be a bit sore for a while and needs a bit of looking after."

"I'll have to get Chris to take a few days off."

"And the rest Nick. Stella's lucky she's so fit and has good core muscle strength. Not to mention the fact that the airbags saved their lives." Dianne continued, "That poor policeman, he had a wife and two young kids."

"Yes, very sad. Best thing we can do is find these people and put them out of action."

"So, how's that going for you?"

"Well, there's still two at large, one's been taken care of."

Dianne butted in. "And was that you?"

"You know I can't comment on that Dianne," Nick sighed, "let's just say that we still don't know who's giving the orders. How's the girl and her father?"

"You mean Felicity and Sebastian?"

"Yes, I mean Felicity and Sebastian."

"Felicity has a broken arm and leg, Sebastian a broken leg. Chris says they were taken back to the safe house in Newark."

"How's Chris, I haven't returned his call yet?"

"He's devastated, he really cares for that girl," replied Dianne sympathetically.

"Yes, I got that impression."

"Where are you now Nick?"

"I'm on a train back to London." Nick was not exactly lying.

"Do you want me to pick you up?"

"I forgot to tell you where I left the Lexus," confessed Nick.

"Age called me and told me you left the car at the Vauxhall Building. One of his chaps drove it to St Thomas's for me."

"That was very nice of him."

212

"Yes, it was. Chris drove me back to St Thomas's and then he drove all the way back to be with Stella. So, do I pick you up?"

Nick didn't want Dianne to know he'd been across the channel. "No don't worry, I'll go back to our digs at the Old Yard and catch up with Nigel tonight. Are you OK?"

"Yes, I'm fine, a bit tired but the rooms here are very comfortable." Dianne paused. "I still have a copper outside in the passage. Is it really necessary?"

"At the moment I would say yes. Don't worry it's their job."

"Ok. Will I see you tomorrow?"

"Yes, I'll get a few things sorted and see you tomorrow sometime."

"Love you."

"Love you too." Nick blew a kiss over the phone.

It was nine-thirty. He had plenty of time to make the calls before he entered the tunnel.

"How did it go?" asked Age.

"To plan."

"Good, that's all I need to know." Age was sitting on the edge of his bed in his pyjamas. His wife Jane nestled into the bedclothes reading a book. "Let's touch base tomorrow, say around midday."

"Yes, will do." Nick hung up. The least said the better.

Nigel's phone went to message as did Chris's. He left a message that he was heading to the old Yard around midnight.

Nick rested, appreciating the supper and cabin service during the passage under the channel. He was tired but his training kept him alert and cognisant of the tasks at hand. He may have eliminated an important chess piece, but the board was far from clear.

67

The lights of Froghalt came into view as the train burst into the Kent countryside. There was plenty of room on the train and Nick was thankful there was nobody wanting a chat as he watched the lights flash by. They would be at St Pancras very shortly and from there a short cab ride from the station. No need to get Teddy out tonight but Nick was keen to hear if the special cab was out of the garage.

Nick got the cabby to stop outside the Red Lion. From there just a short walk behind the Old Yard to the doorway at the back of the building. For the first time Nick noticed a night watchman standing in front of a steel drum, warming his hands on a small fire. "Hadn't seen him before," Nick muttered to himself, then thought no more of it as he unlocked the rear door that would take him down to the basement lift.

Nigel had been in their incident room since late afternoon, expecting to see some of the troops that evening. The lift door opened. Nick walked into the small kitchen and turned the coffee machine on.

"I don't know how to work that fucking thing, Nick."

"Not a problem, I'll fix it. White and two."

"Please," Nigel stood up and walked to the small kitchenette, "and more importantly, how are you?"

"Yeah, fine, it's been a hectic few days."

"It has but how are you, yourself?"

"Sounds Irish to me," Nick poured some milk into a small stainless-steel jug, smiling, "No, I'm good, just a bit worried about Stella and that poor girl, and her father. As if the murders weren't bad enough."

"I guess you got that business done, OK?"

"Yes, it's done," Nick pressed the coffee into the portafilter, "but we may have stirred the possum a bit."

"That sounds a bit Aussie."

"Yes, I often find myself using anecdotes from down under. They tend to soften the tension somewhat."

"Like 'she'll be right cobber'."

"Something like that Nigel, well done." Nick frowned as he steamed the milk as he continued, "Yes, we've stirred up a hornet's nest alright, but the gloves are off now."

"I'm an old copper Nick, as you well know, and I can't get used to carrying a gun. Doesn't feel right."

"It will when someone starts taking pot shots at you Nigel. We're living in a fucked-up world right now."

They took their coffees to the incident room and sat around the table looking at the mess of paper. It was Nick who broke the temporary silence.

"Before she died, she told me they, whoever they are, want to create disturbance and mentioned our corrupt conservative government."

"So, while we've been working on the assumption that these targeted murders were trimming the radicals," Nigel paused to sip his coffee, "they are, in fact, causing general mayhem and division in the community."

Nick carried on. "And at the same time making our conservative government appear incapable of handling the discord and dissention."

"So, what are we dealing with anarchists or Marxists."

"Both, if you ask me," Nick gulped the remains of his coffee down, "might call it a night Nigel. We'll have a chat with Sir Adrian in the morning."

68

The sound of the lift cranking up drifted into the room.

"That's a noisy bastard," said Nigel, "must be Chris coming up."

"No, he's still with Stella at the hospital in Nottingham. That lift is going down."

"Dianne?"

"Not likely, she would have called me first." Nick turned to Nigel, "Did you see the nightwatchman when you came in."

"No, I didn't know there was one."

The lift stopped and the power suddenly cut out. The two were left in darkness with only reflected light from the city filtering through the windows.

"I can smell smoke Nick."

"Me too. Grab what you can Nigel," Nick stopped, "Where's your gun?"

"Beside my bed."

"Grab it and hurry." Nick rushed up to his bedroom to grab a bag and shoved his Sig Elite into his belt. Nigel bolted up the next flight of stairs and within a minute he was back down gun, bag and gaberdine mac in hand. By now there was smoke coming up the lift well.

"The stairs are blocked off below Nick."

"Yes, I know. Phone the fire brigade, maybe someone in the Met has seen the smoke."

Nick leaned out of the window on the fifth floor in horror as he saw the flames leaping out of the windows three floors down. The fire, fuelled by solvents and building materials, was spreading quickly through the renovated rooms and corridors.

The century old timber floors and ceilings were quick to ignite as the flames explored every dry crevice and cranny in the heritage building. The smoke was becoming concentrated and dense in the top floors as Nick and Nigel realised their only option was through the fifth-floor windows and down the ropes.

"Thank goodness for your ESP Nick," yelled Nigel as they both grabbed the coiled up knotted ropes and threw two out from adjacent windows, "but I'm getting too old for this shit."

Flames were starting to leap out of the windows below them as the two climbed out, throwing their bags onto the ground below.

"Kick the rope away from the flames as you go down Nigel," yelled Nick as they grabbed the knots while descending.

"That's easy for you to say," spluttered Nigel, "I'm flat out holding on."

It was only a matter of seconds before they touched the ground, looking up at the flames now enveloping their office area and bedrooms.

"Look at the speed of that fire," uttered Nigel as they both looked up. The sirens of fire appliances pierced the night with screeches and yelps, as the whole building seemed to be fully involved. The heat was getting intense as they grabbed their bags and ran towards the Met building along the iron fence bordering the roadway.

They were turning the corner of the building when several shots rang out from the laneway at the back. Instinctively Nick found cover as Nigel hit the deck. The shots missed their intended victims, but Nick drew his Sig and crept forward running towards the back lane with the light from the fire illuminating the alley and throwing complex shadows around the building site. He saw a figure turn the corner into Derby Gate towards Parliament Street. By the time Nick turned right into Derby a rapid response fire vehicle was turning in followed by a fire appliance. The fire chief stepped out putting on his white helmet as Nick almost bumped into him.

"Did you see a man running out of this lane Chief?"

"Sorry mate, I didn't." The Chief waved to the appliance behind as firemen leapt out and started running hose through the site and up to the blazing building. "Anyone in the building?" asked the Chief.

"No, just the two of us in the north-east wing as far as I know." Nick stood there watching the building engulfed in flame as Nigel joined him.

"Fuck me," uttered Nigel.

"I can't see the nightwatchman, Nigel."

"Nightwatchman my fucking arse." Nigel had a way with words sometimes.

69

Nick picked up the phone, gazing at the blazing building as the firemen worked frantically to save what they could.

"Hey Teddy, how's the cab coming on?"

"Got it back this afternoon Commander."

"Any chance you could pick us up tomorrow morning?"

"What address guv?"

Nick looked at Nigel standing there in his crumpled suit with his mac laying on the ground with the few personal possessions he was able to grab during the quick exit.

"Dorchester Teddy, say around 9?"

"You got it boss, see you then."

"Let's go Nigel, my shout."

"Where's that Nick?"

"I'll tell you when we get there."

Nick called a taxi and when asked the pick-up address, "Follow the flames in Parliament Street, we'll be outside The Red Lion."

"Where to sir?"

"Mayfair."

Nick heard Nigel mumble. "Fuck me."

While they were waiting for the taxi, Nick phoned Dianne to tell her he was OK. He needn't have bothered.

"Nick, it's nearly one o'clock. Couldn't you have waited till the morning. You woke me up."

"Sorry I just wanted to tell you that Nigel and I are OK."

"Well of course you are, I wouldn't have married you if you weren't. Goodnight Nick." Dianne hung the phone up.

"I don't know why I bother sometimes," uttered Nick.

The phone rang. "What do you mean Nigel and you are OK. What's happened." Dianne was now fully awake.

"Not much dear, Nigel and I just leapt out of a burning building, that's all."

"And you're both OK?"

"Yes, we're fine, I'll tell you more about it tomorrow. Goodnight."

"I'm glad you're both OK. Goodnight dear." Dianne hung the phone up again.

The cab arrived and Nick's phone rang again. "What building?"

"Old Scotland Yard but the firemen are doing a sterling job. Goodnight dear."

Nigel and Nick jumped in the back of the cab.

"Dorchester please."

The night manager greeted them at the desk. "Good evening Commander, how can we assist you this evening."

"Two Queen rooms please."

"Very good Commander, do you have any bags for the porter?"

"Not tonight I'm afraid, we left in a hurry." Nick was not to know that both he and Nigel had brown smoke smudges over their faces and the odour of smouldering building on their clothes was more than noticeable.

"Very good sir," the night manager handed over two key cards smiling. "Had a busy evening Commander?"

"You could say that."

Nigel followed Nick with a degree of trepidation having never spent a night in a luxury hotel.

"You must be a regular here, the night manager recognised you."

"Dianne and I dine here every now and then."

Once in the lift Nick turned to his friend. "Relax Nigel, it's only for one night, just sorry I couldn't find a better hotel at short notice."

Nigel couldn't resist a jab. "Well get your act together Nick, I have standards you know."

"You coppers, you break me up."

70

Nigel dressed early, eagerly anticipating the best of British breakfasts as he walked into the Promenade. Greeted by a waiter he was escorted to a plush green velvet sofa and seated beside a low table with two Edwardian chairs opposite.

"Would sir like to view the breakfast menu."

Nigel couldn't help himself. "Yes, sir would, thank you so much." Thankful that he didn't bring his gaberdine mac with him as was his custom, and not quite fitting for his current surroundings, he thought. He would however be making the most of this experience backed up by a healthy appetite.

The waiter returned with the menu as Nigel leant back on the cushion provided, admiring the gaslight style chandelier above the table. Whilst mentally noting the cooked breakfast inclusions and contemplating the number of choices of coffees he was abruptly interrupted by Nick who plonked himself down in one of the opposite chairs.

"No time for that Nigel," remarked Nick as he flipped the menu away from the astounded copper, "we've got a taxi waiting."

Nick led the protesting detective away from the Promenade to the lift where Nigel continued to lament that his once in a lifetime opportunity for a Dorchester breakfast had been unceremoniously snatched from him within the blink of an eye.

Teddy was waiting in his renovated taxi at the grand entrance as the top hatted doorman opened the door for the two departing guests. The doorman doffed the brim of his hat as Nick slipped a ten-pound note into his left hand resting on the opened taxi door.

"Thank you, Commander, have a good day sir."

Nick turned to Nigel as they made themselves comfortable. "The most important person in the hotel Nigel."

Teddy couldn't help himself. "Cor, blimey. Aren't we slumming it these days? Where to Guv?"

"And hello to you Teddy. Nice job on the cab." Nick looked around at the perfect finish by Jankel.

"Yep, even fitted revolving number plates and machine guns up front." Teddy pulled away from the driveway turning left into Park Lane.

"You're fucking kidding me," uttered Nigel in astonishment.

"Yes Nigel, Teddy is having a joke at our expense, but it's an interesting concept."

"Sorry Guv, seen too many movies but I've got the goss on summit you might be interested in."

"What's that Teddy?"

"Well, I got chatting to one of the mechanics at Jankel, who funnily enough's been shaggin' the sister of a mate of mine down at The Blind Beggar."

"Perhaps we could dispense with the nefarious habits of EastEnders Teddy."

"Of course, Guv, anyway as I was sayin', this mechanics on the competition shooting circuit and he was talking to this ex-army geezer over a pint or two a couple of weeks ago."

"And?"

"And you're going to luv this skipper," with no instructions of where to drive to, Teddy pointed the taxicab towards Westminster around Wellington Arch and down Grosvenor Place.

"This army geezer got very pissed. Was working in one of the armouries before 'e paid off. Says that when the troops come back from deployments and exercises, they check their weapons in and then those weapons are inspected and tested."

Nick interrupted, "But that's standard procedure, Teddy."

"Yes, it is Guv but what some of the armourers are doing is replacing parts but sometimes the parts ain't defective. They get tagged as defective to go back to the manufacturer for replacement." Teddy concentrated on the traffic for a few seconds before continuing.

"Somewhere during that process, the tags are marked, and the parts get put aside as they are not on the manifest. Dunno who or where they go but the parts then eventually get assembled into a complete handgun or rifle and flogged off."

Nick joined in, "So no serial number or if there is, there would be no complete gun to match it within defence or police records."

"Exactly Guv, and with so many firearms with interchangeable calibres as well, the guns are not traceable." Teddy slowed the cab down to a crawl in the heavy traffic as he turned around. "Guv, these people doin' the shootin' could throw away or exchange the barrel or chamber and if the gun is found it probably wouldn't get matched up wiv a previous brown bread."

"Forensics couldn't match the bullets to another crime," offered Nigel.

"Exactly, "said Nick, "they're called ghost guns."

"That's what the shagger said, Skipper."

"So, let's say we've got a couple of killers from Germany, the way it's looking," Nigel spoke looking out the window at the bumper- to-bumper traffic, "they get hold of these ghost guns, as they can't bring their own through customs, with spare parts to disguise or confuse the forensics, and then go off on a killing spree while we chase our tails."

"That's about the sum of it," stated Nick as he tapped Teddy on the shoulder. "Anyway, can we track the source of these weapons and parts Teddy?"

"I doubt it Guv, no one's gunna dob in these geezers on pain of deff. We was lucky to get the goss as it was, and let's face it, just hearsay wiv a geezer speaking to a drunk."

Nick reflected for a moment. "We had a similar situation many years ago when we closed our bases in Singapore and Hong Kong. A fair quantity of armaments went missing from the P/Ls when they were audited back home. Gone to local black markets, maybe service personnel involved, maybe local employees. We never found out and when the defence chiefs reported it to the Ministry it was hushed up. The paperwork never saw the light of day."

The cab went quiet for a few minutes as the stunted traffic flow plodded on down Vauxhall Bridge Road. It was Nick who broke the silence.

"Take us to St Thomas's Teddy and we'll catch up with Dianne. Maybe stop for a cuppa and a bit of brekky."

"Thank god," said Nigel, "I'm fucking starving."

71

Dianne was waiting at the entrance to St Thomas's House Library as Teddy pulled the cab up. It was Nick who suggested the Marriott County Hall for breakfast to which Teddy grumbled about doing a u turn and going across Lambeth Bridge as the main entrance to the County Hall was off Westminster Bridge.

"Honestly, what's the fucking problem Teddy. A talented cabby like you would know all the shortcuts."

"Ain't no shortcut guv, lest the Bill nabs me and that ain't 'appening tadday."

Despite the grumbling, Teddy navigated the cab onto Westminster Bridge, veering off to the left, taking the tunnelled portal to the circular hotel entrance in remarkably quick time.

Nigel was muttering under his breath something about being able to eat a rat on the run if he could keep in step. Teddy, of course, knew the doorman and was given a convenient priority spot to park the hackney in the circle.

Nick, familiar with most of the finest hotels in London escorted his tribe through Noes Bar to the Library Lounge producing his Platinum card to the maître d'.

"Good morning, Commander Hood, table of four?"

"Yes please, by the window if possible."

The four were escorted to an appropriate window table past the extensive buffet where Nigel took the opportunity to avail himself of the considerable fare.

There was little conversation until their appetites were sated, and coffees were poured by the attending waiter.

Dianne broke the silence first. "I had a call from Chris Spencer this morning."

The others stopped to listen.

"He's picking Stella up this morning and was wondering where it would be best to take her."

"Why not here," suggested Nick. "I'm a Platinum member and Stella can park here on my account. Chris can stay with her as required. I'll inform the manager of security to have them stay under an anonymous name."

Dianne turned to Nick and took hold of his arm. "That's very generous Nick but it will cost a fortune to stay here for any length of time."

"Well, you're just across the road and can call in every now and then," offered Nick.

"How long is this going to go on for?" asked Dianne with more than an element of concern.

"Not much longer," replied Nick, "they've started to get careless and making mistakes."

Nigel jumped in, "and that's why we can start putting the pieces together at last, but we need Chris and his online resources."

"Well," said Teddy, "the cabs there when you want it."

"And we will," said Nick, "a mobile ops room will be exactly what we need." Teddy bid them farewell, winked at Nick and then he was gone.

Nick turned to Dianne. "Can you call Chris and tell him to come to the Marriott. In fact," Nick continued, "we should all stay here for a day or two at least."

Nigel could hardly contain himself with the contemplation of big breakfasts, room service, swimming pool and comfortable beds.

"I'm not sure we can go back to our residences yet," said Nick, "they may still be under observation, and considering that they found us at Old Scotland Yard they may also have an inside source."

Nick spoke to the hotel manager and arranged adjacent rooms for a few days. Dianne was pleased to be spending each night with Nick again after over a week at the hospital. Chris and Stella arrived late afternoon, with Stella in a wheelchair ably manoeuvred by Chris, and greeted warmly by the team.

Dianne, under Nick's instruction, phoned the hospital to say that she had found alternative accommodation and would be unavailable for the forthcoming week. Before they retired that evening Nick retrieved Dianne's Lexus from the hospital car park across the road. The only people who knew where they were staying were the five of them. Teddy would go about his business and be on call.

The next morning following a restful and rewarding sleep they gathered in Nick and Dianne's suite where they debriefed each other on where they were at. Nick did not divulge too many details, suffice to say that one of the threats had been eliminated.

It was glaringly obvious to Nick that it was possible there could be some attempted retaliation for Helga's demise once her body was discovered. It was now Monday and by this evening alarm bells would be ringing where Helga worked at the commission in Brussels. It was also a fact that Hans and Volka, and possible others, were still at large in the UK and perhaps plotting any unfinished work. In that regard Nick and his team would not be kept waiting too long.

72

At eight -thirty there was a knock on the door followed by two waiters from room service, each with a trolley of beverages and pastries wheeling them into the lounge area of Nick's suite. The chairs had been arranged so that they were sitting facing each other with Stella in her wheelchair in a space provided. Chris had set up his laptop on an adjacent table with a white board, kindly provided by the Marriott, against the wall. Their three rooms had river views across the Thames, over Westminster Bridge to the parliamentary buildings and Big Ben. Despite the proximity to the traffic, the double-glazed windows prevented any noise from the city to disturb their comfortable abode. To the far right the edge of the London Eye was just visible. Immediately opposite was the partly burnt-out North Norman Shaw building which had been their domicile, if only for a short while.

Stella asked if she had missed much. The response was peppered with laughter.

"Just a little." was a unanimous reply.

Chris broke the silence. "I've just got a text from Deputy Commissioner Cynthia Burrows, there's been an incident in the vicinity of the parliamentary buildings."

The team glanced across the river at the column of dark smoke rising from the south end of the parliament buildings. The sound of police sirens wailed as police cars raced across Westminster Bridge. A fire appliance followed by several ambulances could be seen speeding along the embankment towards Big Ben.

A black rigid inflatable boat came thundering under the Hungerford and Jubilee Bridges manned by what was probably anti-terrorist personnel, dressed in black and clearly armed.

"I thought I heard something while breakfast was being wheeled in," commented Nick.

Nick's phone rang as did Chris and Nigel's', almost simultaneously.

"Nick, it's Age. I'll be quick as I'm on my way out of my office. An explosive device has been detonated outside the south end of the parliament buildings as a group of politicians were congregating with the media in the Victoria Tower Gardens for a tour of the Palace of Westminster. Multiple fatalities, media and pollies. That's all I know right now. The Foreign Secretary has called me in. I'll get back to you."

Nigel and Chris got a similar message.

"Best we stay put for the time being," stated Nick. "It'll be a dog's breakfast over there and the roads will be closed anyway."

"Poor choice of words darling," offered Dianne.

"What," responded Nick as he glanced across the river. "Oh yes, see what you mean."

"As usual at your tactful best." Dianne raised her eyebrows as she acknowledged the expressions of the others.

There were a myriad of police boats and anti-terrorism units now on the river and at least five helicopters in the air, some of them from the media no doubt, thought Nick.

"Do you think it's them?" asked Nigel.

"London to a brick, I would say."

Stella had been very quiet, obviously still in some discomfort. "Can't help thinking that whoever these people are, they're trying to portray a picture of chaos and mayhem." Stella shuffled in her chair leaning forward into a more comfortable position. "We're on our way out of the European Union and from outside, and of course the bloody media are playing their part, it looks like we have law and order breaking down, disorganisation, protests in major centres and communities, and a perceived lack of direction from what could be seen as an inept government. Call me suspicious but this has the EU and radical Remainers written all over it."

"I think she's onto something," remarked Chris.

73

Thirty minutes earlier.

Hans and Volka drove their white Ford transit van down the left lane passing Black Rod's entrance. Hans turned into the driveway to the Victoria Tower South Gardens and showed his media pass. The 'UK News' outside broadcast van was there to cover the special media tour of the Palace of Westminster. Hans parked the vehicle on the edge of the grass alongside another broadcast van. Nodding to some of the adjacent media he climbed on to the bonnet and adjusted the transmitter dish on the roof in line with the aerials on the other vans. He had parked closest to where the group would be mustering for the briefing by their host politicians.

The technicians on the adjoining van looked across.

"Where's your presenter, it starts in a few minutes?" asked one of the technicians.

In perfect English Hans replied, "Must be stuck in traffic, we might take a look outside, she may have forgotten her media pass."

"Yeah, they're a dozy lot these presenters," commented the technician, "look good but not much between the ears."

Hans and Volka locked the van and gave the technician a wave as they headed back to the gate, nodding to the attending constables.

"We've lost our presenter," uttered Hans as he raised his eyebrows.

Laughing, the constable waved them through. By now the media throng of around thirty-five journalists and technical operators had gathered in a semi-circle around the group of fifteen politicians. Nobody noticed that UK News outside broadcast had no representatives attending.

The device in the van was a simple one. Two hundred and fifty kilograms of military grade C4, detonators, battery and a mobile phone receiver.

Hans and Volka walked across the road to the south-west corner of the Jewel Tower. Without hesitation Volka dialled a number as the two of them lay flat against the rear wall of the Tower.

The effect of the detonation was lethal as the blast radiated out, killing everyone within a radius of over thirty metres. The media group took the full force of the explosion with some politicians still alive with critical injuries as the blast tore its way through the group.

The carnage was spread over a huge area with body parts of all descriptions scattered over the manicured lawns. Most of the remains were charred due to the extreme temperature of the explosion. Every window in the south facing wall of the Westminster building was broken. Pedestrians were injured, some fatally as they walked on the pavement behind the garden trees, now smouldering and devoid of most of their leaves. The two policemen on the gate lay deceased on the ground.

Some of those furthest away from the blast lay injured and bleeding, crying out for help. People in the adjacent area of Abingdon Street and Millbank walked around dazed and deaf, their ears ringing from the blast and shock wave. Several cars had crashed, with their drivers walking around unsure about what had just taken place.

Hans and Volka walked away through College Gardens as students and teachers from Westminster School pushed past them, rushing towards the smoke and noise.

Hans and Volka had parked their car in Great College Road and were now heading to their hotel to shower and change their clothes in case there was any residue that could be detected prior to boarding their plane to Brussels. Their diplomatic passes would ensure there would be no unnecessary delay at Gatwick airport.

74

The room at the Marriott County Hall was ominously quiet as the group observed the activity on the river and the emergency vehicles gathering around the Palace of Westminster. Traffic on the Westminster Bridge was being turned around at the south end causing no end of confusion for motorists heading north with massive congestion in the Westminster area.

The smoke was clearing as Nick watched with the others from the window. It had been some while since anyone had spoken. Chris broke the silence.

"Best I get back to work boss," as he touched Nigel on the shoulder.

Nigel nodded as he too stood aghast at what had just happened.

Nick thought to himself *"was this retaliation for knocking off Helga."* But he quickly dismissed the thought as this attack had to have been planned long ago. Turning around he addressed the group.

"Right, we need a new base. I can't afford to stay here, and neither can Her Majesty's Government." Turning to Dianne he continued. "Our place at Belgravia is like Fort Knox and if they try something there, we'll be ready for them. Besides, security cameras on just about every home and intersections in our area."

Dianne joined in. "Yes, I agree, we have plenty of room for all of you now the kids have left home. There's a basement where you can set up your incident room."

"Damn it, we should have done this weeks ago," uttered Nick. Turning to Chris, "Your car is here Chris, so you, Stella and

Nigel go together. Dianne and I will go in her car. Drive into the mews behind the house and I'll open the garage doors for you. Best you take the Vauxhall Bridge."

Nick and Dianne left first, leaving Chris and Nigel to grab the remaining paperwork and wheeling a frustrated Stella.

"Damn these wheels, I feel so helpless at the moment."

Chris gave her a reassuring hug as they made their way to the car.

75

The traffic congestion was building on the southside and getting onto the Vauxhall Bridge was a nightmare. The approaches to Lambeth Bridge were gridlocked, with traffic on the bridge stationery. Nick detoured around Old Paradise Gardens and then back to Lambeth High Street and onto Albert Embankment, then under Vauxhall Station and onto the bridge, while at the same time cursing about the traffic. What would normally have taken ten or fifteen minutes took them over half an hour as they pulled into the Mews and triggered the garage door.

It would be another 30 minutes before Chris, Nigel and Stella pulled in to be greeted by Nick while Dianne scampered off saying she would put the kettle on and do something for lunch.

Nick closed the door and followed the car into the basement garage where Nigel promptly got out and inspected Nick's collection of fine motor vehicles.

"And I called those blokes at the Hind's Head a bunch of tossers."

"And I told you I had an Austin Healy 3000."

"Yeah, but look at the rest of them," Nigel raised his hands, "It's a fucking car museum."

"Settle down Nigel, Dianne's got the kettle on."

"Fucking hell Nick, how much of this street do you own?" Nigel took a three hundred and sixty degree visual of the massive cellar.

"Just the one town house Nigel but three of the cottages so we excavated under them and joined up with the townhouse under the gardens."

Climbing the stairs from the garage they were met by Dianne in the kitchen. "Sorry Stella, we don't have an elevator."

Nigel butted in, "Well surprise, surprise, it's about the only thing you haven't got. This place is amazing."

"That's OK," Chris offered, "I'll carry Stella."

"Well," offered Dianne, "We'll have lunch in the conservatory, and the coffee and tea is made so let's relax and talk about how we're going to do this."

76

They had just settled into their lunch when Nick's phone rang.

"Nick, it's Age, we have to talk. I've just been to an emergency meeting with the Home and Foreign Secretaries and there's going to be a big meeting tomorrow with the PM."

"When and where?"

"Where are you now?"

"We're all at my place at Belgravia. We'll make it the base for the moment."

"I'll be there in about an hour, OK?"

"Yes, see you then."

Nick went back to the conservatory.

"That was Sir Adrian. He'll be joining us in about an hour."

"Well, I'll make a plate up for him," remarked Dianne.

77

It was decided that they would wait to hear what Sir Adrian had to say before embarking on any action. Chris was set up on his laptop and scanning the Met emails and messages in the downstairs living room.

Nigel was engrossed in one of Nick's books on vintage automobiles while Dianne busied herself in the kitchen.

Nick and Stella remained in the conservatory chatting.

"How are you feeling?" asked Nick, sympathetically.

"Well apart from this fucking wheelchair," laughed Stella, "not bad really. Doc says I can start standing and walking for short periods in the next few days. You know, get some strength back into the muscles."

"Well, if there's anything we can do," offered Nick. "Might be best if the doc calls in here."

"Thanks Nick. The brain's fine by the way."

"I'm sure it is."

The bell at the main door on Eaton Square rang out the familiar Westminster chime. Nick made for the front door with Nigel smiling. "Of course, it had to be a Westminster chime."

Stella leaned forward, "do I detect an element of cynicism Nigel?"

"Just my way of having fun Stella."

Sir Adrian walked in and greeted everyone with a wave, taking his coat off and laying it across the embroidered sofa.

"How are you doing Stella, anything we can do at the moment."

"No, but thanks for asking Sir Adrian, Nick and Dianne have been very kind."

"Excellent, what I have to say, I can say to all of you." Adrian settled into the sofa moving his coat aside.

"I've just come from a meeting with the Foreign and Home Secretaries and as you can imagine Parliament is in an uproar. It doesn't help either to have me reporting to one minister and MI5 and the NCA reporting to another. Then we have Europol jumping up and down for treading on their toes."

"Coffee, Sir Adrian?" enquired Dianne.

"Oh, yes please Dianne," and turning to Nick, "have you got something strong to chase the coffee down old man."

"Yes, Age. Anyone else?"

Nigel raised his hand.

"As I was saying. Each entity, and I'm talking police, MI5, NCA et al, all have different ideas about who we're dealing with and what the damn motive is. I let the Secretaries have their bit and refrained from exposing too much detail of your investigations. Less is better when talking to pollies. They do tend to go off on their political tangents and then into electoral survival mode when confronted with the bleeding obvious."

Dianne brought a coffee in for Age which she placed on the occasional table between the sofas. She carried a pot with which she replenished the half empty cups.

Age smiled and thanked Dianne as he took a sip of coffee. Nick had poured three small glasses of single malt whisky, placing one on the small table for Age and passing one to Nigel. Retaining one glass for himself, he gulped it down in one swallow. "I needed that."

Age picked up the small glass and sniffed the aromas. "Balvenie?"

Nick smacked his lips, savouring the last vapours of his glass, "Lagavulen actually."

Age pulled a long face, "of course it is."

Nigel shook his head as Stella contained her mirth. Chris and Dianne sat together at the table quietly observing the perceived pretence.

Nick took the opportunity to jump in.

"We were going to meet today, Age, to discuss my meeting with Helga."

Age got the drift immediately and realised the sensitivity of Nick's excursion across the Channel. "So how was it."

"Quite informative really," offered Nick, "we had a little chat, and I can give you two names, Hans and Volka. She also kindly gave me her phone for us to check her call log."

"That was kind of her," commented Age as Nick handed the phone across. "Perhaps Chris here could play around with it for a while." Age stood up and smiling, passed the phone to Chris.

"Thank you, sir."

"See what you can find out Sergeant."

Nigel moved his seat beside Chris as Age continued.

"Let me make a phone call. If this Hans and Volka did the job, they may have left the country. We might even have them on a database, long shot but we'll give it a go."

The phone call lasted thirty seconds tops.

"So right now," Age continued, "the media is gearing up for a frontal assault against the government. The trouble shooters in Westminster are trying to placate the media as over thirty of their people lost their lives in the explosion. Military grade explosives. The bomb squad said they could tell by the smell. Two pollies survived the blast but are expected to succumb to their injuries. A total death toll of sixty-three plus some police and members of the general public. Thankfully no children lost their lives although there were some minor injuries. Small comfort for Parliament as they lost fifteen backbenchers."

"My god," said Dianne.

"Indeed," commented Age as he glanced around the room, gulping his scotch down. Looking at Nick, "another one please."

Nigel also raised his hand.

"I'll throw in another interesting statistic, although we shouldn't jump to any conclusions," Age paused, "the backbenchers were all Brexit voters and out of a mix of fifteen for a walk around the Palace of Westminster I would have expected a few 'Remainers' to be in that group." Age paused again, "just an observation, that's all."

Stella half stood and rearranged her skirt before sitting back down. "If I could throw a few things into the mix here," waiting until she had everyone's attention. "It wasn't that long ago that we had no clue who was doing the killings and which murders were related. We knew they used stolen white transit vans, the most common vans on the roads and when on motorcycles once again the most common, Honda 125s, yellow, and in each case, they had swapped number plates with registered Transits and Hondas."

"Where are you going with this Stella?"

"I'm getting to that Nick," Stella resumed with a sideways glance, "Since we learned that there was more than one perpetrator, we also learned that they were well resourced and organised. They also had access to a range of weapons which we now know are non-traceable ex-military."

Nick's phone rang. "Excuse me Stella, can you hold for a moment."

"'Allo Guv, just a quick one. You know that geezer I told you about from the shooting range, ex-army type."

"Yes, what about him, have you got his contact details."

"As matter of fact I have Commander, he's currently having a nap at the Harwich morgue, cut ear to ear. Thought you should know."

Nick put the phone on the mantlepiece. "Carry on Stella."

Stella, shuffled in her seat before continuing. "The killers of Victoria and Celia spoke German and the woman, Helga, who was at the scene, was known to be German. We originally

243

thought we could be dealing with vigilantes of some kind but were baffled as to the motive. The victims all came from a controversial standpoint, that is extreme behaviour or views. Irrespective of politics, left or right, but always at the end of the spectrum." Stella looked around appreciative of being given an opportunity to be heard. "So, from individual killings of perverts and child molesters to corrupt judicial and political figures, then the far left and right of the fringes of society, religious factions and now media and politicians as victims. What have we got?"

"Is that your question?" asked Nigel.

Chris looked up from his laptop. "What we have got, if you'll excuse me chipping in Stella, is protests and mayhem in the streets of northern cities, Muslim against Muslim against Neo Nazis, bike gangs holding rallies and driving through highly ethnic populated areas, general disillusion with the Court process, anger at police methods, total lack of faith in the ability of the government and opposition to contain and solve the issues." Chris paused and held his hand up to assuage an interruption, "student protests in all major towns egged on by Antifa, probably pissed off that their two major bagmen were topped, Black Lives Matter marching whenever a person of colour is arrested, beaten, shot or stabbed." Chris drew a breath, "if the aim was to disrupt our communities right at the time when Britain is about to go through the last painful throes of exiting the EU than I think it's been somewhat successful."

"I agree Chris." Stella placed her hands together in her lap, "and I could do with one of those whisky's please."

Age's phone broke the silence as Nick reached for the decanter of Lagafulen, pouring a small glass for Stella. Nigel put his hand up but was ignored by Nick with a sideways smirk.

The call lasted a few minutes as Age scribbled down some notes on a piece of paper flicked over to him by Nick.

"OK, Hans Kaberle and Volka Dienstbier boarded a Vueling jet to Brussels from Gatwick three hours ago. They had EU diplomatic passports, nothing suspicious at that stage so they boarded without question." Age stopped in his tracks and glanced at the floor seemingly talking to himself. "Bastards."

Age looked up at Nick and then around the room. "What I have to say must not leave this room. I would normally just speak with our people, but you've all put so much work into this that you deserve to know a few things." Age stood up and rested an elbow on the mantlepiece.

"You may or may not know, except for Nick of course, that the German Chancellor, with help from the French and Dutch, has for some time been working on a combined army of sorts. Britain has resisted and with good reason, as if we want a platoon of French, German and Dutch, and God knows who, goosestepping down Park Lane. We don't of course. But we're facing opposition from the Remainers in parliament who don't want the EU umbilical cord cut at all. The Prime Minister has also got some Conservatives, in name only, within his own party to deal with. Personally, I have some doubts about the Home Secretary as he seems to be joined at the hip with a number of EU Commission delegates."

Age waved his glass at Nick. "That will be my last one. Thank goodness I have a driver." Shifting his stance, he continued. "Plans are quite advanced over the Channel and the Dutch already have a joint tank division in operation with Germany. Not everyone in Europe is convinced an EU army is the way to go and our military chiefs are thankfully dead against it. The proposition of forming an EU army and other military units has been open and fairly transparent within the Union and whilst not our cup of tea it is progressing slowly, but of course we won't be involved because we'll be well and truly out by the end of 2020." Age gulped the tot of whisky.

"However, and this is new to Nick as well, we've just heard rumours of a para-military unit being formed under the radar. Exactly who has ordered or even organised it is unknown. We also know that we have one or perhaps more British politicians who are complicit. We can only assume that such persons were against Brexit, so we only have half of the House of Lords, Half of the House of Commons and half of the British bureaucracy to choose from. Not an easy task by any means. But we were looking into it without creating too many waves. That is until you people started getting close."

Age moved again, resting forward on the back of an Edwardian chair. "Don't take that negatively, this was always going to escalate and Stella your dissertation was pretty well on the ball. Create as much mayhem and disruption to our political and social structures and then the malcontents and spineless politicians will call for another referendum and in the middle of all this crap the vote is surely to swing in the favour of the Remainers as sure as my Richard Johnson points to the ground." Age looked up," I apologise ladies, the sailor came out in me."

The girls smiled.

Nick spoke first. "So where do we go from here Age?"

"I think you do what you do best and keep digging. Can't possibly upset any more people. We still need to expose traitorous pollies and anyone else who's on board with these murdering thugs. You should get some leads from Helga's phone I would think. If your enquiries extend overseas, be careful. If you head across the channel, you could be on your own. I don't want Europol or Interpol coming down on me or issuing arrest warrants on your team Nick."

Sir Adrian donned his coat, adjusted his silk tie and made for the front door. Before leaving he turned, "Thanks for the coffee, Dianne. And Nick, thanks for the tipple." Outside, his Sentinel was ready and waiting.

There was stunned silence until Nigel spoke.

"We need to nail those two bastards Nick."

"Yes, we do."

78

Nigel gave his empty glass a sympathetic look, "What have you got Chris?"

"Helga was busy on the phone immediately after the Kensington murders and the twenty-four hours before she so benevolently gave Nick her phone."

"What happened to Helga?" Dianne asked, "was she arrested?"

All eyes turned to Nick.

"Out of our jurisdiction I'm afraid. If she's got any sense, she'll take a leave of absence." Nick sniffed his glass. "I've had enough I think."

Chris scrolled through the numbers on the screen, "Going to take me a while to source these numbers Commander, although there is a UK mobile number. Plenty of calls received and sent."

Nigel's phone rang. His face dropped and acknowledged the call with, "Right."

"Dianne, can you put the TV on, the media is going ballistic."

As if all the media were reading off the same piece of paper, every commentator was calling for the Prime Minister and members of his Cabinet to resign. Opposition members of Parliament were calling for a vote of no confidence in the government, and a new referendum on Brexit, saying that the mood of the people had changed. Dianne flicked through the channels, and all were repeating the same message together with scenes of the carnage and destruction at the Parliament Gardens.

The group were silent as they watched the revolving reports all calling for the current political leadership to resign.

"This is the culmination," Nick stated, "the end game, the required result. Brexit cancelled, back in the EU, loss of sovereignty overruling British law, consolidation of police and military functions into one EU police force and one EU army, navy and air force. We were warned about this years ago, but no one took it seriously. What started off as a common market and mutual partnerships was only headed in one direction."

"Hang on Nick," Stella moved forward in her wheelchair, "The press don't have the full picture. They don't know what we both know and suspect. The police and probably the NCA haven't joined the dots like we have."

"What are you proposing Stella?" asked Nick.

"How about I give Emily Chancer a call. Bring her up to speed?"

"Could work," Nick turned to Nigel, "What do you think Nigel, give her a few leads?"

"I'm all for it, Nick. We're an unofficial group anyway. I suggest we keep Sir Adrian in the loop, so he's prepared."

"Good idea. I'll call Sir Adrian. Stella, you call Emily. Get her here as soon as you can."

Chris called out, "what about this mobile number Nick?"

"Don't call it just yet. Try and find out who it belongs to first."

Sir Adrian was cautiously approving but told Nick not to use the names of the Germans, however, to say that they are of European origins with links to para-military groups on the continent. Stella convinced Emily that she had a coup for her with breaking news. Within thirty minutes Emily was knocking on the Eaton Square front door.

"Come in Emily," Dianne escorted the journalist to the front sitting room.

Without invitation Emily pounced on a vacant area of one of the sofas and opened her leather bag pulling out a notepad and voice recorder. "What have you got for me?"

"Let's get one thing straight Emily," Nick took the vacant spot on the sofa next to her, "You cannot name your source, but you can say a reliable contact in the intelligence community."

"Sounds fair," Emily pulled out her cigarettes and lighter just as Dianne put her hand gently on hers.

"No smoking in here Emily."

"Fair enough, let's get down to it so I can go out for a smoke."

Emily stayed for an hour before heading out of the front door, lighting up and taking a deep draw of her cigarette. Calling her editor, she rattled off a few proposed headlines while hailing a taxi.

"Where to miss?"

"Northcliffe House."

Emily looked around the cab. "This is new."

"Electric too, no engine noise eiver," said the driver with an evident cockney intonation. "Non-smoking miss, 'av a drag when you get out, yes?"

79

Chris was still drawing blanks with the international numbers but some partial luck with the local mobile number.

"It's a pre-paid phone Nick," Chris played with the buttons, "but there're some messages on Helga's voicemail."

"Bring them up Chris. We'll have a listen." Nick displayed some excitement as they gathered around Chris, "and put it on speaker."

The messages were all from one person over the weekend. Male and very British.

"Helga darling, I haven't heard from you for a few days, call me back."
"Missing you my liebling, call me back as soon as you can."
"Call me Helga, we need to talk."

Nick turned to the others.

"I know that voice but can't place it."

"Yes," said Dianne, I've heard it too. Maybe on the news perhaps."

The others nodded in agreement, but all were equally baffled.

Nick tapped Chris on the shoulder.

"Never mind for now, we'll think about it. Call Interpol Chris. Nigel, can you clear it with Cynthia."

Nigel made the call while Chris got his questions in order.

"Do you have any contacts at Interpol or Europol Nick?" asked Chris.

"Not for this job Chris. Remember Interpol only investigates, they have no powers to arrest or detain. They can issue a RED notice to the local authorities, but Age will have to give us the go ahead for that. We'll keep Europol out of it for the moment."

Stella answered her phone. The call was brief.

"That's Emily, they're giving her the front page. She's asked for anything else by five PM."

"Let's see what Chris comes up with when he talks with Interpol. I'll get Sir Adrian to put a bit of pressure on."

Nick gave Age a quick call with an update on the impending front page on the Daily Mail. Age had his own news.

"The Lower House has gone into an emergency session of Parliament Nick. We're expecting a vote of no confidence in the government this evening. The leader of the Opposition called it, the Speaker approved it and it's on. Usually, they do it the following day. Someone's in a hurry."

Nick called Chris over, "Bring the phone here Chris and play those messages to Sir Adrian."

After listening there were a few seconds of silence.

"Don't lose those messages Nick, whatever you do, make copies, I don't care but do not lose them. Right?"

"Yes of course. Do you have any ideas who that might be?"

"You'll have to leave it with me Nick."

"We've got another number as well. Chris tracked it down. Helga has been speaking to a member of the Opposition, the office of the Shadow Secretary of State for Exiting the European Union."

"Right, I'll get someone on to that pronto. Good work."

"By the way, we've got the front page but that won't hit until tomorrow morning. How long will the debate go for Age?"

"Hard to say but maybe you can get something online by this evening. The pollies will have their phones on, and the advisors will be monitoring social media."

"I'll see if we can get some teasers in the pipeline Age."

"Good man Nick, we've got to neutralise the squeeze on the government as a priority. I'll give the Foreign Secretary as much as I can. It will give her and the PM some ammunition during the debate. I'll call you back shortly."

Stella was already on the phone to Emily before Nick hung up.

"Emily said she would do what she could."

"Let's hope it's enough to calm the pollies down. Just as well she works for a conservative newspaper. If it had been the Guardian, we would have been stumped." Nick grimaced.

"Emily is far from conservative but she's hungry for a headline and at least the owner of the paper is pro-government." Stella lifted herself off the chair for a moment. "Ah that's better, I get stiff if I don't move around. Wouldn't it be better if our media wasn't so biased one way or the other?"

"Nature of the beast Stella. Just got to work with it."

Nick's phone rang.

"'Allo Commander, fought you would like to know I took a female journalist from your place to Northcliffe House."

"And?"

"And she was very vocal over the rag 'n bone. Told whoever was on the uvver end that she can't reveal her source but would like to." Teddy paused, "That wouldn't be you would it, Guv?"

"Really," said Nick quietly as he put his phone down.

"What's up Nick?" asked Dianne.

"A job for Stella, Di." Nick moved across the room and sat on the sofa next to Stella's wheelchair. "Give Emily a call and tell her that our sources tell us that a member of the opposition is possibly an accessory to murder. Tell her to get it online right now."

80

Nigel and Chris worked the phones getting the required permissions to identify the international phone numbers and following up with Interpol who, as Chris remarked, "were very helpful but slow in getting details emailed through."

Nick's phone rang.

"Nick, it's Age. I need you to do something for me this evening."

"Yes of course, what is it?"

"I need you to call that UK mobile number at exactly the moment I say. Is that clear?"

"Yes, what time?"

"I'll call you when I have everything in place."

"Right, we'll just stand by."

"Good man."

Age hung up and looked at the Prime Minister, sitting there with a ghostly pallor, collapsed in a wing back chair, gulping down a neat scotch.

"Everything is in place Prime Minister."

"Thank you, Sir Adrian, but I don't know why we can't get the rest of my team in on this."

"We can't afford any leakages Prime Minister."

The PM stood up and walked to the window, looking out onto a dreary Downing Street.

"I suppose so. What a bloody mess."

81

The Prime Minister took his seat on the bench looking directly across at the person trying to unseat both his position as PM and his Conservative government. The polls were not looking favourable for the Government. Not surprising considering that the polls being broadcast by the mainstream media were generally anti-government. Regardless, his advice was that it'll be touch and go whether they retain power. The advisers and lobbyists were hard at work rallying the 650 members one way or the other, including the new seated members replacing those killed in the explosion. Front of mind for all the members of the House of Commons was their prospects of re-election when they next faced the ballot box.

Smart phones and other devices were allowed on silent mode, so during the huff and puff of debate and the waving of papers, eyes were often looking down, usually at the information and advice from their advisors and staff.

The debate was in full swing with 'fors' and 'against' battling for poll position when one by one the members became silent as notification of the article in the Daily Mail online page was received. Upon receiving an item of information, the Leader of the Opposition stood and raised a Point of Order requesting the Speaker adjourn the debate.

The Speaker was having none of it, stating that regardless of what was happening outside the Chamber, the original motion will be dealt with as per Daily Orders. It took the Speaker a full fifteen minutes to bring the house to order and instructed the House to vote whereby he called for Aye's and No's.

The call of Aye's and No's was not conclusive enough and Divisions were called. The clerks took the votes as the members moved through the lobbies.

"Concerning the vote 'this House has no confidence in Her Majesty's Government'; the No's have it, the motion is defeated, and the Prime Minister and his government remain, with a majority of 48 votes.

All parties, at the direction of their leaders retired to their respective party rooms.

The Leader of the Opposition demanding to know where the headline in the Daily Mail came from and to whom it refers to. Within a few moments his adviser came into the room to inform him that the accusation related to the office of the Shadow Secretary of State for Exiting the European Union. The message came via Emily Chancer requesting a comment from the Leader of the Opposition.

The Conservative members gathered in their party room as word filtered through regarding the nature of the accusation against an Opposition Member and their staff. Once out of the Chamber members were now actively engaged on their phones. Mostly to advise their families whether they would be home that night. It was already ten in the evening and for the members it had been a long and frustrating day.

The noise and discontent diminished enough for the Prime Minister to say a few words on the day's proceedings and asked the inner cabinet members to sit with him at the dais. As the front bench took their seats alongside the PM, he insisted that they leave their phones on so they can take calls from staff or concerned family.

Sir Adrian was standing outside the doors to the party room and made the call to Nick. Inside the party room the clatter subsided as the PM stood to address the members. No sooner had he stood up than a mobile phone behind him sounded. He turned around to face the member who was sitting there looking at his phone.

"Wilford, you may like to take that call outside."

"Thank you, Prime Minister, I won't be long."

Wilford du Maurier opened the door into the lobby area, not taking any notice of those in attendance.

"Helga, I've been so worried."

Before he could carry out any more of his conversation Sir Adrian and several undercover agents surrounded the Home Secretary with one officer taking the phone out of Wilford's hand.

"Wilford du Maurier you are being arrested for alleged involvement in terrorism, sedition and treason." Turning to one of his officers, "read him his rights."

"You do not have to say anything. But it may harm your defence if you do not mention when questioned something which you later rely on in court. Anything you do say may be given in evidence."

Sir Adrian gave the Prime Minister a call. "It's done."

Without answering the PM put his phone in his pocket. "I've just been advised that the Home Secretary has resigned from his position and as an elected representative in the House of Commons. I have no doubt we will hear more during the forthcoming days."

82

Sir Adrian called Nick.

"Well, that's done and dusted Nick. It won't take long to weed out the other cretin in the Shadow Portfolio, but we'll put the other agencies to work on that. All I can say is well done to you and your team."

"Thanks Age, they're a good team and still at it. We've still got to try and get those two killers and whoever is giving the orders."

"Tread carefully Nick and remember if you cross the Channel keep your powder dry. I've had a host of calls from our European friends. I can tell you that Interpol and Europol are currently not happy chappies."

"Nothing we did, I hope?" offered Nick.

"Well, I'm not sure, but something has upset them. My guess is the aggravation comes from the European Commission. Keep going with it and if you intend on a trip to the Continent, let me know before you go. I'll help where I can."

"Well, hopefully the media will settle a bit, they're after blood Age."

"I'll drip feed them some stuff through our channels but keep that Emily Chancer onside. No reason why she shouldn't have the scoop on why the Home Secretary's been arrested and that it's the Shadow Brexit Department that has a case to answer."

"Wilco."

"Now that's a word I haven't heard in a while Nick."

83

The rest of the week was a continuation of enquiries for Chris and Nigel regarding Helga's voicemail. The Home Secretary had admitted to his involvement in conspiring to corrupt the Brexit process together with a staff member of the Shadow Secretary of State for Brexit.

"No wonder we were outplayed during the negotiations," remarked the Prime Minister, "they knew our strategies every time we went to the table."

The Home Secretary denied any involvement with any murders or the explosion at the Parliament Gardens. He refused to answer further questions until fully briefed by his 'legal-council'.

The entire British delegation to the European Commission walked out that week waving the Union Flag and chanting Rule Britannia, packing their bags and flying home.

Stella was on her feet and under instruction from Dianne that both she and Chris remain in the house. Nigel was given the opportunity of a room and with the possibility of fine food and wine, and not wishing to travel between Belgravia and Waterloo each day, he took the single malt option.

Chris was sifting through the mountain of papers and online documents. "You know boss, of all the incidents we've investigated we haven't got one full frontal face image of any of these killers. It's as if they knew where the cameras were. They wore hoodies or baseball caps, always looking down and never at the cameras."

"So, what have we actually got then?" asked Nick.

"Just partials. We know two of them are six-foot approximately, Caucasian, fair skinned, the partials show beards, some without. The only distinguishing feature is blue eyes. I just looked it up, ten per cent of the world's population have blue eyes."

"And Europe?"

"Hard to say, maybe around fifty per cent."

"Thanks Chris, every time I see a white male with blue eyes, I'm going to think he might be one of our killers."

"I'll keep looking Boss."

It was Friday when Nick got the call to come to Age's office.

84

The summoning to the office of Sir Adrian Nightingale had taken Nick by surprise considering that all recent communication and visits had been informal. Nick sensed that they were close to finding out where the orders to kill were coming from. It was definitely 'European government'. Whether a departmental executive decision or a roque bureaucrat they couldn't be sure. Perhaps Age had put the pieces together and would be there to assist with his assets, ready to pounce when the time was right.

Joyce, the personal assistant in the outer office, who had asked Nick to take a seat, motioned him to go through. Age was his usual affable self, standing from behind his desk and walking forward, arm outstretched. Grabbing Nick's hand with a firm grip and placing his other hand on top he ushered Nick to the two facing leather couches. "Sit down Nick".

They sat down opposite each other. Age smiling with almost sympathetic eyes as Nick adjusted his trousers. "We've come a long way, you and me." There was a questioning look in Nick's eyes.

Where's he going with this? thought Nick.

"This is as far as we can go, I'm afraid Nick." Age brought his hands together rubbing them as if crushing something between the palms. "We have to stop, you got close, too close, and now it has to stop."

Nick leaned forward with steely blue eyes staring daggers at Age. "What the fuck are you talking about Age? Yes, we're close, very fucking close. In fact, the bastard or bastards could still be in London, or close by. We can't stop now."

"Remember who you're talking to Nick," Age paused with obvious difficulty, "We do have to stop Nick, we will, I will, you will, and your team will. It all stops here. The killings will stop as well, I can assure you of that. There'll be no more random murders, no radicals eliminated, well not related to our, or should I say, your investigations."

Nick jumped in. "Why Age? The team have worked so hard, tirelessly and so well. Despite the pricks in Whitehall trying to shut us down. Despite the NCA fucking up time and time again. It's as if the people we're supposed to be working for were fucking us over every time we turned the next corner."

"That's exactly right Nick. Did you ever wonder why, when you were making such good ground that suddenly the rug gets pulled out from underneath you? Two steps forward, one step back?" Age leaned back extending his left arm across the back of the couch. "It's in the hands of the pollies now. It's their mess and they've got to clean it up themselves."

"Well Age, I have to admit I was getting very pissed off. I knew something was wrong a long time ago and it was two pronged most of the time. Finding the killer and trying to work out who was fucking us over."

Age stood up giving Nick the impression that the discussion was coming to an end.

"Take that extended holiday you and Dianne have always wanted Nick. You've done your bit for Queen and country. You could have been here in my chair if you had wanted to, but you were addicted to the field work, the chase, hunting the bad guys. I've lost count of the times you've knocked back a promotion."

Nick smiled. "Diplomacy, Age. Never had a great deal of it. The art of telling someone to go fuck themselves in such a way that they take it as a compliment. It never felt right, still got a bit of the lower deck in me I suppose."

"Nothing wrong with that. We all know that the Chiefs and PO's run the ship." Age paused and put his hand on Nick's shoulder, "I'm serious Nick. It's time to take a back seat and leave the bad guys to the next generation. Don't worry, despite current government cutbacks I've made sure you get a redundancy. It means you get your pension plus a tidy lump sum, more than enough for you to live a comfortable life down there on the south coast."

Nick looked Age in the eye. "I'm very pissed off."

"I imagine you are Nick. I've known you for too many years to expect you to just walk away," Age paused again, "but you must. I'm not just saying that as your boss but as your friend."

"Just walk away?"

"Yes Nick."

"So, whoever's been doing all this shit just walks away Scot free?"

"I wouldn't say that exactly. I've got people from Interpol and Europol meeting with me here in a few minutes. As I said it's political now. Maybe we'll get to the bottom of it and with a bit of luck they'll finish the job."

"You think so?"

"I would say that we all have a boss. We all answer to someone, somewhere. Even me. Keep in touch Nick," Age extended his hand.

There was no way Nick was going to end forty odd years of friendship by just walking out, disappointed as he was. He extended his hand as Age grabbed his with a firm shake.

"Take care my friend." Sir Adrian's smile was genuine as the handshake remained. "By the way, do you still have your diaries?"

"No, I don't, I got rid of them some time ago."

"That's good, I'd hate them to fall into the wrong hands." *That's the first time Nick has ever lied to me,* thought Age. "Well then, behave yourself now."

263

"No promises there, Age. You know me." Nick released his grip and stepped away.

Age turned towards his desk as Nick left the room, "I do Nick; indeed I do."

Nick nodded to Joyce, Sir Adrian's PA, as he left the outer office and made his way towards the one exclusive lift to the boss's office. Pressing the lift button, he waited as the indicator lights showed the progress.

That's the first time Age has ever lied to me, he thought.

85

Nick stood back waiting for the doors to open, allowing any occupants to exit first. The three occupants, two in smart European style suits strode out carrying briefcases followed by a short older man in a black overcoat and black felt fedora with a grosgrain ribbon. He noticed the man's pasty grey complexion and cold steel staring eyes. Nick instinctively, and politely, took one step to the left and stepped into the lift momentarily meeting the gaze of one of the men in a suit. Nick pushed the ground floor button while at the same time looking at his reflection in the mirrored interior of the lift. That face was familiar. He had seen it before but where? The short-cropped hair, broad shoulders, athletic build. Even though the glance was only fleeting their eyes met momentarily. Two pairs of icy blue eyes, both with a hint of recognition. The one exiting the lift last, glancing back and smirking as the doors closed. The man in the black overcoat maintaining a steady forward gaze, unflinching and barren.

Nick travelled down in the lift racking his brain as to where he had seen that face and those steely blue eyes, almost like looking in a mirror. He suddenly got a bad, almost nauseous, feeling and pressed the stop button and reversed the elevator back to the private floor of Sir Adrian. The lift door opened, as he pushed his way through quickly, almost running to the desk of personal assistant Joyce Merewether. The reception area was empty.

"Joyce," enquired Nick, "who were those three men who arrived as I left just now?"

"That is Mr Blake, the older gentleman, from Interpol I believe, and I don't know the name of the other two."

"What does Mr Blake do with Interpol?"

"He's in charge of something or he wouldn't be here Nick, I don't know anything else, very hush, hush." Joyce paused as she turned towards the door to Sir Adrian's office. "I get the impression that Sir Adrian doesn't regard Interpol in favourable terms Nick. In fact, they've had a number of arguments over the phone recently."

"You mean he calls regularly?"

"In the past few months, yes."

"Does Sir Adrian still have the doorway into his private room?" Nick pointed to the panelled wall at the end of the reception area.

"Yes, I have the electronic door lock switch under my desk."

"Is it silent?"

"Yes, it just releases the internal lock. You just push the panel."

Inside Sir Adrian's office the two men in the tailored suits stood with their backs to the door, feet apart and hands folded in front at waist height. Their leather bags resting at their feet. The man in the black overcoat stood in front of Sir Adrian's desk motionless. The brow of his hat did nothing to hide the venom within his icy stare.

"My instructions are very clear Sir Adrian; you will terminate Commander Hood and his team. I don't care how you do it but close them down. They have become an aggravation to the Union and what we are endeavouring to achieve."

"Are you barking mad. You can't just walk into the office of MI6 and start barking orders." Without waiting for a reply, Sir Adrian continued. "Let me make myself perfectly clear I don't answer to you or whatever you stand for now get out before I kick you out."

"Oh, but you do answer to me Sir Adrian and I don't have to tell you of the consequences if you don't."

"Is that a threat. Who in the hell do you think you're talking to?" Enraged, Sir Adrian stood up with his hands on his side of the desk, pressing the silent alarm, while placing his hand close to the handgun mounted under the desktop.

"Well, I was hoping it would not come to this Sir Adrian," his cold eyes widened as his lips tightened, "None of us are immune to the people we answer to. It is a 'just cause'."

The men at the door reached into their jackets and withdrew silenced Glock 19 Gen 5's, pointed at Sir Adrian.

"A 'just cause' you say," Age was starting to lose it, "You people are insane. Do you think that you could come in here and just assassinate the head of MI6?"

"And yet, here we are. From now on MI6 will answer to the European Union."

"Well, Mr Blake," Sir Adrian said calmly, "you've actually done us a favour."

"How so?"

"You've saved us the trouble of tracking you down."

Blake pursed his lips to speak but was cut short.

The door to the ensuited private room opened slightly, allowing Nick to fire two quick head shots from his Sig killing the suited men at the door instantly. Blake pulled out a small calibre handgun from his coat pocket but before he could get a shot away Sir Adrian pumped two shots into his chest and one in the head. *Just in case Blake was wearing a vest*, thought Age. The room was sound-proofed, and all shots were fired with little audible evidence to attest to what had just taken place. There were, however, several cameras independent of the main security monitoring system that would clearly show the sequence of events. The video files, very likely, were never to see the light of day.

Joyce released the door-lock to Sir Adrian's office allowing two officers, with guns drawn, to enter the room as both Nick and Sir Adrian placed their guns down and held their hands in the air in compliance. Once satisfied the two officers shouldered their weapons clearly recognising Sir Adrian and Nick.

The three bodies had bled profusely as the group surveyed the scene. Sir Adrian tut-tutting as he looked at the amount of blood on the carpet. Picking up the phone, Sir Adrian spoke to Joyce calmly and quietly. "All is well thank-you Joyce. It would be best if you didn't come in, but could you call our 'cleaning company' we have a bit of a mess to clean up here."

Joyce promptly called the agents responsible for discretely dealing with such issues.

Sir Adrian turned to the two officers that intervened. "Thanks chaps, as you can see Commander Hood and myself were able to deal with this incursion just before you entered. Could I ask you to wait in the reception area with my PA while I have a word with the Commander."

The two officers left the room. Nick was first to speak.

"What the fuck was all this about Adrian?"

"Long story old boy," replied Age, "as I said to you, even I have to report to someone, but not these pricks." He paused as he looked around the room, "well, this is one piece of shit out of the picture, and we can assume that these two are Hans and Volka."

"Let's hope so but who do they answer to?"

"I'm fucked if I know Nick, but I suspect this was not the Mr Blake from Interpol that I've been speaking with."

Age and Nick sat down on the two, leather wing back chairs in the bloodless area of the office.

"Do we have another British minister involved?" asked Nick.

"Perhaps. I doubt those spineless bastards would have the brains or intestinal fortitude to approve of the work this prick was doing." Age paused again, "Look, it could be someone in our government or even a person or entity who's got the pollies in their pocket. Could be related to a defence contractor, I don't know, but they're under our radar and obviously some kind of protected species." Age continued, "You have to remember something about governments Nick. They can create a crisis or make one appear to be worse. They will rely on the media to spread fear and apprehension, which they will; then those in power will develop a strategy to save the population from that which they created."

"Is that a theory Age."

"Take it from me, it's a fact Nick. This 'just cause' was for the European Union to save Britain from itself. Today it was about control and consolidation of European power. Tomorrow it could be an armed conflict or even a virus. That's why we're here Nick."

"What's next for us Age?" Nick looked quizzingly at Sir Adrian.

"Well, you Nick, are going to do exactly what I told you to do. Buggar off and get a life. Spend some time with that lovely wife of yours and get some use out of those sports cars in your cellar."

"You know about those?"

"Of course, I do, you idiot, how do you think you got those building approvals done when you bought the cottages in the Mews." The two men stood up together as Age continued. "You must think I live in a bubble Nick or got my job from a card in a packet of corn flakes."

"Not at all Age," laughed Nick, "but won't someone be wondering what happened to these three cretins."

"I suspect they will, but will they poke their heads above the trenches and pose the question? I doubt it. Whoever's

269

missing the company of these three miscreants will most likely keep their head down. As soon as they ask the question, we will have the person behind this business. I doubt it's the Home Secretary, he hasn't got the brains for it."

Nick nodded and once again extended his hand in a gesture of farewell.

"That's the second time you've saved my life Nick. Now piss off but drop me a line every now and then." Age placed his hand on top Nick's as they extended their grip, neither wishing to let go, "you never know, there might be the odd job or two."

Nick gave Joyce a quick hug as he passed through the reception area. As he approached the lift it opened and two men in beige overalls, carrying cleaning equipment and buckets walked out. Nick smiled at them. "You're going to need more than that, I'd call for back up if I were you."

86

Nick was nearly home when his phone rang. It was Age.

"Someone's going to get their head rolled Nick. Those people we took care of were part of a para-military group out of Germany. Blake was, as we suspected not Blake, his name is, or was Max Elpers, Colonel in the Bundeswehr and seconded to the Union. His forebears were known Nazis during the war. Elpers and his boys creamed the original Interpol and Europol delegates at their hotel. Three bodies in three rooms, shot three times, two in the chest and one in the forehead."

"Fucking hell Age."

"It's worse, one of our cleaners gave them guns on their way up. He's now in custody and will be there for a long time, conspiracy to murder."

"Who were they working for?"

"Someone in power Nick, and money will be involved, I'm sure."

"So, am I in or out?"

"You're out Nick, call in tomorrow sometime and do the paperwork, and I mean that in the nicest way. Go home and make love to your wife."

"I would," thought Nick to himself, *"but I've got a house full of fucking guests. I'll have to tell them all to piss off somehow."*

Nick parked the car in the underground garage and came through the basement, up the stairs and into the lower sitting room.

"It's over guys, the other agencies are taking over now. It's back to our old boring lives."

"What just like that?" asked Chris.

"Yes, Chris, exactly like that. The threat's been eliminated, and our role is over. You and Nigel can take any evidence and material back to the Yard and hand it in I guess."

"What an anti-climax," cried Stella.

"So, bangers and mash for me tonight," Nigel looked very dejected.

"Oh, and I was just getting used to all this subterfuge and crimefighting," said Dianne throwing her hands up.

"Well not so fast," said Nick looking around the room, "I think a celebratory dinner is called for. There's a great little Italian place not too far."

"I'm in."

"Me too."

"And me."

"And me makes five," laughed Dianne, holding up her hand.

87

"They pensioned me off." There was no hello as Nick took the call from Nigel Connelly. "The Commissioner called me into his office just now and basically told me to fuck off. We've been having a lot of cut-backs Nigel, he said, and doing it this way we can give you a lump sum with a redundancy package. What could I say...thank you very fucking much?"

"What a co-incidence Nigel, my boss just gave me a golden handshake as well." Nick stopped in the foyer of the Vauxhall Building. "What's happened with Spencer and Stella?"

"Chris is back out Chelmsford way. I'm not sure about Stella. What are you up to then Nick?"

"Time for a holiday I guess." Nick paused and took a breath as he gazed around his old workplace, "Look I've got to catch up with Dianne and work a few things out. Keep in touch Nigel."

Nick pocketed his phone as it rang again. "Hi Nick, it's Stella. Had a great night last night. I'm really sorry, I thought we were almost there."

"We were Stella, that's why it was shut down, at least our role. The NCA and whoever else, have closed down the lot as far as I can see."

"So that's it, it's over."

"Seems that way, what's happening with you?"

"Chris proposed last night when we got home. I said yes, of course. He's been sent to Chelmsford and there's a spot at the university there so I might take it up. Promise me you'll call in and say hello sometime." Stella's tone in her voice lowered. "Do you think they'll ever catch the people, Nick?"

273

"Well, it's on the cards Stella, and yes, I'll call in sometime. Good luck to you both, I'll look forward to an invitation."

"Yes, Nick and, thank you." Stella hesitated for just one moment and hung up, smiling to herself as she walked into the bridal shop.

"Where to Guv?" asked Teddy as Nick stepped into the back of the cab.

"Let's go to your favourite Rub-a-Dub Teddy, I need a fucking drink."

88

Dianne opened the door to their townhouse to be greeted by rose petals scattered over the floor of the front hall. They continued as she followed the trail into the dining room where Nick was waiting with a glass of sparkling French wine. He had dusted off the silver candelabras and lit the candles, casting flickering shadows on the elegant Wedgewood tableware. The gentle aromas of a carefully prepared dinner wafted from the kitchen as he walked towards her offering the glass. Taking his own in his hand he lifted the glass and Dianne responded as the glasses chinked together.

"What's all this about? Have you got a promotion?"

"You could say that. I am officially Commander Nicholas Hood, retired."

"You've resigned?"

"In a fashion my love, services no longer required I believe is what the letter will say."

"Are you happy?"

"I guess, but I would have preferred to have finished the last," Nick stopped momentarily, "er, project."

"Well then, what's next?"

"What would you like to do?"

"How about that holiday you keep promising and never do anything about?"

"Ok, but something else I need to do first."

"What apart from taking that saucepan off the stove?"

Nick put his glass down and grabbed Dianne. "No this." He took her glass from her hand and clumsily put it onto the dining table as he bent her over and pressed his lips firmly on hers.

"Nicholas," she gasped, "get that saucepan off the stove right now and be a good sailor and take me to bed."

Nick was fixing himself breakfast when Dianne came downstairs fully dressed and ready for the office. "I should be home around three this afternoon Nick, unless one of my ladies decides to be early." Nick got a fleeting peck on the cheek and then she was gone.

Throwing himself down on the sofa he switched the TV on, flicking through the channels to find something of interest. He shouldn't have bothered, with the same news broadcasts on numerous channels. It was that or kid's cartoons which seemed to offer more inspiration than the news.

He closed his eyes. For the first time since he could remember he had nothing at all that resembled a job list for the day. No calls to make, no case to investigate, no plane to catch and certainly no one to kill, that he could think of, although he was seriously considering making a list. The phone rang.

Considering the landline was a silent number it would have to be someone either he or Dianne knew.

"Hello." Nick was used to neither identifying himself or the number on a cold call.

"Nick is that you? Tom Jordan here. How are you buddy."

"Tom, my goodness, it's been years, how are you?"

"Buddy I'm well, I'll be in London in a week or two and knowing how busy you are I thought I would see if we could catch up."

"Can't see a problem with that Tom, what are you up to these days."

"I'm retired old buddy, touring the world playing golf, you know the story, living the American dream. By the way Nicho said to say hello."

"Admiral Nicholson. What's he up to?"

"Getting on a bit Nick but he still tells the story about your Aussie bar-b-que on the quarterdeck of the Halsey back in '86

276

when he got so concerned with the flaming grill that he called the fire-fighting party to stand by in case it got away from you."

"It was the marinade Tom, too much rum. Good old days. By the way how's Barb, will she be coming as well? I am sure Di would love to catch up."

"Yes, Barb will be with me, she spends her whole life working for these international charities, if she can't find one, she starts one, you know Barb. What about you, how's work? Or can't you say."

"I paid off yesterday, officially retired but between you and me I'll have to find something, or I'll go stir crazy."

"Hey guess what? I had a call from Dimitry Voskolov a few days ago. He asked me what you were up to. Mind you in his line of work he should know that. He said he'd give you a call. Said he had something interesting to tell you."

"Well, if I know Dimitry, and I do, it will have something to do with fast women, fast cars or fast boats."

"Funny you should say that he says he's got himself a new boat. Anyway buddy, I'll give you a call when we fly out, we'll be in England for a few weeks at least. It's been years since I was at St Andrews."

"That's in Scotland Tom."

"That's right, I forget that you live on such a small island Nick. I'll be seeing ya'll buddy."

"Yes Tom, see you later."

Well, thought Nick, *that was a blast from the past and Dimitry wants a chat as well. Retirement could be looking up.* Nick wasn't the least bit interested in fast women but fast cars and fast boats, well they were something else.

89

Dimitry Voskolov disembarked from the Lufthansa A380 after a most comfortable first-class flight courtesy of the Yedinaya-Rossiya party. In fact, after nearly fifty faithful years of service to the Kremlin and, being a lifelong friend of the president, the benefits were finally realised. A trouble shooter in many respects with not only the theatre of the FSB, previously the KGB, and very much in the same business, and with the SVR. Dimitry was happy to assist the political elite by recently re-distributing some Chechnyan assets after one of the criminal oligarchs fell afoul of the regime. For Dimitry his impending retirement was fortuitous in that he had planned to move to warmer climes and cash in his hidden assets to some Swiss banks with the blessing of the party. Of course, he was able to offer a few party elites some remuneration for their friendship and protection during his retirement years especially as he was privy to many lucrative in-party transactions over many decades.

The assets of Chechnyan Bratva were something of an embarrassment and not something the party would like on their books or even absorbed by any of the party quangos. One such, now deceased, member of the Bratva was known as the Kahnkala Soldat Udachi, 'soldier of fortune'. Guilty of many assassinations and killing of his competitors, he was also operating one of the most profitable drug cartels on the Asian continent. Amassing a grotesque fortune big enough to run many small countries, he was in the process of building a small army including military style vessels operating in the Black Sea,

Caspian Sea, Mediterranean and Arabian Sea to protect his drug trafficking.

During the course of his illegal operations, KSU as he was known, had paid off a number of coastal party officials to ensure that his cargos were given little attention in the ports. Most of those party officials on his payroll were now either deceased or breaking rocks in government installations in the Siberian province. Dimitry was allocated the responsibility of rounding up the beneficiaries of the illicit operations and as his president said to him, "Dimitry there is a 'smushchenyi' that we cannot even consider placing in our service. To even admit that it was built under the nose of our administration is out of the question. Take it. I suggest humanitarian, it makes me look good, but it must act independently."

"Where is it my friend?"

"It is in Singapore at the Sembawang shipyards Dimitry. You will appreciate that there is no crew, they have been, er, re-distributed."

"Of course, if it is the Party's wish, it shall be done."

"Very good Dimitry, you have done your country proud; I have made you a very rich man so ten per cent per annum for the party will suffice, enjoy your retirement."

Dimitry had a private limousine courtesy of the Posol'stvo Singapura to meet him and take him to the Fullerton Hotel in Collyer Quay. He was now a billionaire in his own right and the proud owner of a luxury yacht called Khameleon. *Strange to name a boat after a lizard*, he thought. *This is not such a pretty name for a luxury cruise boat.*

As most billionaires would, he chartered a helicopter to take him to the north of Singapore Island to view his acquisition at the Sembawang Shipyard. In his mind he imagined a large white ship like he had seen in the glossy European magazines. He had Googled 'Khameleon' but nothing was registered that he could see. Perhaps if it had been registered then his president may have had it removed, he thought.

The Airbus H155 helicopter landed in a grassy block off Old Middle Road joining the old stores basin with the North Road Wharf. Khameleon was berthed outboard of the finger wharf directly opening onto the Johore Straits with the new estates of Senibong Cove on the Malayan mainland opposite. A shipyard official greeted Dimitry and drove him onto the wharf in one of the dockyard staff cars.

"There must be some mistake?" asked Dimitry when he saw the massive ship alongside the wharf. "My boat is a luxury yacht not a warship."

"This not warship, this ship Khameleon. Quick we go on ship. I show you."

The vessel was a pale grey in colour and gave the impression of being a hybrid. Part military ship, part luxury cruiser. Dimitry had been on many navy ships, but this one had him guessing. Approaching six hundred feet long and four decks high above the hull Dimitry had to hold himself upright, holding onto the bonnet of the dockyard car. On closer inspection he noticed the sleek lines, the tinted black windows, a helicopter sitting on the foredeck that resembled the bow of an aircraft carrier. There were no guns, at least not visible however he could not resolve within himself the sheer size of the vessel. The bow itself towered above them some ten metres or more.

"Come, we look inside. You not seen before? It very nice boat. No crew, they disappear. Now you come and can take away. Pay bill as well." The dockyard officer was very excited as it appeared that the account for berthing was still outstanding.

Dimitry and his guide ascended the accommodation ladder on to the main deck whereupon the dockyard officer produced a set of keys and ushered Dimitry to a set of glass sliding doors near the stern of the vessel. Even through the glass doors Dimitry could see the opulent wealth displayed in the furniture and fittings.

"Please I must sit down. I'm sorry but I need to rest a moment." Dimitry staggered to a couch.

"Of course, Mr Voskolov, please, you sit down, I will get you a drink." The officer scurried off and returned with a small bottle of Perrier. "When we look around, we have papers to sign and then ship yours and when you get crew ready, you go."

"That's a good point Mr Lu. How many crew do I need?"

"This ship needs about 45 crew, captain, engineers, you need good cook too for good food."

When Dimitry recovered composure, Mr Lu was waving a newspaper across his face. "You not look too good Mr Voskolov, maybe I fetch doctor."

Back at the Fullarton Dimitry helped himself to the mini bar in his room. Several small bottles of vodka later, and some medication from the hotel doctor, he was able to gather his faculties realising that what he thought was a luxury cruiser was in fact a significant ship. Money was not the issue. He had billions of dollars in many currencies in Swiss Bank accounts and other smaller quantities in banks around the world, none of them in Russia. He reflected on Mr Lu's advice regarding crew, and following a recommendation was able to speak with a shipping agent. It was getting very complicated. He needed some help.

It was early evening when Nick's home phone rang again. Something that did not happen often.

"Nicholas my old friend, it's Dimitry."

"My goodness Dimitry, this morning it was Tom and now you. What are you up to? It's been so long."

"My dear friend, I am in a jam, thick jam, can you help me, just for a few days please my friend?"

"If I can. I seem to have a bit of free time on my hands, where are you?"

"I'm in Singapore Nicholas, can you come?"

Nick turned to Dianne who was deep into an issue of The Lancet. "Di, Dimitry needs a hand for a few days. Do you mind?"

"Dimitry, on the phone? Hello Dimitry" called out Dianne.

"Oh, such a lovely lady Nicholas, you were always so lucky with the ladies."

"Shut up Dimitry, where will I find you?"

"I was hoping you would say yes Nicholas. I have already booked you with Singapore Airlines, first class. A car from the Fullarton Hotel will pick you up. I pay for you Nicholas. I pay for everything."

"You're too kind Dimitry, when is the flight booked?"

"You leave in five hours Nicholas. Please don't miss your flight."

Nick jumped onto the couch with Dianne. "You don't mind, do you?"

"No, of course not. I've got a fair bit on this week, babies and all that stuff you know. When do you leave?"

"Dimitry says I'm booked on a flight in five hours."

Dianne laughed "Well off you go, piss off." She flipped a few pages over as Nick raced up the stairs. Dianne shouted after him, "and I want a nice souvenir. I'm thinking jewellery Nicholas."

90

On arrival in Singapore, a uniformed chauffeur was holding a card with his name and escorted him to a Bentley conveniently parked at the front of the terminal. His single bag arrived at his side courtesy of a porter and Nick dropped a British five-pound note in his hand.

He was pleased to be staying at the older Fullarton rather than the Fullarton on the Bay. The older hotel was once the Singapore Post Office dating back to the colonial days. Today an expensive and exclusive property with a large open foyer in the centre of the building with café style tropical lounges surrounded by a range of selective fashion and jewellery shops. Nick made a mental note to find a nice gift for Dianne as a matter of urgency.

Reception had a message from Dimitry which requested that he travel to Sembawang at his earliest convenience and that a limousine would be available, apologising that he could not pick him up personally. Thankful that he had been able to sleep in his first-class pod, Nick decided to shower and freshen up first. Requesting the car be available in one hour, he made his way to the luxury suite facing the harbour.

The car ride to Sembawang via the Central Expressway was a comfortable thirty-five minutes, even more comfortable in a Bentley. Resisting the temptation of complimentary Krug Champagne Nick relaxed in the back seat taking in the scenery. A very different landscape from his early navy days, in and out of clapped-out yellow diesel Mercedes with clear plastic seat covers, from bars in the Sembawang strip to Nee Soon shanties. He did however take time in those early days to conduct more civilised outings to the Britannia Club and then across the road to the Raffles for the odd Singapore Sling.

The dockyard security waved them through without bothering to check. Anyone travelling in the Fullarton Bentley would no doubt be someone of importance and not to be embarrassed by a simple boom gate. Nick's jaw dropped as they pulled up on the wharf alongside a vessel that resembled a warship in the form of a super yacht. "Fuck," was the only adjective that came to his lips. He thanked the driver who replied that he would wait until instructed further.

Dimitry hurried down the gangway. "Nicholas, my good friend. Come, come I have much to show you."

"Dimitry, what the fuck is going on here and what are you doing with this beast of a ship?"

"It is a long story Nicholas, but all will be revealed in good time. Quickly I have someone I would like you to meet."

They arrived at the top of the gangway, stepping onto the immaculate teak decks. The black caulking standing out against the timber decks, everywhere demonstrating a high standard of craftmanship. No stranger to ships and the talents of shipwrights Nick was amazed at the combination of luxury and nautical genius as he admired the fit out of this unique vessel. This was a ship in every sense of the word.

Walking into what appeared to be the main deck lounge, a figure appeared from below decks.

"Nick, what a surprise. Dimitry said I was going to meet someone on board."

"Tom, now why am I not surprised."

"My friends, please, I want to show you my new acquisition." Dimitry ushered them forward, "I will explain as we go."

Nick and Tom were staring in amazement. Their years of naval service allowed them the ability to appreciate and recognise many of the features of seagoing vessels however

284

nothing was going to prepare them for the customised credentials of this floating gin palace.

Dimitry stopped. "My friends, destiny has smiled upon me, and my immediate thought was to share my good fortune with you. What I have here is too much for one man, one person." Dimitry sighed as he motioned them to sit on the luxurious leather couches. "My dear president considered this ship to be an embarrassment for the party. The previous owner is no longer with us, and the manner in which he accumulated his wealth was unscrupulous and evil." Dimitry sighed and lifted his hands as if in prayer. "Despite what you have heard about our government, the conspicuous exhibition of wealth and opulence is not of our mantra, even if it does occur in some deep and dark corners. No, the ties to the now defunct drug and criminal cartel have been severed and the real estate has been seized by our government. However, the cash and luxury assets cannot have any connection with our administration. I was given the formidable task of dealing with them as I wish and to keep them distant from the party." Dimitry's facial expression screamed c'est la vie as he slouched forward in the leather couch.

Nick and Tom were sitting totally speechless wondering where this conversation was going. Dimitry continued.

"I need your help my friends. There is one proviso; my president suggested it be used for humanitarian work if I keep it, in case it comes back to him, and what do I know about humanitarian stuff, I used to kill people. I don't know how to crew a ship or even how I could operate such a vessel. I can't sell it, that would attract too much attention and when I show you what this ship really is you will understand. Come with me."

Dimitry stood up and signalled them to follow as he shuffled ahead. The central passageway from the main deck lounge led forward to a single stairway. The furnishings were ornate and opulent as one would find on a luxury ocean going liner. At the top of the stairs one deck above was a plain grey steel door. There was a numbered keypad into which Dimitry entered five digits. The locking mechanism on the door released and Dimitry pushed the door handle and opened the door.

"This, gentlemen, is what I believe you call a CIC, Combat Information Centre." Dimitry ushered them in. Nick and Tom stood in amazement.

"Good grief," exclaimed Tom, "this is like the CIC in our latest destroyers."

"This is where I started my naval career," uttered Nick, "we called them Ops Rooms in the old days, I used to be an ops room Chief. It's not unlike the CICs of our new Type 45s."

"You could run a war from this room." offered Dimitry.

"Damn right you could Dimi; or start one. This could be deadly in the wrong hands," stated Nick.

"Fortunately it's in ours." Dimitry looked at the flickering lights, "The power is on Nick, can you bring up some of the displays?"

"Yes, I think so?" replied Nick, "the tabs are in Russian which is to be expected but some of the equipment is familiar, Sperry, Thales, Raytheon, there's even Microsoft." Nick switched on the command consoles. "It's Windows based, so we should be able to change the language, that would make it easier to operate, well for me anyway, my Russian is not what it was."

The four consoles on the central desk came to life as did the larger displays on the forward bulkhead. Nick leaned across the desk towards Dimitry. "As I said my Russian is a bit rusty, what is the Russian word for windows system?"

"система Windows, Sistema."

"And control panel?"

"панель управления, upravleniya."

"And language?"

"язык, yazyk."

Nick played with the system for a few minutes. "Got it, I'll just restart, and we should be set up." The screens came back to life and the trio set about interpreting what systems were installed on the ship.

"Hey, look at this," Nick pointed to one of the screens on the forward bulkhead, "This is a virtual tour of the ship systems. My goodness Dimitry, this boat, or should I say ship, has integrated systems. She has at least four independent radar and communications systems."

"What does that mean Nick?" asked Dimitry with Tom standing there with his mouth wide open.

"If the CIA knew about this shit, which I doubt, they'd be shitting themselves."

"Well, according to the control panel, there's phased array radar and EW and a shitload of other stuff from the UK, USA, Russia and China, and all able to be operating independently," said Nick.

"You've lost me Nicholas,"

"Dimitry, this means that this ship, by its electronic signatures, can appear to be any one of the four major powers or their allies by virtue of which system they're transmitting. We could sit off the coast of China and to them we would appear to be one of their own. The same could be said for the USA. We could sail through the Baltic and the Russians would think we were a Soviet asset. Where in the hell did this person get this equipment?"

Dimitry shrugged. "He had politicians around the world in his back pocket, I guess they fell off the back of a truck."

"Yeah," said Tom, "some truck."

Nick pressed start on the menu engaging the virtual tour as if it was an advertisement of a luxury hotel resort. The screen displayed a plan of the ship from above and zoomed into the bow area where there was a helo pad and massive landing deck. The helo pad opened to reveal a lift well and hangar space with an Airbus H155 passenger helicopter sitting in the hangar. A phalanx style weapon was situated on a platform, concealed under the deck.

The image then zoomed to the rear deck whereupon the centre of the stern opened to reveal a docking area. Inside were two landing craft with an armoured AWD, all-wheel drive vehicles, a mini submarine and tender boats in varying sizes. The deck above the docking area had another helo pad which also had a hangar in the main superstructure. Again a concealed platform with another phalanx type weapon located within the hangar. Inside the hangar was another helicopter, this one more of a military type.

"AH1-Z Viper," said Dimitry impassively, "better than ours."

The cursor moved to the bridge area, revealing the wheelhouse displays and equipment. It then highlighted the masts with the types of radar and satellite navigation aerials. Nick paused the virtual tour. "Dimitry, some of these radars are weapons control systems."

"You're quite right Nicholas, I'm told the ship is fitted with a number of defensive weapons. Continue with the tour." Dimitry smiled.

The cursor pointed to specific locations around the ship. Four .50 cal machine gun positions and one .70 cal machine gun.

"The Phalanx style weapon was a gift from South Korea I believe, a prototype," explained Dimitry. "I believe the ship designers borrowed some ideas from 'Octopus', you know, the man from Microsoft."

The virtual tour then dissected the ship into each level showing the communications centre next to the CIC, captain's stateroom on deck 03, and a viewing deck on the top level, deck

04. Next on deck 03 was the bridge and ten master staterooms and below them on deck 02 were fifty spacious double guest cabins.

At the rear of decks 02 and 03 there was an open deck recreation area, each with a spa and pool. Deck 01 was the recreation deck, dining rooms, galleys, lounges bars, library, service areas. Deck 1 was the main deck with the large entrance lounge, meeting rooms, offices, aft hangar and helo deck. 2 deck was the first below deck with access to the forward hangar and rear docking area.

There were also crew recreation areas and galley, a fully equipped medical centre with operating theatre and a twenty-bed hospital. 3 deck was crew area, canteen, briefing rooms, equipment spaces and immediately forward of the docking area was a room marked 'armoury' and another 'magazine'. Deck 4 was a combination of crew spaces and boat spaces that also functioned as recreation decks for access to the boats, watercraft and vehicles.

Each boat space had drop down sides that provided landing platforms and recreation areas that opened out to the water. Deck 5 and below were machinery and engine room spaces.

"Wow," said Nick, "this is some ship Dimitry but what would you like us to do. More suited to a war zone than humanitarian?"

"I was hoping you could tell me what to do with it," remarked Dimitry.

The three of them sat around the command console looking each other in the eyes.

It was Tom who spoke first. "Whoever owns this ship, and right now it seems to be you Dimitry, would have to have a very good reason for having the weaponry. Just docking with this shit could get you arrested, in fact the Singaporean government could march in at any moment."

"Oh, that won't happen," quipped Dimitry, "that has been taken care of, but I think they would prefer we depart sooner than later."

"I'm not surprised," offered Nick, "this ship is more of a liability than an asset."

"It is difficult," said Dimitry, "I accept that."

"Difficult, is an understatement," argued Tom.

"Unless" interjected Nick, "unless it was registered as a 'special use' vessel." Nick paused and stood up as he studied the display screens. "If this ship was used, as you said Dimitry, for humanitarian efforts." Nick turned to the others, "Say disaster relief, crisis assistance. Dimitry is seen to respect his President's wishes as instructed."

"Like operated by a charity or trust?" posed Tom.

"Exactly," joined Nick, "Barbara has had experience with charities hasn't she Tom? What if a charity or foundation was set up to utilise this ship for relief work? Say, leased to a trust from the owner......that's you Dimitry...The crew and us would also be available to deal with security issues, protection for personnel."

Tom stood up, excited at Nicks suggestion. "Barb has been champing at the bit to run her own rodeo."

"And Dianne has been wanting to do medical relief work in poor countries." Nick clicked his fingers. "How much money is there really Dimitry? Because a ship and crew like this would suck up money like it was going out of fashion," asked Nick.

"It is embarrassing my friends. The billions invested with international banks returns millions every day, it just keeps building. It keeps me awake at night."

"I'll have to speak with Dianne," said Nick, "but let's face it, we're all retired, the girls would have an opportunity to realise their personal goals and we could have a play now and then. Cruising the world does have its merits."

"I knew you would help Thomas, Nicholas, my friends." Dimitry embraced the other two with a bear hug as they separated and shook hands.

"Getting the right crew could be a problem," said Tom.

"I'm sorry, I can't call the Kremlin," said Dimitry, "they would not understand and besides, you would not want a Russian Captain. Trust me."

"No," said Nick, "They wouldn't understand, but I know a certain Commander who would, and he has an ocean-going, master's ticket. Last I heard he was skippering an oil rig tender in the North Sea. I'll give Jason a call and get back to you."

"Right," said Tom, "I'll have to head back to the states and get Barbara sorted. By the way what's this ship called?"

"Khameleon," said Dimitry, "you know that lizard that changes its colours and has eyes that see in every direction."

"I like it, "offered Tom, "isn't that what it does?"

"Yes, I agree," said Nick turning to Dimitry, "perhaps if you tell the dockyard it's being converted for humanitarian purposes, and slip them a few dollars, then we might be able to stay here a bit longer."

Dimitry stayed on the ship promising to extend their stay at Sembawang and bid the other two farewell as they departed in the chartered limousine, waiting so patiently on the wharf. Tom and Nick stayed the night at the Fullarton before flying back to London.

Dimitry headed down to the main lounge for a vodka. "Damn," he muttered, "I didn't tell them about the private jet."

Nick was exceptionally pleased with himself for remembering to bring back a present from the jewellery shop at the Fullarton.

91

Barbara was ecstatic at the prospect of having a charity with a wealthy benefactor, a ship, and the prospect of rendering humanitarian aid across the globe. Tom was frank about the other possible nefarious aspects of the ship however assured her that he, Nick and Dimitry would treat those assets with the same integrity that they had exhibited in their chosen professions. *That covered a multitude of sins,* thought Tom.

Dianne jumped up and gave Nick a huge kiss on the lips when he presented her with a Dolce & Gabbana gold pendant necklace and suggested it might be time for her to carry out her life-long passion of rendering philanthropic medical help to impoverished people. Tying up loose ends with her practice was a simple phone call to her practice partners. The apartment, mews and house on the south coast would remain as is. They anticipated that they would transit as demand would have it.

Within seven days Tom, Barbara, Nick and Dianne were back at the Fullarton in Singapore, bags packed with essentials only. Barbara and Dianne hit the shops at Marina Sands while Tom and Nick gave Dimitry a call. He answered his phone as he was walking into the spacious Fullarton open lobby in the magnificent Neo-classical building. Just across the road, close to the mouth of the Singapore River, the Merlion, a mythical creature with a lion's head and the body of a fish, was gushing water into the harbour.

The three greeted each other in the lobby before proceeding to the Town restaurant taking a window table overlooking the terrace and river.

Coffees were ordered, and as insisted by Dimitry, three shots of Beluga Gold Line vodka. "Za zdorovye, cheers, bottoms-up," and a customary chinking of the glasses. Dimitry looked around at the palatial surroundings and laughed, "No razbit ochki, no fireplace, how uncivilised."

"This is the tropics Dimi, nor much call for fireplaces here," commented Nick as he placed the shot glass on the table. "Here we go." Dimitry did the same however somewhat loudly and heavily.

"I'm sorry, force of habit. I would like to crunch it under my foot as this is such an important time."

"But you won't, will you Dimitry?"

"Nyet, my friend I will not. But I want to, so much. Waiter, three more."

The next three Beluga vodkas arrived. Then in unison "Khameleon, Za zdorovye."

There was a crunch. "I'm so sorry I dropped my glass." Dimitry shrugged, "and I accidentally stepped on it."

The waiter rushed over with a small silver brush and scoop.

"My apologies," said Dimitry with feigned remorse, "I don't know how that could have happened."

There was laughter around the table.

"My friends, where are the girls?"

"They went to Marina Bay Sands." replied Tom.

"I want them to have a gift. After all I have so much money. Tom, call them and tell them to go to Hermes. I will call the shop right away." Dimitry pulled out his Black Amex, called Hermes and gave them his card number. "The ladies will arrive soon; they can have anything they want." Replacing the card in his wallet. "We must toast again. Oh, I keep forgetting."

"What," said Nick and Tom together.

"The jet."

"What Jet."

"A Bombardier Global 7500."

"Where?"

"It's at Changi at the moment."

There was silence as Nick and Tom looked at each other and then at Dimitry.

"Is there anything else we should know Dimitry?" asked Nick. "I was working out of a London taxi last week, so anything is an improvement on that."

"I think that's about it," replied Dimitry with a smile and shrug.

"One more thing Dimitry?" asked Nick.

"My friend anything, anything at all."

"Well Dimi, the last case I was on left a few of my associates getting a right royal shafting by the establishment."

"You want someone *'usyplen'*, how do you say, euthanized?"

"No, nothing like that, although I'll keep it in mind. No, I'd like to send them a little something to thank them for what they've been though."

"Nick, you have a blank cheque. Here, I will write an account number. Use it as you wish and please be generous, eh?" Dimi handed Nick a piece of paper with an account number and password.

92

Nigel Connelly was eating his regular Thursday night fish and chips, settling in for an evening of Netflix crime shows when there was a knock on his door.

"Mr Connelly, Nigel Connelly."

"Yes."

"Well, I am glad I've caught you at home."

"You are?"

"Yes, I certainly am. I'm Naomi from the War Services Veterans Lottery Foundation. A few months ago, you purchased a ticket in our lottery, and I'm pleased to tell you that you've won first prize."

Expecting it to be something like a set of saucepans Nigel shook her hand. "Well thank you, that's lovely what did I win?"

"Well, first prize is a semi-detached house in Wych Elm Road in Hornchurch, a full house of furniture and appliances, landscaped garden, conservatory and swimming pool. And that's not all."

Nigel felt weak at the knees and reached for a kitchen chair and sat down.

"More?"

"Yes," continued Naomi, "You also get a choice of one of three cars, a fifteen-foot caravan, and twenty thousand pounds of gold bullion. I'm available to meet you there tomorrow if you're available?"

"Available," replied Nigel, "available? I can go there tonight luv, although I'll be sad to leave this place." Naomi shook his hand as they both laughed.

Stella Wilde opened the card wishing her and Chris the very best for their engagement and forthcoming wedding. It was signed by Nick on behalf of his wife Dianne, Her Majesties Government and a chap called Dimitry. Inside the card was a key taped to the inside with the address of The Penthouse at The Old Schoolhouse in Moulsham Street, Chelmsford. The message, *"Thank you so very much, enjoy your life together, see you at the wedding."*

Constable Kevin Constable was woken early by his wife asking what the motorhome in their driveway was doing there. Dressing quickly Kevin opened his front door to see the Swift 4 berth motorhome sitting proudly in front of their home. He approached the side door observing an envelope tied to the door handle. His hands were shaking as he opened the sleeve. Inside was a card. *Mentioned in Despatches – enjoy, Nick Hood and team.*

A representative from the Police Union knocked on the door of Catherine Hensley, widow of the late Constable Graham Hensley, killed in a motor vehicle accident on the A1 near Grantham. Catherine was presented with a cheque for £500,000 and advised that the money was from an anonymous donor with deepest sympathy.

Teddy Firkin greeted the morning in his dressing gown. What was left of his hair ruffled from his night of tossing as he boiled the kettle and poured the steaming water into the teapot. Popping the tea cosy on the pot he placed the pot, cup and saucer onto a tray. Passing the fridge, he grabbed a small jug of milk, added it to the tray with a couple of sugar cubes. As was his habit, he placed the tray on the table against the window looking down onto the courtyard between his house and the maintenance shed where he serviced his own taxis. He was surprised to see a car transporter parked just inside the gate with his mechanics and drivers climbing over the gantries holding electric taxis.

"What the fuck is going on down there?" he yelled from the window.

"Your new taxis have arrived Guv," yelled one of the drivers.

"What new fuckin' taxis?"

93

The four decided on a typical Asian experience at Clarke Quay, settling into a waterfront table, surrounded by lanterns and illuminated dragons. Dimitry passed on the invitation saying he had to catch up with a friend, or so he said. The typically humid evening was made bearable by a slight breeze and continuous beverages. Icy cold Tiger beers for the men and tropical cocktails for Dianne and Barb.

"Now look here," commented Dianne, "I know you boys want to spend your time playing with Dimitry's toys and swanning about in the playgrounds of the rich and famous, and I am sure you haven't told us everything, but Barb and I have been talking."

"That's right," interjected Barb, "I'm more than happy about developing a strategy for a humanitarian, not for profit charity, and I could get that up and running quick and lively."

"Exactly," continued Dianne, "but it has to be up front and kosher all the way."

Nick and Tom sat back doing exactly what would be the most pragmatic thing to do at this time, listening.

"I can see the advantage in having a crew with your skills," Dianne admitted, "and I'm sure if we find ourselves in awkward situations then I could not think of being in any better company than you old cronies and your associates."

"Yes," commented Barb, "but we mustn't lose sight of the mission and if Dimitry is accurate in stating his financial position there is a huge amount of good that can be done."

"I haven't seen the ship yet, but Nick has told me about the medical facilities on board and I must say I'm excited," said

Dianne, "but if we're going to sail into the great beyond and do some serious work, we'll need to stock up on everything from face masks to pharmaceutical supplies." Dianne paused, "and I'll need some medical staff. I can't do it all by myself."

"Ah," said Tom, "Nick has a skipper in mind, and we've both spoken about employing ex-military personnel and that would include military nursing staff and medics."

"That's right, "said Nick, "the idea will be to have a multi-skilled crew for not only manning the ship but also shore operations."

"And I suppose that would mean dealing with any trouble along the way," interjected Dianne.

"That's right," replied Nick, "there are so many highly skilled military personnel that leave the forces having so much to offer an operation such as this."

"Let's have a toast," proclaimed Tom, "this time without breaking any glasses."

Nick's phone rang.

"It's Age, I hear you're in Singapore, and you've got yourself a ship?"

"I'm not even going to ask how you know," replied Nick.

"When you get operational, I'd like it if you stuck around that area. There's a bit of shit going down China side, and it would be handy if you and your team were in the vicinity. Oh yes, a word of advice."

"What's that Age?"

"Don't hang about too long. Get 'crewed' up, out of Singapore, and in open water by the end of the year. I'll be in touch."

Coming soon

Khameleon – Tsunami

And

Jake's Awake
from The Diaries of Nicholas Hood –

www.mikedfry.com

About the Author

Mike Fry was born in Eastbourne UK and moved to Australia with his family in 1964 at the age of 15. He started his working life with the Royal Australian Navy in the radar division in 1966, leaving in 1975 as an anti-submarine air control instructor. This was followed by a variety of career paths in retail marketing, airport rescue, airline sales and marketing, skipper and owner of a paddle wheeler and guesthouse owner on the west coast of Tasmania. During his time in Tasmania Mike wrote many tourism articles for magazines and newspapers while still maintaining his interest in navy and defence related issues. He served as Chairman of the regional tourism organisation as well as other positions on boards and committees. While operating the guesthouse Mike also operated off road and fishing tours. Mike now lives in Hobart with partner Carolyn, spending time writing, woodworking in his shed, and enjoying time with his daughters and grandchildren.